"WHY, MISS PERRY, ARE YOU SUGGESTING I SHARE INFORMATION WITH YOU?"

Somehow his hand had found hers again; they rested together atop the ruled surface of the noctograph. "That sounds suspiciously like cooperation."

When one of his fingers began to stroke the back of her hand, her heart began to beat faster. "You swore you should not be my foe."

"Nor shall I. I shall be the ears where you cannot go, and you can spend the time in . . . virtuous works."

She choked back a laugh that trembled a bit.

"And in return," he stated, rising to his feet and pulling her up to face him, "will you be the eyes for us both?"

"That sounds as though we would be one flesh." Still, he held her hand, and her fingers could not seem to release his much thicker ones.

"Perhaps later," he murmured. "In the meantime, I rather think we shall be unconquerable. Don't you?"

FORTUNE FAVORS *The* WICKED

THERESA ROMAIN

ZEBRA BOOKS
KENSINGTON PUBLISHING CORP.
http://www.kensingtonbooks.com

All Kensington titles, imprints, and distributed lines are available at special quantity discounts for bulk purchases for sales promotion, premiums, fund-raising, educational, or institutional use.

Special book excerpts or customized printings can also be created to fit specific needs. For details, write or phone the office of the Kensington Sales Manager: Attn.: Sales Department. Kensington Publishing Corp., 119 West 40th Street, New York, NY 10018 Phone: 1-800-221-2647.

Zebra and the Z logo Reg. U.S. Pat. & TM Off.

First Printing: April 2016
ISBN-13: 978-1-4201-3865-8
ISBN-10: 1-4201-3865-0

eISBN-13: 978-1-4201-3866-5
eISBN-10: 1-4201-3866-9

10 9 8 7 6 5 4 3 2 1

Printed in the United States of America

Acknowledgments

Thanks and squishy hugs to my husband and daughter, who supported me and each other while I wrote this book, and to Amanda, critique genius and eagle fancier.

As always, I'm deeply grateful to my editor, Alicia Condon, who makes my books better, and to my agent extraordinaire, Paige Wheeler. Thanks and admiration to the wonderful artists, production staff, and publicity and marketing folks at Kensington Publishing Corp. who put their hearts into making books.

Last but never least, thanks to you, dear readers, for joining me for another story.

Chapter One

From the Slovene lands to the South Sea, no place in the world smelled like one's first whiff of London. The world of the London docks was acrid from coal smoke, pungent from yesterday's spoiling fish and the sludgy water of the Thames.

When Benedict Frost was a boy of twelve, new to the Royal Navy, these had once seemed the scents of home, of freedom from the small cage of shipboard life.

Now, as a man of twenty-nine, he would rather encounter them as a farewell before a journey—and the longer the journey, the better. If a ship were a small cage, England was nothing but a large one.

With determined strides, Benedict disembarked from the *Argent*. He wouldn't need to stay in England more than a few days. The *Argent* was leaving port before the end of the week, and he'd be back in his familiar berth when it did. Before then, all he needed to do was to deliver his manuscript to George Pitman and arrange payment. The precious handwritten pages were heavy in his satchel; in his right hand, his metal-tipped hickory cane thumped on the solid wooden planks underfoot.

"Frost!"

He took another step.

"Oy! Frost!" The unmistakable tones of a sailor: wind-coarse and carrying.

Benedict halted, donning an expression of good cheer at being thus summoned. He didn't recognize the voice, so he said only, "Oy, yourself. How goes your day?"

"Thinking of a treasure hunt. How about you? Goin' to seek the royal reward?"

The what? Benedict covered confusion with a devil-may-care grin. "Not this time. A man's got no need to hunt treasure if he makes his own." He ignored the snigger of a reply, adding, "Good luck to you, though."

With a wave of his cane that fell somewhere between a salute and a *bugger-off*, he continued on his way.

But something was off about the docks. Step by step, it became more obvious. Where was the usual ribald clamor? What had happened to the sailors negotiating with hard-voiced whores, to the halloos and curses as cargo was unloaded? Instead, quiet conversations clustered behind broadsheets, the cheap paper crackling as sailors passed it from hand to hand.

"Theft o' the century, they're callin' it," muttered one as Benedict walked by.

"Aye," agreed another. "You'd want balls of brass to steal from the Royal Mint."

Or balls of gold, Benedict thought. Ever since the war with France had begun, England had been bleeding gold—so much gold, the whole system of currency had recently been revised. Still, creditors were reluctant to take paper money or silver.

Benedict couldn't fault them. He wasn't interested in paper money either.

And so he listened a bit more closely to the conversations he passed, easing free of his sea legs with long strides that carried him westward from the docks of Wapping. Miles of pavement, a test of his memory of London. On every street, the city shifted, with roughened naval types giving way to sedate professionals. But the sounds were the same. Newspapers rustled, and that odd phrase echoed from person to person: *the theft of the century.*

Since the year was only 1817, this seemed a premature declaration. But as Benedict stowed away more overheard details, he could not deny that the crime sounded as audacious as it was outrageous. Four guards had been shot, and six trunks of the new golden sovereigns had been stolen before any of the coins entered circulation. The loss was estimated at fifty thousand pounds.

And that was it. There had been no further clue for weeks, not a single incriminating coin spent. The Royal Mint had just offered a substantial reward for the return of the money.

So. That was the royal reward of which the sailors had spoken. England would soon become a nation of privateers, hunting for coin in the name of the Crown.

Benedict turned over the possibility of joining them. He had attained the frigid summit of Mont Blanc; surely he could spend a few balmy May days to locate a hoard of coins on his native soil. The reward offered by the Royal Mint would allow him to increase his sister Georgette's dowry from *pitiful* to *respectable*.

Tempting. Very tempting. The mere thought of a treasure hunt eased the hollow ache of being in London's heart. Why, it might be like . . . like not being in England at all.

But his manuscript would offer the same reward while still allowing him to depart on the *Argent*. Just as he had told the sailors: he had already drafted his own treasure. Now it was time to claim it.

He strode forth, cane clicking the pavement with his renewed determination, in the direction of Paternoster Row and the office of George Pitman, publisher.

Two weeks later

"He wore a cloak with a hood coverin' his face," the serving girl held forth to an eager group of listeners. "But I looked beneath the hood and saw his *eyes*. They were demon eyes, red as fire!"

Behind her veil, Charlotte's mouth curved. She could not help but roll her eyes—which were non-demon features, closer to the color of a leaf than a flame.

Alone of the reward seekers in the common room of the Pig and Blanket, Charlotte had heard Nance's tale time and again. It was different with each retelling, and therefore each account revealed something different about Nancy Goff herself. About what she thought important, or shameful, or likely to win her the coins of a stranger.

Somewhere within that coil was the truth.

Which was why, for a second endless day, Charlotte sat alone, listening, in the corner of a Derbyshire inn's common room. The Pig and Blanket was ordinary in every way, from the middling quality of the ale and food to the indifferent cleanliness of the tables.

Ordinary in every way, that is, save one. A week ago, in this inn, Nance had been paid with a gold sovereign. Since no one had gold sovereigns yet except the Royal Mint and the thieves who had stolen six trunks of uncirculated coins . . . well.

It was the first clue related to the theft, and it was a good one. And like seemingly half of England, Charlotte had followed it. All the way from the squalid rented room she had just taken in Seven Dials. She was in far less danger among the neighborhood's thieves and cutthroats than she was in her luxurious town house, or promenading the rarefied streets of Mayfair.

In Derbyshire, she was still in danger, but of a different sort. Thus the veil.

And the solitude.

"I knew he was a wrong one," preened Nance, tossing the brunette curls she had today left uncovered by the usual cap. A pretty young woman of about twenty years, she swanned about the common room of the Pig and Blanket, distributing drinks and scooping up coins. "Had that look about him. It was as much as I could do to carry his ale without spillin' it. So afraid, I was! Shiverin' in my boots."

This last was spoken in a tone of such relish that Charlotte smiled again. Ten years ago, nearing the end of her teens, she'd had the same sort of vigor.

Would she have told a story ten times, embroidering it more with each telling?

No, she would have told it eleven. Twelve. As many times as someone would listen, and in her dark-haired, bright-eyed enthusiasm, she might have looked much like Nance. Even now, she wanted to join in; even now it hurt to sit at the side of the room, alone. It hurt to cover her face with a veil, to miss the shadings of expression that flitted across the faces of others when they were interested. Bored. Curious. In thrall.

Despite the crowds packed into the common room to drink in Nance's dramatic tale along with their ale, the other seat at Charlotte's table remained empty. Somehow the sweep of blurry gray net across her face made her as fearsome as the demon-eyed stranger who had given Nance the gold coin.

The veil was a nuisance, like peering through smoke. But years of notoriety had taught Charlotte that sometimes the annoyance of a veil was preferable to the greater inconvenience of being recognized.

With a wiggle of her significant bosom, Nance scooped up a stray coin from a table. "'Twasn't only his demon eyes that gave me that sort of shivery feelin'. No, it were the cloak, too. Nobody covers up like that in spring, does they? Not unless they has somethin' to hide."

Behind her covering veil, Charlotte chuckled. Nance was a shrewd girl.

The inn's door was shoved open, marking the entrance of a new visitor. From her seat near the corner, Charlotte had a view of everyone who entered the small foyer before passing by or turning into the common room.

This was an odd sort of shove at the door, slow and deliberate and interrupted by several thumps. And the figure who accompanied it, washed by golden afternoon sunlight before the door closed behind him, was no less unusual. He was broad and large and dark, wearing a naval uniform. Through her veil, Charlotte could not pick out detail enough to determine his rank. But whether an admiral or a lieutenant, a sailor had no business in landlocked Derbyshire—unless he, too, were hunting the stolen coins.

Nance must have thought the same, for she cut off her tale and began swiping the nearest table with a grimy cloth and an expression of pious concentration. A few coins would set her to talking again, like an automaton being wound.

Thump.

Pause.

Thump.

The boisterous common room had gone quiet, watching the new arrival progress across the room. Before each step, he smacked his cane against the floor like a gesture of emphasis. *I have arrived, damn you. Look my way.* And who could not? His determined features were like a thundercloud on this spring day: one ought to be wary lest a storm drew close.

Until he reached the center of the room and spoke in a low, pleasant tone. "Greetings, all. I heard such a welcoming din as I approached that I couldn't help but enter." His brows lifted in a puckish curve. "There is no need to end your party on my account. I'm quite a pleasant fellow, I promise you."

His reassurance was enough to coax the din to recommence, first in a slow trickle, then like the tumble of the nearby Kinder Downfall after a torrential rain. Once Nance took the man's order for ale, then picked up the thread of her tale about the cloaked visitor with demon eyes, it was almost impossible to hear the thumps of the cane on the wide-planked floor.

Until they sounded before Charlotte.

"I beg your pardon. Might I sit at this table?"

The broad figure was planted before her, the sailor's tone quiet and courteous.

But for a man to ask to sit with a lone woman to whom he had not been introduced—this was so bold that for a moment Charlotte could only blink. "Here? With—me?" Of course with her. It was the only empty seat in the common room. "Yes, all right."

To forbid him a place at her table would be to draw more attention than to agree. And within her left sleeve, the hidden penknife was reassuringly solid.

"You are very good, madam. Thank you. I don't mean to bother you, I assure you. Ah—are you quite alone at this table?"

"As you see."

"Right," he murmured. "Right." With a deliberate gesture, the sailor drew out the empty chair and settled his large frame within it. The cane that had announced his presence with solid thumps was now balanced across his thighs.

Not that Charlotte looked at his thighs; she was only looking at the cane. Lord. She'd had enough of men, and their thighs, and every other one of their parts.

Nance flounced over and slopped a tankard onto the table, naming a price that had both Charlotte and the sailor jerking with surprise. Every hour, the prices at the Pig and Blanket went up. How much was this due to the owner's rapaciousness during this moment of fame, and how much to the serving girl spotting the rare chance to line her own pocket?

A shrewd girl; very shrewd.

But one could never be shrewd enough, and Charlotte's brow creased with worry.

"Thank you." The sailor took a few coins from his pocket, tracing a thumb over them, then handed two to Nance. This won him a grin and a curtsy before she flounced off.

He cocked his head. "It was no gold sovereign, but she liked that well enough. Ah—did you want anything, madam? Shall I call her back?"

"I need nothing at the moment. Thank you." Atop the smooth-rubbed wooden table was a single pottery tankard in which remained an inch of yeasty ale. She had sipped at it for hours, until the innkeeper's wife began to cast resentful glances her way. Soon Charlotte would have to buy something else—another ale, maybe, or a bowl of stew—in order to keep her seat.

Her little sigh set the cloudy net veil to dancing before her face. How warm the day was; she wished she could sweep off her veil and deep-brimmed bonnet. She was perspiring under their unaccustomed weight.

All right, not only because of their weight. Too long had she hidden without taking action, and the knowledge prompted a dew of worry. But was it safer to stay or to leave?

"Thank you for the seat." The man's voice broke into her thoughts. "I've been traveling unexpectedly for some time, and the chance to sit is welcome. Benedict Frost is my name."

"Of His Majesty's Royal Navy, I see. Have you been traveling by land or sea?" Charlotte had learned the markers of rank; in her profession, one had to pick out the important men at a glance. Now that he sat close to her, she could make out the details of dress she had missed before. His high-collared blue coat looked well enough, but the gold buttons and the white piping about them proclaimed him a lieutenant.

In her previous life in London, she would have chilled him with a quelling flip of her fan, then passed him by.

Now . . . she wondered about him. The cane; the careful touch at the coins; the surprised lift of his brows when she spoke. Was his vision dim? If she could sweep aside her veil and look at him—really look at his eyes—she would be able to tell in an instant.

Not that it mattered for his sake. But for hers, it would mean that she wouldn't have to hide her face from him.

"I've traveled by both land and sea within the past fortnight." He sighed. "And river. On wheel and on foot, and if there are any other ways to travel, I've probably found them, too."

"Horseback? Hobby-horse?" Charlotte thought for a moment. "Ostrich cart?"

"Ah, there you've got me. It has just become one of the great sadnesses of my life that I have never traveled by ostrich cart."

Considering Charlotte had just made it up, this was no wonder. She had missed friendly conversation of this sort, so she added, "From where have you traveled, Lieutenant?"

"Most recently from France, then London. But I'm no longer active in the navy." A flash of white teeth against tanned skin. "I've still the right to wear the uniform, though, and ladies seem to like it."

Some roguery made Charlotte ask, "What of the men?"

"Probably some of them do, too. But I admit"—he leaned forward with a conspiring air—"the true reason I wear it is because a man in uniform is always in fashion and need not concern himself with the changing styles."

"Ah, you are practical as well as attractive."

He pressed a hand to his chest. "You honor me, madam."

"I simply repeat your own ideas."

"You assume they are correct, though. You've only my say to support my practicality or my effect on the female sex." He grinned, a sliver of sunshine.

Ha. She had more than his word for the latter; she had her own response. She had a weakness for strong men, for men who grinned at her as though she were delightful. A sunrise smile always made her want to open like a flower—a response that had led more than once to her plucking.

Benedict Frost cut a figure of rough elegance: hair dark as soot, and as curling as Charlotte's was stubbornly straight. A strong jaw, a sun-browned complexion. Broad shoulders and ungloved hands. A cane that demanded a person look at him; a voice low enough to allow him to listen.

"Though I have naught but your word," she replied, "the fact that you admit it is in your favor. In a coaching inn, no one knows anyone else. We all must go on faith that we are what we seem."

Not that he should have a bit of faith in her, as she added, "I am called . . . Smith." She could not give him the name familiar to the locals. And too many in London knew the assumed name of Charlotte Pearl; a sailor who hadn't been in the navy for some years might well be one of them.

He took a long drink of his ale. "Well, Mrs. Smith, I'm pleased to make your acquaintance. But I haven't the leisure for going on faith."

"I don't think the situation is so dire as to require *that*," she said lightly. "These crowds are not here because of faith, Lieutenant Frost. They are here because of evidence."

"The evidence of the serving girl," he agreed. "And please, *mister* will do."

This mention of the serving girl was timed excellently, for Nance had been persuaded by a table of soft-bellied cits with Bloomsbury accents to relate her encounter with the cloaked figure. Again. "Eyes like a cat, he had!" the young woman exclaimed. "They glowed in the dark."

Never mind the fact that her previous retellings had mentioned the afternoon sun picking out the coarseness of the mysterious customer's cloak. He had left the gold coin at an hour much like the present one, divided in time by seven days. If only Charlotte had been here to see the truth for herself.

"The coin was real enough," said Frost. "Yes, we have that evidence." He spoke quietly, held his hands deliberately: first tracing the arc of the table before him, then sliding them to find the tankard. They were careful hands, a careful voice. As of one trying to hear rather than be heard.

He could not see—or not well. She was quite sure of that now, and relief drew from her a tension that left her shoulders aching.

"She thought it a guinea at first," Charlotte said. "Nance, the barmaid. She hasn't mentioned that in her tale lately, but she swore to it when the Bow Street Runner questioned her yesterday morning."

The London officer had grown more and more impatient as Nance's tale failed to yield identifying clues. Perhaps this was why each retelling now popped with a surplus of detail.

"Hasn't mentioned it for a day, hmm," mused Frost. "So she's ashamed. Maybe that she did not know the difference between one gold coin and another."

"Or," Charlotte continued, "maybe she's ashamed of the fact that she *did* know the difference, took a coin she knew to be stolen, and then lied to a Bow Street Runner. One or the other must be the case."

"There is not much one won't hide to escape trouble. Or for the promise of reward." He took another long pull from his tankard.

Charlotte had been unable to do more than sip at her ale; she had let herself grow fastidious during her London years.

All part of the job.

"Your name isn't really Smith, is it?" he asked.

Charlotte pressed a hand to the anchoring wall at her side, the rough mortar and brick cold through her glove. "Why . . . should you think such a thing, Mr. Frost?"

"Because you don't ask the question everyone asks

when they meet me. And that makes me think you don't want to answer questions yourself."

He seemed so large, and they were quite alone near the corner of the room. Everyone else was watching Nance. Charlotte had created her cocoon well.

"You need not answer questions either," she rushed. Why, she had not even asked his name; he had volunteered that on his own. She would not ask, for to seek an answer was to look behind a person's veil. And she could not return the favor.

"It's all right. You are wondering." He rested his fingers around the tankard. "The answer is no, Mrs. Smith. I cannot see at all."

As she fumbled for a gracious reply, he turned his smile upon her. "Now that's been addressed, how is the stew here? I'll need a good meal before I seek my fortune."

Chapter Two

"The stew is as good as the ale. Make of that what you will." The intriguing Mrs. Smith's tone was warm as she replied to Benedict, with a bubble of laughter in it. "And I must add, since you tell me you are blind and therefore might be unaware of this detail, that you are quite right about the effect of your uniform on certain females. Mrs. Potter, who owns the Pig and Blanket with her husband, has granted you the only smile I have ever seen cross her sour features. If you wish to return it, she is across the room and to your right."

And that was that. She noted and accepted his blindness, and that was all she had to say about it.

Huh.

"It is most gratifying to know I can turn a woman up sweet. Or at least that my coat can. Thank you," Benedict replied, grateful to his veiled companion for far more than her appraisal of the cookery at the Pig and Blanket.

Feeling his way through the world was a skill that had taken years to hone. As was the ability to smile when one felt not at all like smiling, and to ask for help when one would rather curse the darkness.

He had not felt much like smiling since his dreadful interview with George Pitman. But just now, it was not so difficult. He even pointed a bit of the smile to his right, in the direction of the unknown Mrs. Potter.

"Not at all." Just when he thought she had no more to say, she added, "You are correct that my name is not Mrs. Smith. But if you would continue to call me that, I should be grateful."

"Very wise of you to keep your counsel. One will not find a stolen treasure by trusting every random encounter with valuable secrets."

"My identity is not a valuable secret, Mr. Frost. Nothing of the sort." The bubble of laughter had popped.

"I meant to imply nothing of the sort. I am certain your identity is a matter of complete dullness. Only the plainest people with the most tedious of lives go about veiled under a false name." Before she could ask how he knew of her veil, he waved a hand. "You— there's something in front of your face. It gets in the way of your voice."

"It gets in the way of a damned sight more than that," she muttered, just low enough that he could pretend he hadn't heard a lady curse.

The word carried a little shock, almost like coming upon a lady undressed. And there was no question that she *was* a lady, though she was alone and passing under a false name. Her voice was well-bred, well-educated. Accent was everything in England; the way a person spoke or dropped their aitches was enough to open or shut the doors of society.

God. This country was such a cursed prison.

Cursed streets, cursed thieves, cursed coaches that didn't run precisely on time to the schedule one had memorized.

Most of all, cursed George Pitman, because of whom Benedict was still in England and not scudding across a springtime sea.

Oh, the publisher had enjoyed Benedict's accounts of his travels. Found them everything he'd been promised through their earlier correspondence. Was perfectly happy to publish the piece on commission.

As a novel.

There's no way a blind man could have done these things, Pitman said. The chair behind his desk creaked as he leaned back; the scent of cheap tobacco arose from his clothing, assaulting Benedict's nostrils. *You've got a wonderful imagination, Frost, but this is a fiction, not a memoir. Anyone could see that.* And then he laughed. *A blind man could see that.*

The precious manuscript pages, marked out with the guiding lines of Benedict's noctograph, had not been left with Pitman. Nor with any other printing house; they had laughed him out almost as soon as they met him.

There would be no fortune of his own making. Not if it were up to the publishers of London.

Had he thought he wanted stew? His throat closed, choking him.

With a deep breath, Benedict summoned calm. Not-Mrs. Smith was speaking to him. "I have heard it said that one's other senses become more acute when sight is lost. Have you found it so, or is that rubbish?"

I've found that to be utter shite. But the question was posed with courtesy, and so he answered it in kind.

"I have been told that, usually by sighted people intending to offer unwanted comfort. But the effort I've invested in making my way about a sighted world has convinced me otherwise. Rather, I have trained myself to notice things others need not."

"Such as a veiled woman."

"I doubt I am the only one who noticed you, madam." Surely anyone who caught sight of a veiled woman would be curious.

Benedict had never dropped the habit of wondering what people looked like, even after four years of living by his ears and wits. Mrs. Smith possessed the voice of a beautiful woman. But beautiful in what way? Was she buxom and dark? Slim and golden? Buxom and golden? Slim and dark?

There were so many ways a woman might be beautiful, and he missed seeing them all. If he had met her at another time, in another place—at an ambassador's party, maybe, or even among the long shelves in the bookshop that had once been his parents'—he might have been flirt enough to read her features with his fingertips.

"I hope you are," she replied, and for a moment he thought she was granting him permission to do just that.

"I . . . beg your pardon?"

"I hope you are the only one who noticed me, I mean. I am here to listen, not to draw attention."

Ah. Yes. That made more sense than a mysterious, cultured woman craving the attentions of a rough stranger. "Would that I could achieve the same," he said lightly. "But when one enters a room by smacking a cane on the floor, one must expect to be looked at."

"It is certainly an effective way to announce one's

presence. There are—I imagine—men and women aplenty in the *ton* who would adopt the same method at a ball, if they only thought of it."

"My sister is twenty and covets a Season of her own. Perhaps I will recommend the use of a cane to her as a method of becoming notable."

His metal-tipped cane, solid and dependable as a third hand, didn't clear a path through the world so much as it revealed its shape. Different floors had their own unique feel; the movement of air about a room told Benedict something of its size. This common room, for example: its air was humid and close on his face and ungloved hands. A great crowd surely sat within, then, each pair of lungs a bellows and each heart a tiny hearth. People could be felt, just as floors could.

Stillness could be felt too, when a crowd became silent bit by bit. How could he learn their secrets if his mere presence brought them to silence? How could he gain the royal reward amidst useless clamor and gossipy whispers?

He ought to have begun by using his friend Hugo Starling's letter of introduction to the local vicar, instead of taking his chances with a public house. What clue could he hope to gather on his own that a longtime vicar would not be able to tell him more quickly? Hugo's friends, the Reverend John Perry and Mrs. Perry, were expecting him sometime today.

He might as well leave at once; there was no purpose to sitting here longer. No reward would come his way from sitting with a woman, no matter how presumably lovely she was.

He shoved back his chair, flipping his cane to its

spot at his side as he stood. "I must be leaving, madam. I wish you good luck on your search."

"So soon, Mr. Frost? But you have taken no food." She paused. "Of which you are aware, of course. Excuse my obvious remark; I'm only surprised. You seemed determined to fortify yourself before joining the horde of treasure seekers."

"But you did tell me the stew was as good as the ale—and I've had better to drink on board a ship three weeks at sea." A roguish grin. "I'll find something else. There's nothing more to be found here."

He had to be careful, so careful, to smile and put people at ease. Otherwise he would become a caricature, like the growling hero of *La Belle et La Bête.* His sister, Georgette, had loved those old *contes de fées* as a child, even reading them in the original French. An advantage of having parents who owned a bookshop.

An advantage of being able to read words on a page. Those who took such a thing for granted were fools.

"I hope," said the satin-rich voice of not-Mrs. Smith, "that there is more to be found here after all. I intend to brave the stew and wait a few more hours."

"You are going on faith now? Better you than me."

"Right." She said this more quietly. "Right. Well. One does what one must."

"Thank you for the opportunity to make your acquaintance." He bowed a farewell.

The path back to the door was easy to follow; he reversed the steps in his mind and wound his way to the foyer, then the door of the inn. There was no need to thump his cane on the floor this time, listening for echoes. He might leave without making a spectacle of himself.

And he had to leave—to find Hugo's friends, to learn what they had to share. Then go somewhere, do something to find those damned gold sovereigns. And once he did, once he had collected the reward, he would make the life he and Georgette deserved.

The world might think a blind man couldn't write a book about travel. But even the most doubting ought to realize: there was no one better at finding a path others had overlooked than a man who couldn't see.

As soon as Frost departed, another man—stinking of ale and tobacco—took his place at Charlotte's table. "Allow me a bi' o' yer company. A pretty lady shouldn't be left alone. No' in a place like this."

He was a young, bulky man in a farmer's home-spun garments, with enough stubble that one might generously call it a beard rather than simple untidiness. His Derbyshire accent was thick, but she didn't recognize him as a local. Not that she knew the inhabitants of Strawfield by sight anymore; a decade's worth of faces had come and gone since Charlotte last lived here.

She sighed. "How do you know I'm pretty? Or alone, for that matter?"

"Because the fellow who were with yer just left."

"He wasn't with me."

"So ye *are* alone." He shrugged. "I'll keep an eye on yer."

"Not necessary."

"C'mon, miss. Is that friendly?"

"Is it *friendly* to impose one's presence on a woman to whom one has not been introduced?"

He blinked, then slurred a reply. "Ain't ye a treat. If yer wan' to be introduced, le's call someone over to do the pretty."

"No. Don't." When he stretched and turned as though preparing to call across the great room, she sprang to her feet.

He must have caught the movement from the corner of his eye, for he turned back to her, lolling and laughing. "Don' be shy. Nance in't shy." With one beefy hand, he caught Charlotte's left wrist. "Maybe she can join us. Nance!"

God save her from the half drunk. Men could be reasoned with when they were sober, and when they were completely inebriated, one could push them about. This scoundrel was at the dangerous point in between, the point where men forgot their manners and lost their tempers. His fingers were crushing the bones of her wrist.

She had been fine as long as no man took notice of her. Now it was as though Benedict Frost had laid a claim on her, then rejected her. Now instead of being her own property, she was open for claiming. Or so this . . . creature . . . thought.

She didn't blame Frost. He'd needed a place to sit. No, she blamed this ale-soaked would-be rogue.

"Let me go," Charlotte said through clenched teeth. "Or you won't like what happens next."

"Oh, ye'll like it." The fool must have misheard her. Already Nance, summoned by the call of a customer, was pushing through the crowd toward Charlotte's table. Curious customers were following the barmaid with their gaze.

Charlotte had to get out of here before anyone realized the insignificant unknown figure was—

hereabouts—nothing of the sort. She looked for the Bow Street Runner, a scrubby bearded man made conspicuous by his brogue. At the moment she neither heard nor saw him.

Very well. She was on her own.

With her free hand, she pulled the penknife from her left sleeve and pressed it to the heel of the man's hand. "Do you like your thumb?" she said sweetly. "One of us is going to keep it. If you want it to be you, you'd best move your hand away at once."

He tightened his grip, and a thread of blood appeared across his knuckle. "You bitch!" He gaped, releasing her to suck at his wound. "You bitch! You cut me!"

"You cut yourself when you tightened your grasp." She looked at the knife in some disgust, then wiped the drop from its blade onto her sleeve and stowed it again. Thank goodness she'd worn her dark blue serge. "It's a poor excuse for a man who blames a woman for his own faults."

"Bitch whore," he spat.

"Bitch *courtesan*," she muttered. "It's a completely different occupation."

When he started to rise to his feet, reaching within his coat—for a blade of his own?—she declined to educate him further in the niceties of kept-woman vocabulary. Tossing a few coins on the table, she turned on her heel and left.

Not fled.

Just left.

For she had wanted to leave. Truly. She had been ready. Somehow she needed to find the person who had given Nance the coin, and she would not do that by listening to the young woman spin a useless hodgepodge of demons and cats and cloaks and premonitions. All Charlotte had really learned in two wasted days was that the girl was eager for coin and praise.

She knew the type well.

And it wasn't because of the half-drunk beefwit that she strode away so quickly. She wanted to breathe fresh air, nothing more. This was not so unusual, the speed of her pace. She had always been a fast walker.

As she walked along the too-familiar main street of Strawfield, brushing past slower-moving villagers, her eyes watered. The sun shone at a pale distance, and a chill wind teased her veil.

This was why her eyes were teary. It was only the sharp air. Not some excess of stupid feeling. She was far too jaded to mind being treated as that man had treated her. She was not bothered by using her knife.

Ducking into a space between two buildings, she tugged free her veil and bonnet, tucked them under her arm, and covered her head instead with the light wool shawl that had hung about her elbows.

Thus freed from the unwelcome film of the veil, she blinked into a world of sudden color. The sky was a painful blue, the trees in full leaf. The buildings were gritstone-dark and the deep red of old brick, with roofs of slate or thatch or split-wood shingle that made them look as though they'd popped from the living ground. On the village green, tents had sprung up like mushrooms. The Pig and Blanket was full to bursting, and some villagers were renting out rooms in their houses. Every day there were more and more treasure seekers.

The edge of the village was not far; from there, she'd cross the corner of the Selwyn lands. The rough land of the Northern Peak was at its greenest right now, before sheep cropped the grass to its roots and the remnants scorched in late-summer heat.

Somewhere, in the worn stone crevices of the moors, there had to be more coins. Six trunks full.

None for the master, none for the dame. Six for the little girl who lived in the vicarage—if Charlotte had her way.

She clambered over the stone wall that divided off the Selwyn lands, cutting a corner that shaved ten minutes from her walk. It seemed foolish to hurry when the situation she'd left also awaited her at her destination: a veiled expression, a careful silence. Bland food and lonely corners.

Though for a few moments, when speaking with Frost, she hadn't been lonely. She hadn't even needed to be harsh. She'd just . . . been.

That hadn't happened to her often since she was Nance's age, or maybe even younger. The life of Charlotte Pearl was, for all its luxuries, not one that permitted relaxation.

She squinted into the distance. Was that a party of treasure seekers on Selwyn land? Surely it was; the faraway figures carried picks and spades. Much luck to them. If Edward or Lady Helena or one of their servants caught them trespassing, they'd be hauled before the magistrate.

Charlotte presumed upon Edward's good graces by crossing his land. But then, she was a very old acquaintance. A few footsteps across his grass was the least of what he owed her, not that she wanted anything of him. Not now.

The trio had drawn a bit closer, close enough for their forms to become more distinct than blobs carrying hand tools. The way the man in front moved was so familiar. Of whom did he remind her?

Randolph.

She moved without thought, hauling herself over the second waist-high stone wall. Breaths swift and hitching, she slid to the ground behind the shield of the old wall. Her hands trembled, and she clenched them into fists with a reproof to herself. *Stupid.* It could not be Randolph. Not here, not with a spade slung over one shoulder. A marquess, with all his vast resources, would not be bothered hunting gold coins. Or even pretending to hunt, while he searched instead for the woman on whom he felt he had a claim.

Right. That was right. Of course it was not Randolph. No shout had followed her over the stone barrier.

Gritting her teeth, she ventured a peek over the wall. The men had drawn closer now, and the one she'd mistaken for Randolph looked nothing like him. They shared a brawny build, but this laughing man was as pale as the marquess was dark.

She slid back to her hiding place. *Steady, Charlotte,* she murmured to herself, over and over, until she no longer needed the stone wall at her back to keep herself upright.

It was perfectly natural to think one saw familiar faces at every pass. In one's birthplace, one expected it.

Even if the faces one saw, or feared seeing, had been left far behind with a great deal of secrecy, expense, and effort.

She allowed several minutes to pass, along with the trio of laughing men, before standing and continuing on her path. Another minute's walk brought her to

the garden behind the vicarage, across which a maid
had strung lines and was pinning up sheets.

Charlotte halted. "Barrett? Why are you hanging
the washing? I thought my parents hired this out."

A cap-covered head with a pair of dark eyes peered
above the makeshift line. "Miss Perry! I didn't expect
you back so soon."

Not that Sarah Barrett had reason to expect Charlotte to act in any particular way, since this was
Charlotte's first visit to Strawfield in four years. But
she and Barrett were almost of an age, and the
sturdy, frank maid had grown up alongside the two
Perry sisters.

"Mrs. Fancot," Barrett said in a tone of great scorn,
her Yorkshire accent thick as pudding, "forgot to take
down the vicarage washing before last night's rain
shower. Sent it over t'us today all damp and said
she'd charge for another week's washing if we wanted
it done over."

"How extortionate," Charlotte said, as she was
clearly expected to do.

"That's what I thought. So I tol' her never to mind,
and that she wasn't the only washerwoman in Strawfield."

"Isn't she?"

"No, she isn't." Barrett sniffed. "And it's time she
remembered. Mrs. Reverend, she gave me a free
hand to see to these matters, and see to them I will."

Charlotte took up a handful of wooden pegs, handing them to the maid as needed. Barrett wrestled
sheets with an easy grace Charlotte could not achieve.

Now that she thought about it, she really didn't
know how to do anything useful.

But Barrett had done well for herself. The vicarage

and its living were too small to support a housekeeper, but Barrett was the nearest thing. She had the help of a lower housemaid and a few kitchen servants, and she had always known everything that passed in the vicarage.

"How is my father today?" Charlotte ventured.

Barrett dropped the clothes-peg she was holding. "Oh! Sorry, Miss Perry." She disappeared behind a bath sheet. When she stood with the recovered peg, her cheeks were flushed. "His health is fine. He just worries; that's all. You know how he does."

"Yes, I know."

"It's this guest coming; he wants everything perfect."

"He is doomed to disappointment, then."

"And he's been horrid busy with all these new people about, looking for that gold. Someone tumbled over the Downfall this morning—"

"Good God." The local waterfall was not large, but it threaded through crushed and scattered rock.

"—and his friends were all set to have dragged him into the front parlor for the vicar to pray over."

"The doctor gets the cases with hope, and the church gets the hopeless ones," Charlotte said. "I trust you did not allow a corpse to be dragged into the house."

"Well, he weren't quite a corpse. But no, they took him into the stable and your father went out to 'im."

This made sense. The vicar could afford to keep no carriage, no horses. The stable was nothing but a box for storage of all the oddments of vicarage life that fit nowhere else. The tools given to the church because they could no longer be sharpened; the cracked vases donated because they could hold no water. Each gift, no matter how useless, had to be accepted with thanks.

"Is . . . ah, the man still in the stable?"

"No, his friends dragged him off again. Might be that he'll live after all. Power of prayer and whatnot."

"Right," murmured Charlotte. "I don't suppose the friends gave the vicar so much as a shilling for his trouble?"

"They seem to have forgotten that part," Barrett said through teeth clenched around a wooden peg.

The influx of reward hunters was a boon for those in Strawfield with something to sell. For those with something to give—like the vicar, like the church— it was nothing but a rip in an already threadbare life.

"I wish they'd take something from me," Charlotte said. "My parents, I mean." Not that she had much to give now. But for the past decade, the Reverend John Perry and Mrs. Perry had refused to accept so much as a coin from their daughter. Partly pride; partly duty; an even greater measure of shame.

Which made Charlotte just another of the locusts swarming the Strawfield vicarage, taking much, giving nothing.

For now. Not for long.

Before she could ask another question, Barrett said, "If you don't mind my saying so, Miss Perry, you oughtn't to cut across the Selwyn lands. Lady Helena will get in a powerful rage if she catches you."

"Did you see me hiding, then? I thought I saw some of her groundskeepers." A plausible excuse for cowering against the stone wall. "Silly of me. They were only a trio of reward seekers with digging tools."

"Lady Helena won't like that either," commented Barrett.

"And is her husband not in residence?" That would be Edward, who had married an earl's daughter and filled his house with sons. Charlotte saw him too often in London; she disliked seeing him here, too.

"No, he's visiting a friend. Some nobleman," Barrett tossed off, as though dukes and barons and their like were all of equal unimportance.

"Very good. That's very good." Handing the clothes-pegs back to Barrett, Charlotte continued around the vicarage to the battered front door. She knocked, waited, then turned the handle. There was never a servant at hand to answer the door. It would have been a family joke, had either of Charlotte's parents been possessed of a sense of humor.

Once inside the wood-paneled entryway that stretched into a narrow corridor, she called out. "Papa? It's I, Charlotte."

The reply sounded from the small parlor to her left. "Of course it is. Only one person in the world calls me Papa since your sister's passing, God rest her precious soul."

Always such a barrel of cheer, her father was.

Charlotte peeped in to greet him. The front parlor was the finest room in the house, and she tried not to see it with London eyes that would pick out every smudge and faded spot on the flowered wall-papers. The hooked rugs Charlotte and her older sister Margaret had made as children. Her father, faded and thin as those worn carpets.

The Reverend John Perry set aside his thick book and spectacles. "You must remember to keep silence in the corridor outside your mother's study. She so dislikes having her translation interrupted." Before she could reply, he clucked with dismay and unfolded his lean figure from his favorite chair. "You must change your clothing, child. Make yourself respectable! Lord Hugo's friend is arriving today. Don't you recall?"

"Yes, Papa. Of course I do." She could not help but fix it in her mind, having been told seventy-five times since her own arrival two days before. Lord Hugo Starling, younger son of a duke, was the most fashionable acquaintance her father had ever made—if one excepted Edward and Lady Helena Selwyn and Charlotte herself, which her parents always did.

One of England's most respected young scholars, Lord Hugo had written to the Reverend John Perry after admiring one of Mrs. Perry's classical translations. The resulting correspondence had ranged across many subjects; Charlotte had no idea of their scope. But when she had arrived at the vicarage, the reverend had informed her with no small pride that one of Lord Hugo's friends had written a manuscript, and that the friend required a place to stay in Derbyshire. As he was constitutionally unsuited to public houses, he would stay with Lord Hugo's trusted correspondents—nay, *friends*!

He had waited for Charlotte to collapse with delight, but she had little interest in this matter. She didn't plan to be in Derbyshire long enough to become acquainted with this likely eccentric.

"I recall everything you have told me," Charlotte recited as her father's long, thin hands began to twist. "It will be fine, Papa. I shall behave."

She only hoped this friend of Hugo's would behave himself, too. Just in case, she would continue to keep her penknife about her. Maybe she'd give one to Maggie as well.

"I don't like this plan of you sharing Maggie's room." Twist, twist, went one hand about the other, as though wringing out wet laundry for Barrett. "It's not proper."

Margaret's namesake and the reverend couple's sole grandchild, the ten-year-old occupied a sunny chamber on the upper floor of the vicarage. It was not considered as fine as the spare room kept for the rare guest, but Charlotte would be glad for the company. "Maybe not, but what's the alternative? It would be even less proper for Mr. Starling's friend to share my chamber."

The reverend closed his eyes. "Do not speak of such things, child. You never know who could hear you."

Right. Yes, that was the only problem: the risk of being overheard.

She could not share in her father's distress over propriety, yet it speared her. Her poor father; he looked so thin and gray. He ought to be settling into a sedate retirement in a seaside resort like Bath, not caring for a child. Or hosting his wayward daughter.

"You look tired, Papa. Do sit, and I'll make certain that all of my belongings are removed to Maggie's room, and that all is in readiness for your guest. What is his name, by the bye?" Her father had called him only *Lord Hugo's friend* for the past day, but this would hardly do once the man himself were present.

"Ah. He's a soldier! No, a sailor? I can never recall how those types are called. He was the sort that sails around, I think."

"A sailor, then." To cover her suddenly nerveless

fingers, Charlotte set down her discarded bonnet and veil and began to tug at her shawl. "Would he by chance be a lieutenant?"

"I believe so, though he doesn't care to be called by his rank. Frost is his name."

Shite.

Failing at untying the knot, she tugged the shawl over her head and yanked it off. "Well, I look forward to meeting him."

This was not exactly false, but not quite true either. She would have to meet him again knowing he sought the stolen sovereigns, and he knowing she did, too. Knowing he had found her veiled and giving a false name.

And knowing he was blind, about which her reverend father seemed not to be aware. Had Frost lied about writing a manuscript? Was he truly friends with the son of a duke?

If he was, how the devil did such disparate worlds collide in this tiny vicarage in a nothing village in a rough bit of the Peak District?

Because of gold. Because of the royal reward. She'd never have come back here—she couldn't think of it as home—if not for the chance to get five thousand pounds for herself and Maggie. And once she did, she'd be a proper maiden aunt to her niece, living in an equally proper village somewhere. Charlotte Pearl, and Charlotte Perry, and Mrs. Smith—they could all vanish. Good riddance to them.

She swooped up her shawl, bonnet, and veil, intending to take them up to Maggie's bedchamber, but a knock sounded at the front door.

"It is he! Earlier than I expected." Her father's knobbly limbs seemed to fly about in all directions.

"That knocking must not be allowed to disturb your mother. She is at a delicate stage in her translations—oh, shall I ring for tea?"

"First we ought to answer the door. Shall I fetch a servant to answer it, or shall I do it myself?"

"Answer it, answer it. Barrett is never about. She *would* hang the washing out to dry, though we've a guest arriving. What will he think, seeing sheets everywhere like a flock of sheep?"

"I do not think he will mind." Charlotte stowed her items under a chair. Summoning a polite smile, she headed toward the door through which she had just passed. A proper greeting was all ready on her lips, with a faint hope that maybe Frost wouldn't recognize her voice at once.

But when the door opened, and she saw the tanned, craggy face she had not expected to encounter again, she found her smile changing from polite to genuine. "Hullo, Mr. Frost."

His brows lifted with surprise, and he smiled, too. "Why, Mrs. Smith. This is an unexpected delight. Are you employed here at the vicarage?"

"About that. Right." Rather than letting him into the small house, she stepped out to join him on the stoop. "Before you enter, there are a few things I ought to tell you."

Chapter Three

"—hereabouts I am known as Miss Perry, maiden daughter of the Reverend John and his wife. I do not live at the vicarage. The good people of Strawfield believe that I spend much of my life traveling to dull corners of the world doing virtuous works."

Benedict nodded, half listening to the words as he sank into the lilt of her voice. Without the ability to admire the traits beloved by most red-blooded males—the curve of a breast, the line of a thigh—he was drawn to the line of a voice as it rose and fell, or the curve of a woman's scent about him. Mrs. Smith-turned-Miss Perry smelled of the breeze, heavy with the promise of rain.

He breathed in deeply, feeling clean-scoured after the winding walk through village to vicarage, broken by many pauses to inquire his way of whomever crossed his path.

For the first time, Hugo's letter of introduction to the Perrys felt like good fortune rather than just another cane on which to rely.

She paused, evidently waiting for a reply, and

Benedict stepped in with a question of his own. "You tell me what the people of Strawfield believe. But how much of that is true—or how much am I meant to believe is true?"

"You are meant to believe what you like, Mr. Frost. It's quite true that I am the daughter of this house, that I was born Miss Perry, and that I return here seldom."

"So the bit about the dull corners of the world, and the virtuous works? Is that *not* true?"

When she replied, he could hear the smile in her voice. "That depends on which parts of the world one considers dull, or the sort of work one considers virtuous."

"Miss Perry, I confess myself intrigued by your notion of virtue."

"When in Strawfield, do as the Strawfielders do, Mr. Frost. My notion of virtue is unassailable at the present moment."

At the present moment, maybe. But Benedict was increasingly curious about all those other moments.

"Mr. Frost." She drew in a deep breath. "I didn't tell you my true name at first because I never expected to see you again."

"Wouldn't that make more sense the other way 'round? People often share the truth in moments of no risk."

"But that does not apply to me. Not here. Charlotte Perry must be connected only to this vicarage and to the blandest of purposes."

Charlotte. At last, his new acquaintance had a Christian name to go with her multiple surnames. He could tell she was of middling height for a woman, and the soft sounds of *Charlotte* coaxed to mind a flaxen fluff of curls, a pert nose, and great blue eyes.

He was probably wrong about all of that. But still. *Charlotte.* He liked knowing her name.

And convoluted though her explanation was, he understood. "While you are in Strawfield, you don't want any of the villagers to recognize you unless you are playing the part of the vicar's daughter."

"Correct. My reasons for being here are the same as yours, Mr. Frost: I seek the stolen coins so that I might claim the royal reward."

"Ah, then we are allies in our shared purpose."

"Or foes in competition with each other."

Damnation. He could not tell if she were jesting or not. "What shall I call you, then, now that I am possessed of the full complement of your names?"

She paused. "Call me Miss Perry while we are at the vicarage. I do not expect we will meet each other anywhere else."

Hmm. He would see about that. "Well, I have the same name everywhere. If you like, you can simply call me Frost. And now may I meet the others in your family?"

"Of course." Her hands made a flutter; air eddied across the backs of his own bare hands. "We've been out on the stoop for too long already; let us go in. Take one step forward, then one up."

Benedict did so. The air closed about him; he extended his fingertips and brushed the frame of a door. "Next?"

"Straight forward for—oh, about three yards. Then a turn to the left. My father awaits you in the front parlor."

"Very good. Lead on, Miss Perry."

She reached behind him to shut the door, then stepped away. The thump of his cane on the floor—it gave the shallow wooden echo of parquet—revealed the accuracy of her words. They were in an entry corridor. Three yards, she told him, then trusted him to find his own way.

Very good indeed.

Charlotte preceded him into the parlor and spoke a few words of introduction. With a gentle pat of pages, her father closed a book.

"Lieutenant Frost, honored to make your acquaintance. That letter of Lord Hugo Starling's—" His voice wavered, as though he were swooping down in a bow, then back up. "Marvelous. A marvelous account of your accomplishments."

Benedict hadn't actually been *told* the content of Hugo's letter. Judging from the vicar's careful bow, it seemed to have omitted an important fact. "Vicar, the honor is mine. Thank you for welcoming me into your household. You'll forgive me, I hope, if I seem not to address you directly? I am quite blind." He gave a laugh that sounded almost genuine. "I suppose Hugo forgot to mention it. He is always doing so."

"You call Lord Hugo by his Christian name . . . Of course. Yes. Any friend of . . ." The Reverend John Perry occupied a slim, tall space. Rustlings told Benedict he was fidgeting with furniture or shuffling his feet on the carpet. Was he unsettled because his guest was not as expected, or was this always his way?

"Did you—ah, truly write a book?" The vicar posed the question delicately.

"I hoped it would be a book. Thus far it is merely a

manuscript. An account of my recent travels through Europe."

"And you—ah, wrote it yourself?"

"Every line of it." Benedict took pity on the reverend's confusion. "I use a device called a noctograph. Later I can show you how it works, if you like. It allows writing in complete darkness."

"Mama would find that helpful for finishing her work when the candle burns to a stub," Charlotte mused.

"It's a wonderful device. If Mrs. Perry is fond of working into dim hours of the day, she might find a noctograph useful," said Benedict. "Is she present? May I make my hostess's acquaintance?"

"Yes, yes! Of course you may," blurted the vicar. "Only—that is—one would not wish to disturb her in her study—"

"My mother will be delighted to meet you as soon as she realizes you have arrived, Mr. Frost. Which might not be at once." Rescued once again by Charlotte.

Benedict smiled. "I'm familiar with scholars, being a friend to Lord Hugo as well as having been raised above a bookshop. A fit of genius is not to be interrupted under any circumstance short of fire or flood."

"And I'm not certain about the flood," replied Charlotte. "In the meantime, would you care for some tea?"

"No, thank you. I was well fortified at the Pig and Blanket."

"What of your trunk? Will it be arriving soon?"

"Held at the Pig and Blanket. The owner promised to have it delivered before the dinner hour."

Reverend Perry spoke up. "Ah, you will want some time to refresh yourself before the meal!" A whisper.

"Charlotte, I do not know whether your mother ordered a dinner."

"I saw to it, Papa. All is settled; we dine at five."

Miss Perry had said she was rarely present at the vicarage? Benedict had only been within its walls for a few minutes, and already he could not imagine how they got along without her.

"Mr. Frost, let me show you to your chamber," she said. Did the vicar make a sound of protest? If so, she spoke over it with a quick farewell that Benedict echoed. He was not going to pass up an opportunity to traipse about with Charlotte Perry.

Once they retraced their steps into the corridor, the close walls trapped her scent. She still reminded him of the breeze, of bright grass, and the promise of rain.

More prosaically, he guessed that she had walked through a field. But prose sometimes fell short.

"My mother's study is at right," Charlotte said. "If she is within, then the door is closed and is not to be opened unless, as you suggested, fire or flood overtakes the earth. She is as fluent in ancient Greek as she is in English, perhaps more so. Her translations are noted around England."

"Indeed. They caught the notice of Lord Hugo."

She seemed indifferent to the name that so impressed her father. "Right. The dining room is farther on, and here are the stairs to mount to the upper floor. Shall I count them?"

"Please."

A few murmurs ensued. "Eighteen," she concluded. "And they're shallow, so place your boots with care.

We've lost more than one tea tray when a servant made a slip."

Arse over teakettle, quite literally. "Noted. Thank you."

He noted, too, that back stairs were not in use by the servants. The vicarage must be an older design, with a single staircase in use by all. The rooms were small, too. On the upper floor of the vicarage, Charlotte directed him to a washroom and demonstrated how to work the pump, the handle of which required a tricky twist. She noted for him the location of the two bedchambers for family, then guided him into the chamber for guests.

"Let me think . . . how shall I orient you to the room? If the door is south—"

"The door faces north."

She was silent for a long beat, during which he imagined her rolling her eyes. "Very well. The door is north. Therefore the fireplace is west. There is no fire at the moment since the day is fine, but you must ring for one whenever you wish. A servant will lay one at night, of course."

From there she oriented him to the essentials of the room. The bed, the washstand with pitcher and ewer. The writing desk and chair.

As she ended this explanation, he heard the faint creak of the door across the passage as it opened and was quickly shut again.

"Is someone else at home?" he asked. "I heard a door."

"That would be Maggie. You shall meet her at dinner. She is my parents' grandchild, a fine girl of ten years."

"Your niece?"

"Indeed. My late sister Margaret's child and name-sake."

A sighted man might have missed the tightness in her voice. But such a man would have instead noted some expression of grief, perhaps. This was a sentence that had hurt her to speak.

"I am sorry for your family's loss," he said.

"Thank you." With the barest of pauses, she spoke again, rapidly. "The bell-pull is at right. To the north of the bed. To close the bed-curtains or window-curtains, you can simply—"

"Miss Perry. Please. Stop. You have explained all I could desire, and more." As though he would need to adjust the window-curtains! Not since his sight failed, darkening day by day, had he cared whether the sun was covered or not.

She stilled. Sat on the bed, the mattress's ropes creaking. Then sprang up again. "I'll leave you to rest until dinner, Mr. Frost."

She was agitated; she had been since mentioning her sister and her niece. He wanted to put her at her ease again. "Wait, please."

Her tread across the floorboards halted.

"What color is . . . everything?"

"Pardon?"

"The counterpane. The curtains. What does it look like?" He hesitated. "I lost my sight only four years ago. I . . . miss the details of appearance."

Her steps came closer again. "I gave you an incomplete picture, didn't I? All line and no color."

"Spoken like an artist."

"Good heavens, no. But I've spent a fair amount of time around those volatile creatures." She cleared her throat. "Ah—are you fond of art yourself? Or . . . were you, once?"

"No more than most. Painting is lost to me now. Though if I can arrange for a friend to distract a museum guard, I still enjoy running my hands over a good sculpture."

The throat-clearing turned into a splutter—and then a laugh. "What higher honor for an artist than to have his piece groped?"

Benedict smiled. He was quite sure artists enjoyed having their pieces groped as much as any other man. And from the way Charlotte posed the question, he suspected this was exactly the joke she intended.

Footsteps crossed the floor, and then she stood at his side. "Neither of us is an artist, but we'll rub along well enough. With my description of the room, I mean."

"I knew exactly what you meant," Benedict said drily.

"Where to begin? Well, the washstand is a dark walnut. It's scarred on the top where it has been scraped hundreds of times as the pitcher and ewer were dragged free, emptied, and replaced. They are glazed white, and the window is draped in olive. Outside of the window, one has a view of the Selwyn lands. We are on the edge of the moors, but he has some fine grazing land."

"And Selwyn is?"

She spoke lightly, drawing away. "Edward Selwyn is the local squire, as well as one of those volatile artistic creatures I mentioned. The Selwyns are the most notable landowners hereabouts."

He stretched out a hand and found a bedpost. "And the bed? What does it look like?"

"The coverlet is patchwork, pieced in floral patterns and pale silks. The frame is the same dark walnut as the washstand, but in better condition. The knobs in here often get polished."

He had to work to keep a straight face. "Of the bedstead, you mean. Of course."

"Why, what else could I possibly mean?"

"I cannot fathom." This was flirtation—but why him, why now? He almost asked to touch her face. She was the missing piece in this chamber, a sculpture unfelt amidst bed, washstand, desk.

But if he began to touch her, he would not want to stop. How tempting it would be to trail his fingers over the planes of her face, to trace the line of her neck and collarbone. To cover her breast with his hand, to breathe in the scent of her bare skin. She was no maiden, not with her secrets and sly bawdy jokes.

If he asked to touch her, she might say yes.

He must not ask. He sought money, not a tumble. There was no reward in attaching a woman to one-self, whether for a day or a week or a lifetime.

"Would it be too forward . . ." He pressed at the bridge of his nose. "Would—what do you look like?"

"Does it matter, Mr. Frost?" She sounded wary.

Perhaps he ought to have said no. But: "Surely it matters at least as much as the nicks atop the wash-stand, and you told me of them readily enough."

"A solid rebuttal." She sighed. "You have taken the measure of my height, I am sure. My hair is as dark as yours, and as straight as yours is not."

So, his hair was still dark. Benedict remembered his father's head threaded with gray well before the age of thirty, and he had wondered if his was changing similarly.

The shade of one's hair seemed an odd thing not to know.

"What color are your eyes?" he asked.

"Green, though not a stunning shade thereof. And before you ask, I do not have freckles. My nose is of a middling size, and I have all my own teeth."

"What an attractive recital," he murmured. This jumble of facts left him no idea what she looked like, though it was clear his impression of cloudy mildness was entirely wrong. Charlotte Perry was the Derbyshire breeze in human form: invigorating and stronger than one was prepared for.

"Have you any other questions before I leave you?"

"None that I dare ask at present." He pasted on a roguish smile. Let her puzzle that one out.

A sharp knock echoed up the stairwell, and Charlotte took a quick step toward the doorway. "Likely that is your trunk from the Pig and Blanket—and the servants are all over the place with laundry and dinner. As it often is here. Shall I descend to speak with the innkeeper, Mr. Frost, or would you like to?"

"I don't wish to interrupt if it's a family caller. Here. I'll follow you to the stairs and can come down if needed." He counted off the steps from bedchamber to staircase, touching the wall only once to remind himself where the passage wall was split by a doorway.

Charlotte descended the eighteen narrow steps ahead of him; from the corridor below, her voice mingled with that of her father's. The vicar's voice ended: ". . . cannot let the knocking bother your mother," and the front door was hauled open.

"Vicar, y'er needed!" The voice was indeed that of the Pig and Blanket's owner, a man with the local accent and a slight wheeze. "At once, y'er needed at the inn. At once."

Charlotte spoke up, sounding puzzled. "Mr. Potter. Have you brought Mr. Frost's—"

"I need the vicar." The man cut her off with a ragged insistence. "Nance, my serving girl—she's been stabbed. Constable's been told, and the Bow Street Runner, and a doctor, and there's nothing they can do to help her. Vicar—come say a few prayers over the poor lamb, will you, in case she perishes."

Chapter Four

From the upstairs corridor, hinges creaked, though not loudly enough to cover a soft cry.

"Maggie heard that," Charlotte murmured, a cold prickle racing down her spine. "Excuse me, Papa. Mr. Potter, you have my deepest sympathies. I shall pray for Nance's recovery."

She was fluent in polite language; she could speak it, could curtsy even, as her attention flew to the girl upstairs. Her feet followed as she cursed each one of the eighteen shallow steps, brushed past the tall figure of Mr. Frost, and eased into the small bed-chamber she would be sharing with the girl who called her Aunt Charlotte.

Maggie sat beside the bed, a thin figure in a tidy printed gown. Her legs were folded sedately, but her wild tumble of light brown curls still shook, betraying her swift movement to the door and back.

Next to her was curled the familiar old figure of Captain, a rangy brindled hound of some fifteen years. Captain was stiff and slow, her brown-and-browner coat now graying. Maggie petted the dog's head, her own face downcast and hidden behind her fallen hair.

Charlotte seated herself on the bed. It was narrower than Mr. Frost's, but overspread with the same sort of quilt. She and her older sister had pieced them both as teens, months of delicate work throughout which Charlotte had hated every tidy stitch. She was glad for them now, though.

Her feet touched the floor beside Maggie. If she dared reach out, she could lace her fingers through the girl's hair. She could pet her, comfort her, maybe, as Maggie petted Captain.

Or maybe the one she'd be comforting was herself.

"You heard what Mr. Potter said, didn't you, dearest?" she asked.

A mute, miserable nod.

Charlotte sighed and ventured a pat on Maggie's shoulder. A half-grown girl seemed so fragile, her bones slight. But ten years was much too old to allow oneself to be cradled, or to be wrapped in a doting embrace.

So Charlotte only patted her again, feeling far away.

"Will Nance be all right?" A small voice issued from behind the wall of curly hair. "I thought she was nice."

Charlotte could well imagine what Maggie thought of Nance. She remembered being ten years old, stick-thin and awkward with promise. At that age, a blowsy, vibrant young woman such as Nance seemed the loveliest creature in the world.

"She was nice, wasn't she? *Is* nice," Charlotte corrected herself. "Mr. Potter said someone hurt her badly. But he has called a doctor, and Papa—Grandpapa—will help her to be at peace."

Maggie's only response was to pet the dark velvet of Captain's ears. The aged hound thumped her tail and settled her long head in Maggie's lap.

Though Charlotte had named Captain at the age of thirteen when her father brought home the puppy, the skittish hound had always been Margaret's dog. The elder Perry sister had named the second puppy, an Irish Water spaniel with a curly liver-brown coat and a tail that whipped like that of a donkey. Frippery was calm and loyal, with a menacing bark and no bite whatsoever.

He became Charlotte's chum for loping around Strawfield and slipping onto the Selwyn lands to explore the caves there. Margaret was happier at home, where Captain was often to be found curled at her feet alongside her work basket of quilt pieces.

Frippery had been gone for years. Charlotte had been long away. Margaret had sickened within a year of her marriage, following her young husband to the grave.

All that was left was this girl with her name and the hound that linked them. And the same vicarage, where her parents grew grayer and more absent each year.

The walls were still papered in the tiny flowered print from Charlotte's own youth, but a new shelf hung above the bed. Books were stacked upon it, and a small tin horse. Time marched on. Maggie was changing. It seemed unbearable that Charlotte should not know Maggie's favorite book, or that she had not shared the girl's joy over acquiring the toy horse.

Charlotte blinked her eyes dry, then swallowed

hard. She must sound calm and pleasant. "You know I'm to stay with you in your room, don't you?"

Another quick nod. "Why are you here?"

For you. For us. "I had—been away too long." This was not quite an answer, but it was close enough for the present. "Do you remember the last time I visited?"

"I think so. I was only six then." Childish fingers combed through the coarse fur of the hound's back. "You plaited my hair with silk ribbons?"

"I did. With green, to match your eyes." Charlotte closed her lips on further words. How many nights had she climbed into bed in the four years since, praying to dream about that brief visit? *Lord, please, let me see her again, if only in sleep. Let me remember the feel of her hair, the softness of her cheek.*

How it felt to seat her in my lap, to hold her like the precious girl she has always been to me.

"I thought you were nice." Lifting her hand from Captain's back, Maggie pushed back her unbound hair. Tentatively, she glanced over her shoulder.

Young Maggie Catlett was going to be a beauty, some had said. Rot and rubbish. She was already a beauty. Had been a beauty from the day of her birth.

"I thought you were nice, too." Charlotte smiled.

Maggie turned forward again—but she scooted a few inches across the floor, closer to Charlotte's skirts, despite Captain's whine of protest.

"I am not sure how long I can stay," said Charlotte. "But may I write to you once I go? I should like to have a friend with whom to exchange letters."

The girl nodded, then tipped another curious glance over her shoulder. Her brows were straight and thoughtful over Perry-green eyes. "Why do you not write to Grandmama and Grandpapa?"

Somehow Charlotte managed a laugh. "Oh, they know enough about me already."

Too much, really. For the past ten years, since Charlotte had first left Strawfield, it was enough for her parents to know that she was alive and sufficiently far away so as not to embarrass them. She did write to them, but rarely did she receive a reply. She wondered whether they read her letters at all.

Plucking at a loose thread in a quilt block—one of her own resentful stitches, no doubt—she said, "I shall brush and plait your hair tonight, if you like. You may choose the silk ribbons; I've brought many colors from"—*London*, she almost said—"my travels."

"And will you tell me about the places you've been?"

"Oh . . . you might find them dull. But I'll tell you stories. How is that?" The stories would be the bare bits of truth of her life, as much as would be appropriate for a child's ears. She could speak of evenings of wine and wit, of a house papered all in gold and furnished in red, and of a princess with many suitors who could choose none.

She could not bear the idea of lying to Maggie about what she'd made of herself. Nor, however, could she tell the girl the truth.

While she stayed in this room, she must try not to show too much feeling. She must not let the weight of every missed day with Maggie bow her shoulders, or strip from her the joy of the present. If Charlotte could find the stolen coins—if she could claim the reward of five thousand pounds—there would be no more regrets.

Her London life had paid well, but only well enough to finance her escape. Her house in Mayfair was now an empty shell, almost everything else converted into money, handed out in bribes. She had returned to Strawfield with a few trunks, not much more than what she had taken to London a decade before. Barely a woman at eighteen, immortalized on Edward Selwyn's canvases, fallen in heart and body.

Charlotte's chest felt heavy, and she breathed deeply to settle the old weight into its familiar position. "I must go now, to see how dinner preparations are getting on." As good an excuse as any for giving them both a bit of space. "Your grandpapa will be tired and sad when he returns home. We can at least feed him well, hmm?"

She rose from the bed, then crouched next to the girl. Stroking back the hair that fell over Maggie's face, soft as silk thread, she asked, "All right?"

The piquant little face frowned—then Maggie nodded. "May I bring Captain down to dinner, Aunt Charlotte?"

"She's not usually allowed in the dining room, is she? Best not. But she can wait in the corridor just outside. It's nice to know an old friend is nearby, isn't it?" Charlotte smiled.

When Maggie managed a small return of the expression, Charlotte rose to her feet and exited the small chamber.

Benedict Frost stood outside the door of the spare chamber, wearing an expression of doubt that clashed with the assured lines of his uniform. "Miss Perry?"

"Yes." She closed the distance between them. "What can I help you with, Mr. Frost?"

He lowered his voice, no more than a faint tickle

of sound in her ear. "An answer. Please believe I do not mean to pry; I only seek not to blunder."

Chill wariness touched between her shoulder blades. "Of course," she replied equally low.

"Is Miss Maggie aware that you are her mother?"

Benedict did not regret asking Charlotte the question, though he guessed it would break the easy flirtation into which they had fallen.

Charlotte's hand clutched his sleeve, a spasmodic gesture of alarm, and pushed him into his own chamber. "No," she whispered, shutting the door behind them. "No, she does not know. How could you be . . . how did you realize?"

He couldn't say, exactly. As he'd made to return to his chamber once Charlotte entered Maggie's, he had overheard her speak to the girl. Her voice was different, like a string plucked that ran straight to her heart. It harmonized with the way she had spoken of her supposed niece earlier.

"I heard in your voice how much you loved her," he tried to explain.

It was a tone of yearning for something that was already present, a yearning so deep it could not be satisfied. He couldn't think of anything he had wanted that much in his life. Wanting in the negative—to leave England, to undo his blindness—was not the same thing as treasuring another creature so deeply that one's voice shimmered like gold.

The frantic grip on his arm relaxed. "If she hears love in my voice, that cannot be a bad thing. But she is not to know of—the other. Known as the child of my sister, who was wed, Maggie is legitimate. Her life's path will be easier."

He wanted to take up her hand, to hold it in his own. "And yours?"

"The best thing I can do for my daughter is to be her aunt." The words were heavy with sadness—but also determination.

He flicked his fingers out, just a whisper of a touch against the back of her hand. "You are brave, Miss Perry."

"I am what I have had to be, Mr. Frost." Her hand turned beneath his, and for a second they were palm against palm. "As are you."

And then the door opened, and she left.

"I hope it was no inconvenience to travel to Cheshire. I have summoned you here as an admirer of your work." The Marquess of Randolph leaned back in the chair behind his study's desk, regarding Edward with hooded eyes.

"Yes, my lord," Edward Selwyn murmured. "I mean— no, my lord. No inconvenience. I am honored."

So honored, he hardly knew what he was saying. The Cheshire seat of the Randolph marquessate was everything he had imagined luxury to be. Where the floors in his Strawfield home were wood or slate, these were marble. His own walls were carved wood or hung with paper; the Randolph chimneypieces were marble and the walls were swaddled in painted silks.

And best of all, in a place of honor behind the marquess's desk, hung one of Edward's paintings. It was a small figure in oils inspired by Botticelli, depicting a

Venus pudica arising from the sea. One of Edward's early works, but still a favorite of his.

"I am honored," Edward repeated, trying to sound both respectful and confident, "that my art has come to your attention. It would be my pleasure to paint your portrait, my lord."

Randolph's pockets were deep, and there was no denying the man was powerful. This, at last, could be the patronage he had been waiting for. He'd be the next Gainsborough, the next Lawrence.

"A portrait isn't precisely what I had in mind." A decanter of brandy and a pair of glasses sat on the marquess's desk. Randolph poured out a generous measure into each glass, then handed one to Edward. "I was thinking of an exhibition of your work. A private one."

The brandy stung Edward's nose. He'd arrived only an hour ago and was hoping for a cold luncheon of some sort. It was early, surely, for drinking brandy. But marquesses kept to their own schedule.

He took a small sip. "Excellent brandy. And an excellent idea, too, to arrange an exhibition. I know a gallery in London that would—"

"I haven't settled on a place yet, but I rather think it will . . . not be London."

Edward blinked. "Well . . . the Royal Academy exhibits in London. If the purpose is to. . ." He coughed. "To promote an artist's work, then that would be the most logical—"

"Ah. Well." Randolph folded his hands. Edward noticed the marquess hadn't touched his brandy and quickly set down his own glass. "What I'm looking for, to be honest, is information. About your model."

Somehow the nobleman's stillness guided Edward's

eyes back up to the painting behind the desk. To the Venus, dark-haired, her straight locks like a waterfall over her bare body, revealing as much as they cloaked. About her neck winked a necklace in diamonds and emeralds, her only garment.

"If you tell me what I need to know," added Randolph, "then I'll see to that exhibition."

Edward hesitated. Since his marriage to an earl's daughter eight years before, he had grown used to having few secrets. Really, there was only one.

Randolph lifted his glass at last. "Regardless of its location, I promise the result will be to your advantage."

A new Lawrence. A new Turner. As good as Gainsborough.

Edward took up his own glass and clinked it against Randolph's. "What would you like to know?"

Chapter Five

Dinner represented Benedict's first acquaintance with both Maggie and Mrs. Perry. Upon entering the dining room, he made a bow to the vicar's grandchild as though she were a grown woman, recalling how much his sister, Georgette, had enjoyed being treated so during her girlhood.

"Mr. Frost," Maggie replied. "I am giving you my finest curtsy."

"I have no doubt of it." He smiled, then turned toward the doorway as another set of footsteps entered the room.

"Ah, the blind traveler," said an unfamiliar female voice. "Welcome to my husband's vicarage, Mr. Frost. Let me think—the usual sort of greeting won't make you feel welcome if you can't see it. Shall we shake hands?"

"If you like, yes." Benedict extended a hand. "Though your words of welcome are fine enough for me."

Knowing the vicar's wife to be dedicated to scholarship, he had expected an ethereal creature with the dreamy voice of the perpetually distracted. Instead, Charlotte's mother possessed a matter-of-fact tone and a remarkably firm grip.

"Be seated, everyone," said Mrs. Perry. "Frost, stick out your left hand and you'll take hold of the chair. That's right. We can begin our meal now. No reason to wait for the vicar with all this food ready to eat."

Benedict thought a man attending to a serving girl's last moments of life ought at least to come home to a hot dinner and the sympathy of his family. But rather than gainsay his hostess, he found the chair to which he'd been directed, and a slide and scrape of furniture ensued as the three generations of females took their places. Charlotte and Maggie, he gathered, were across from him, and their hostess sat at one end.

Service was the usual *à la française,* with all the foods laid out on the table. He caught the aroma of roasted beef, of some vegetable in a peppery, buttery sauce.

"Mr. Frost," said Charlotte, "shall I describe the dishes around the compass?"

"Do you recall which way is north?" He could not resist teasing her.

"Oh, good heavens—that is too difficult for one who hasn't a lodestone in her head. What of describing the table like a clock face?" When he agreed, she said, "There's a joint of mutton at nine o'clock to you, and a fish at three."

On she went, describing the vegetables, and Benedict did a creditable job serving his own dinner just as the others did. Once he missed the dish of peas and scrabbled for nothing, but someone pushed the dish toward him without a word.

It was a simple dinner, but well-cooked. And it was rather nice to be taken care of. On board a ship, one had nothing fresh to eat, little leisure, and even less space. Nothing to oneself save one's thoughts.

When Benedict had consumed about half the contents of his plate, the vicarage door opened. The usual fumblings ensued: greatcoat removed, hat stowed, boots scraped. Then came a heavy thump, as of a piece of furniture being moved. Quiet words, then the shutting of the door again.

A few seconds later, the light tread of the Reverend John Perry entered the dining room. "Oh—you have begun your meal without me."

"Everything was hot, Vicar," said his wife. "You wouldn't have wanted us to waste the good work of the cook, I'm sure."

"Right, right. No, of course not. Frost, a servant brought your trunk over from the Pig and Blanket."

That explained the thump. Benedict offered thanks, then added, "How is . . . Nance?" He realized he didn't know her last name.

"She's at peace now, poor girl." The vicar settled himself in the empty seat at the head of the table. "There will have to be an inquest. The coroner is convening a jury. I shall be called as a witness."

No one could have missed the strain in his voice.

Or in Maggie's. "Are you in trouble, Grandpapa? Will you have to leave us?"

"Not in trouble, my girl. My help is needed with answering questions." The vicar collected a plateful of food along with his thoughts. "I can't think what the coroner will want to know, though. I'll describe the scene, I suppose. The prayers—will they want me to remember the prayers I said, Mrs. Perry? I do not recall . . . I was agitated, you know, and I might have stumbled over the words."

"I cannot imagine your exact words relevant, Papa," said Charlotte quietly. "They will want to know only that you were there at the time of her passing."

"But her hands—Potter wanted me to fold her hands across her breast once she expired. Can it matter? I hesitated—but I should not have, to offer Potter comfort. I did so, of course. He was right."

"Her family will have to be notified," said Mrs. Perry.

"She has no family," said the vicar. "She was orphaned three years ago, and that was when she began her work serving at the inn."

"Her family is Strawfield," said Charlotte. "She will be greatly missed by the habitués of the Pig and Blanket."

"One of them likely did the . . . the act." The vicar chose his words carefully. "The terrible act. Nance had little to say about that—she had weakened and fallen out of her wits. I couldn't make sense of what she said."

What did she say? Benedict wanted to ask, though he supposed it would be callous.

"I wish I had gone with you to translate, then," said Mrs. Perry.

"It was not another language," corrected the vicar. "No, she only said 'cat eye' and 'cloak' a few times, and she shivered. Cold, I suppose, as the life drained from her . . . ." He trailed off.

Charlotte broke in. "You must be hungry for your dinner, Papa. We'll talk of it later."

"Must we?" The reverend sounded tense, reluctant.

"No, not if you don't wish to." Charlotte paused;

when she spoke again, the color of her voice was warmer. "Maggie, would you care for peas or potatoes?"

"I want to pet Captain." This, Benedict had gathered, was a beloved old hound.

"After dinner, dearest."

This was the last Benedict heard from the girl at table. Since he did not hear her chair drawn back, she must have stayed. Maybe even ate her food.

Maggie didn't mind having someone to look after her, it seemed. With the grandfather anxious and the grandmother more concerned with the ancient past than the present, Benedict wouldn't be surprised if Maggie spent more time with servants than with her relatives.

He had done the same himself. In boyhood, surrounded by books that seemed to mock him for his difficulty deciphering their wiggling, shifting letters, he'd often fled to the kitchen.

Yes, he had been sick for home his first time aboard ship, but not in the sense that he wanted to return to live amidst his parents' books. No, he missed being in a space where one felt at ease, surrounded by the clink of crockery and the splash of dishes being cleaned; of voices calm and orderly. Of errands, fetching and carrying, and the praise heaped on one for completing a task well that one did not have to do.

That old kitchen was a boyish vision of home, but it was the last one he'd had. He wondered if he'd ever have a vision of home again.

"Mr. Frost." The vicar's wife interrupted these thoughts with her efficient accent. "You have written a book, your friend said in his letter."

"Lord Hugo," Perry corrected. "His friend is Lord Hugo Starling, though Mr. Frost calls him by his Christian name." His tone was equal parts awe and reproach, and Benedict smiled.

"Indeed. Lord Hugo and I met in Edinburgh, the year after I was blinded. We were both studying medicine—he because he has quite the quickest mind ever, and wanted to be filling it with a new subject. I, because I knew I could no longer serve in the navy and wanted something to do with myself."

"But surely," said Mrs. Perry, "you could not practice as a physician. Not without your sight."

"Correct, ma'am. I knew I would not be able to do so, but it was better than sitting in my quiet chamber in Windsor Castle."

"A castle," murmured the vicar. "You lived in a castle, and you are a friend of Lord Hugo Starling."

Benedict cleared his throat. "Yes, well, that all sounds a lot grander than it really was. Castles are dank and their chambers are small, and as a Naval Knight of Windsor, I'm bound there in return for my pension."

"Yet you seem not to be in Windsor Castle at present," Charlotte pointed out.

"This is quite correct. I've been granted a leave of absence. More than once." *Thank God.* Yes, he was grateful for the room and board and a few pounds on which to live—but it certainly came attached to strings aplenty.

"My time in Edinburgh was courtesy of such a leave of absence," he explained. "But eventually I felt the urge to do something more than pick up knowledge for its own sake. Which was why I left off studying after a year and began hunting for something else to do."

"And on what did you settle?" asked Charlotte.

"Traveling."

"What good is that?" Mrs. Perry, this time.

"What good is the world, you ask? I cannot say until I have been to every corner of it."

He could hear the smile in Charlotte's voice when she asked, "Which corners have you been to? And what did you find there?"

"Ah, interesting items are to be found tucked away in corners. Though the ones I've been to are not so rare. Truthfully, the book I've written—well, I shouldn't call it a book, as for now it's only a sheaf of hand-written papers—is notable only in that it was written by a blind man."

"That cannot be," Charlotte replied, "for it was written by a former sailor who also studied medicine. There are not many such people about."

He liked hearing himself described so. *Tell me more*, he wanted to say. *What else have you noticed about me?*

"How did you write the manuscript without the benefit of sight?" asked the vicar's wife.

"A noctograph." Perry sounded pleased to con-tribute something. "A marvelous device that allows one to write in the dark."

"Indeed?" Mrs. Perry's voice took on a lilt of interest. "I should like to learn how it works, Mr. Frost."

"I will show it to you after dinner," promised Bene-dict. Since his trunk now rested within the entry of the vicarage, he again had all his possessions about him, including the noctograph.

And his manuscript, which had, over the past

fortnight, begun to seem far less precious in the face of the London publishing world's dismissal.

But maybe theirs were not the only opinions to which he should give weight. As Charlotte had said, how many physician-sailor-explorers could there be in the world? His was a unique tale.

He simply had to find someone who wanted him to tell it.

After dinner, Maggie retrieved the dog, Captain, from outside the dining room door and took her—for Benedict had been informed Captain was female—outside for a walk. As the click of canine claws sounded on the parquet of the entryway, Benedict mounted the by-now-familiar eighteen stairs, bumping his trunk up each one. Settling it at the foot of the bedstead whose knobs had been so frequently polished, he unlocked the trunk and felt through tidy stacks of clothing. Tucked within to cushion it was the noctograph.

He carried it back downstairs, directing his steps toward the sound of voices. They had moved into the parlor in which he had met the vicar earlier.

When he entered the room, he smiled by way of greeting. "Who would like the first look at the noctograph?"

"Mrs. Perry must see it first," said the solemn voice of the vicar.

"She is sitting beside my father," added Charlotte.

Without his cane or a few moments' leisure to feel his way about, Benedict was unsure of the arrangement of the room's furniture. He stepped in the direction of the vicar's voice, noctograph extended, praying like hell that no ottomans or tea tables arose to bark against his shins.

None did, and Mrs. Perry's capable hands took the device from Benedict. "Show me how it works, Mr. Frost."

All business and no sentimentality. He much preferred that to the reverse. And in truth, he liked demonstrating the workings of the noctograph. It had allowed him, for the first time in his life, to master the written word.

Soft footsteps crossed the room behind him; Charlotte had approached, then, to peer over his shoulder. He showed the family trio what appeared at first to be a wooden lap-desk. Once opened, it revealed a straight-ruled metal frame behind which paper could be slipped. The paper itself was of a special sort, inked all over so that any pressure made a marking. Using a stylus and the guidance of the metal rules, one could mark out words in neat rows.

"I have been told that my writing is tidier now than it was before I lost my sight." By way of example, Benedict clipped in a sheet of inked paper and scratched out a few words. *Dear Georgette.* "My sister," he explained. "I must write to her and tell her of my safe arrival."

"Does she worry about you?" asked Charlotte.

"She is much my junior, so I think the reverse is true far more often. If she sends a reply, perhaps one of you will be good enough to read it to me?"

"Of course," Charlotte said as Mrs. Perry again took possession of the noctograph. "I should like to read some of your manuscript about your travels, too. There are so many corners of the world I have never seen."

A careful dance about her story that she spent her life performing good works around the globe. He was curious how much of it was a fiction. "You're welcome to read it," he said. "Maybe you could read some out to me. I'm not sure at this distance in time how I put down my experiences. I have the deuce of a time editing my work, as I'm sure you can imagine."

"I must order one of these for evening work," decided Mrs. Perry. "You know, Mr. Frost, Tiresias was blind."

"I'm sorry, I do not know the name."

"The mythical Theban prophet of ancient Greece. He was struck blind by a goddess, but in return he received the gift of prophecy."

"Would that I had been granted such a gift," Benedict said lightly. "I receive only half pay from the Royal Navy and a small pension from the Naval Knights."

"Along with a room in Windsor Castle," added the vicar.

Mrs. Perry ignored these interjections. "It's a fascinating tale. Either the ancient Greeks had finer imaginations than we do, or the world was far more interesting in their time. Tiresias was blinded after being asked to settle an argument between Zeus and Hera as to whether—"

"May I see the noctograph now?" interrupted Charlotte. "Thank you, Mama. Just hand it over your shoulder—yes, I have hold of it."

Now, why had she interrupted her mother?

Perhaps she was overcome by curiosity about the noctograph. He liked the idea that she was fascinated by the ways in which he adapted the world to suit himself.

The newly expert Mrs. Perry spent the next few

minutes showing Charlotte how the noctograph worked. Then the older woman asked, "How did you lose your sight, Mr. Frost?"

Since the question seemed to be asked not with prurience but with the same scholarly curiosity that marked her every other query, he did not mind answering. "A tropical fever encountered in the Americas. I do not know its name, but it felled people in different ways. Some went lame; some died. I had great pain in my joints, and then in my head. And then my vision began to deteriorate."

They were all silent for a moment in the face of this dispassionate recital. Charlotte was the first to speak. "Do you still suffer from the other pains?"

"No, they went, too. Which was a small consolation."

His calm stripped from his words the nightmare of those days. Of the ship turned into a floating sickroom, of the slightest bit of sun like a knife to his eyes, and more and more covers hung over the tiny window to block out a pain that could not, in the end, be stopped. Darkness crept inward until the world was a tunnel, its end spotted and dim.

Beyond, there was no more light at all.

All the way back to England, he grieved. For the loss of his sight, for the end of his days sailing about the world.

When the ship docked, he put an end to such wallowing. With the help of his captain, he applied for a pension. On receiving the first installment, he bought himself a hickory cane with a metal tip and began learning his way through the world by sound.

And the more he learned of it, the more he wanted to learn. *What good is that?* the vicar's wife had asked.

He could not answer that, but there was value in the search for an answer, surely.

There had to be. There had to be value in any type of search, for otherwise what was the point of so much of life?

Now that the young barmaid, Nance, had lost her life, he wondered anew. There was more to seeking the royal reward than asking questions and poking about in crannies.

There was danger in this particular search, and not of the sort from which one could protect oneself with feigned blitheness and a metal-tipped cane.

Chapter Six

After having a look at the noctograph, Charlotte left the others inside and stood on the stoop, searching out Maggie. Daylight was fading, and the road was a dusky ribbon. The short strip of lawn between vicarage and road was covered with coarse grass, across which Maggie backed, waggling a stick before Captain.

Charlotte spread her shawl and sat upon it. "Stay away from the Selwyn lands," she called.

The girl nodded. She tossed the stick, and Captain's head listed with interest—but the old hound's flesh was weak, and she could do no more than trot in the direction of the thrown stick, beloved young mistress alongside.

Four years before, when she'd last visited Strawfield, Charlotte had made the mistake of bringing along a puppy. It was a curly-coated *Pudel* she had coaxed from a German admirer; she had been fascinated by its unusual appearance. After tying a great blue silk bow around its neck, she'd presented the fluffy black and white dog to Maggie. *He will keep you company, dearest, in case anything happens to Captain.*

Maggie did not stop crying until the puppy was taken from the vicarage.

Charlotte brought it to the only other person who could be permitted to know of the *Pudel*'s origins: Edward Selwyn, whose visit to Strawfield unhappily coincided with hers. He promised that his children would love it. This earned him the sort of withering glance such a remark deserved, and he laughed. "My *other* children."

Another withering glance. She had asked Edward time and again never to speak of such matters, especially since his marriage to the frosty Lady Helena.

The other dog of Charlotte's youth, Frippery, had loved her. Captain had for Charlotte only the sort of vague fondness a dog had for anyone who treated it well. And Maggie's was the human equivalent: that dutiful liking a child possessed for a relative one hardly knew.

If Charlotte could make Captain love her, though, perhaps Maggie's love would follow.

"May I throw the stick for her?" she called.

Maggie hesitated, shoving unruly hair back from her face. "I'm not done yet, Aunt Charlotte. I want to throw it some more."

"Oh." Charlotte smiled, hiding the pain that was much larger than the small size of the girl's *no*. "That's fine. You throw very well."

Maggie tossed the stick into the air and caught it, then ran closer to Charlotte. "I taught Captain some tricks. Want to see? She can lie down whenever I say the words."

Many other times, too, Charlotte thought, as the old hound rolled onto her belly.

"Oh, look! She must have heard what I said." Maggie walked back to stand above her pet. "Up, girl! Up to catch the stick, Captain!"

As Captain heaved herself up, the front door opened, and a booted tread descended onto the stoop. "That dog outranks me. I feel I ought to salute her."

Charlotte smiled. "Hullo, Mr. Frost. I don't think Captain will care if you salute her, but Maggie would like it."

"Your mother is not yet ready to surrender the noctograph back to my keeping. May I join you?"

"Please. I have spread a shawl on the grass, if you would care to sit beside me."

Without pause or hesitation, he took the single step down and strode toward her. He was a noticing sort of man, and a remembering sort, too. It seemed no detail went unfiled or forgotten, and he made his way through the world with unassuming grace.

Twenty-four hours ago, she had not known this man. Now he was in possession of her greatest secret.

Well, one of them.

She did not know what sort of person he was. But she thought—she hoped—that he would hold her trust as the fragile, precious thing it was.

When he folded himself onto the shawl beside her, her breath came a little more quickly, her stays tight about her breasts.

"Miss Perry," he murmured, "I rescued some gristly beef from the kitchen before coming outdoors. May I offer it to the hound?"

Thus winning the heart of both beast and girl. If

only Charlotte had thought of that. "What a good idea. Of course. A dog of Captain's age should have treats aplenty."

He pulled forth a napkin-wrapped bundle. "Miss Maggie! Sir!"

"I'm no 'sir'!" Maggie tossed the stick again, then darted to the shawl and peered down at the pair of adults, panting slightly from her exertion. "Why did you call me 'sir,' Mr. Frost?"

"I called your dog by that honorific," Frost said gravely. "She is a Captain, and therefore she is my superior and I must refer to her with respect."

"Sir." Maggie laughed. "That's a silly thing to call a girl."

"Maybe so. But would Sir like some beef?" He pushed forward the small packet. "Your aunt thought she would."

"Aunt Charlotte! What a treat for her! Oh, thank you. She wouldn't eat anything earlier today, but she'll like this." Swooping down on the beef, Maggie carried the small package several yards over to the stiff-legged Captain. The hound's heavy ears lifted, and she nosed through the napkin to find the meat.

Maggie laughed to watch her—not a sound of humor, but of someone taking delight in watching a beloved creature feel joy.

Charlotte chuckled for the same reason. "Mr. Frost," she said low enough that Maggie couldn't overhear, "that was sly of you to imply the beef was my idea. I thank you."

"My pleasure. As a traveler, I'm in people's lives for only a moment, so I might as well hand along any goodwill that comes my way." His tone was a little wistful—or maybe she was only imagining she heard the feeling that dwelled in her own heart.

"There's nothing she loves better than Captain. I believe she thinks of that dog as a living link to her mother."

There, she'd said the *m*-word as though it were nothing significant.

"My sister," she added. "Of course. The late Margaret Perry Catlett."

"I knew what you meant."

Charlotte slapped at an insect, then picked at the tasseled edge of the shawl spread beneath them. Captain seemed revived by the food and followed Maggie's tossed stick at a tolerable lope, the girl following behind until she was nothing but silhouette and laugh.

When Frost turned his face to hers, his expression held a pinch of roguery. "When your mother began telling me about the blind prophet Tiresias, you turned her away from some anecdote. I'm curious as to why. Would you be willing to tell me?" The way he posed the question meant she had simply to say *no*, if she wished.

This made it much easier to say *yes*. "Although I warn you that it's rather scandalous. Mama doesn't always think of such things, but I knew it would give my father the vapors."

As a vicar's wife, Mrs. Perry ought to spend more time with villagers and less time with ancient prophets. Every time Charlotte visited, though, the balance had tipped further awry, and her parents seemed more distant from each other. Now they were cordial housemates who had little in common. Surely it had not always been thus? Or maybe she remembered through the rosy glass of her own youthful blitheness, when all seemed full of promise and potential.

"I cannot swear not to do the same. I'm easily shocked. I might need you to hold my hand to comfort me afterward."

She had thought him possessed of a *pinch* of roguery? Benedict Frost had it by the cupful.

"Yet somehow I feel you will survive." She drew up her knees, folding her arms around them. "The story—which, I am slightly shocked to admit I learned from my mother—is that Tiresias was punished for some trespass against the gods by being transformed into a woman."

"On behalf of present company, I find that insulting."

"Yes, I never liked that either. But the ancient Greeks thought even less of women than does our present society."

"Well, that is not so lascivious a tale as I feared."

"Hoped for, you mean?" Charlotte teased. "That is not the part that will give you the vapors. Once Tiresias was a man again, he was asked to settle an argument between Zeus and Hera as to whether . . ." Was she blushing? Surely not. Nothing had made her blush for a decade. "As to whether men or women derived more pleasure from the marital act."

Frost leaned back upon his elbows and laughed. "And I thought Londoners would bet on anything. Those old Greeks may have them beaten. I probably shouldn't ask what the answer was, but I've got to."

"Women. Tiresias was blinded by Hera for noting

this, but Zeus gave him the power of prophecy to make up for it. Though I imagine it depends on the man."

"I imagine it does."

She ventured a quick look at him before remembering she didn't have to be circumspect about that sort of thing with Benedict Frost. So she let her gaze rove over him, boot to knee to the long, strong line of his thigh in its uniform breeches. Flat abdomen, broad chest and shoulders. A strong-featured but sensitive face, with eyes as dark and deep as they were unseeing.

Had he taken lovers since losing his sight? She was almost sure of it. His careful notice was a caress, his mischief sweetly erotic.

She wrapped her arms more tightly around her legs. It would not do to forget herself: she was Charlotte Perry, maiden aunt to the granddaughter of a vicar.

"Are you cold, Miss Perry? Would you like my coat?"

I should like to see you shrug out of it. "No, no. I'm quite all right." Certainly her cheeks were heated. "Have you been in Derbyshire before?" It was a nothing question, a distraction as she let the breeze cool her face. In the road, Maggie had taken hold of the stick and was teasing Captain with it again.

"Never. I've traveled little around England. It's been all London and all roads to somewhere else."

"Such as Edinburgh?"

"Yes." He tipped his head. "Tell me, what do you like about this place? What makes Strawfield distinct?"

This was a question more difficult to answer than it first seemed. Was not everything different between the Peak District and, say, London? What did such a slow place have to recommend itself?

Well, there was Maggie, gamboling with dauntless energy from one side of the grass-flanked road to the other. But Maggie would make any place precious.

"I like the grass," Charlotte decided. "It's rare in cities—and in truth, it's rare here, too. So much of the Peak is scrubby moorland, but grass unrolls like a living blanket during its short season."

"And what else?" Frost sat up, unwittingly matching her indolent posture of arms draped about the knees.

"People who like stars may find many to see here. And sunsets—they aren't covered over with coal smoke."

"What color is the sky now?"

She squinted, deciding. "It's like the edge of a bruise, just where purple goes to blue and peach." Too much poetry and contemplation was not safe for the soul.

He grinned. "Miss Perry, you are a natural-born memoirist."

"It's a gift," she agreed. "Describing the world in terms of blankets and injuries. And tell me, how does the world strike you? You heard a feeling for Maggie in my voice that I thought no one would ever notice. You must be surrounded by hidden wonders."

"Nothing that wouldn't be obvious to anyone who gave the world the same attention I do." He tilted his head. "I can tell that Maggie and Sir are coming back our way, and that the dog has begun to favor one of her legs. Her steps are uneven through the dry grass."

"Poor Captain. She is much older than Maggie, and she is footsore."

"But after she is rested, she'll have all the room to roam that she could wish. I have never lived anywhere with much space. In my parents' shop, I always felt as though I were about to be crushed under bookshelves."

"A scholarly way to die. My mother would be honored."

"Yes, well. Hugo would probably like it too, but I—I was never much of a reader. And when I went to sea, my world was a sling in a wooden box on an endless ocean."

Within Charlotte's long sleeves, the fine hairs of her arms prickled. How fine it sounded to slip across the world in truth, as she had so often pretended to do. "I wish I could leave England someday," she murmured.

A blunder. She realized this at once—and so did Frost, for he said lightly, "What of your time in dull bits of the world, doing virtuous deeds?"

"Yes, well, you knew that wasn't true. But it is a convenient sort of thing for my parents to tell the curious. It shuts questions right down; no one wants to hear about a tedious spinster and her dismal virtues."

In their rare letters, her parents never asked any questions about how she passed her years. She wondered if by now, the fiction had taken on heft enough that they had begun to believe it. Certainly they had long ago stopped thinking of Maggie as hers. The girl was Margaret's, and she was theirs.

Charlotte supposed this was a good thing for Maggie, though it made Charlotte herself an interloper in her daughter's life.

Maggie ran up just then, breathing with the hard clean gasps of a strong young body enjoying its exertion. "Would you like to throw the stick for Captain, Mr. Frost?"

"I'd be pleased to, Miss Maggie." Benedict accepted the clear compliment along with the stick, heaving it off to a respectable distance.

Maggie sped after the stick, Captain plodding slow-footed behind. "A fair throw," Charlotte commented, trying not to mind that Frost had been permitted to join in the game of fetch when she had not.

"Was it? That's good. Throwing sticks is more of a sighted person's game."

"And what is your preferred game?"

"At present, locating fifty thousand pounds worth of stolen gold sovereigns."

For a little while, Charlotte had forgotten all about that. "Yes, that is mine, too." She tried to laugh, but the words were too heavy. "I know I shouldn't, but I've begun to build plans upon the reward, as though it's already in my hand."

"You cannot be the only one doing so, Miss Perry. You are certainly not the only one determined to find the coins. The death of the serving girl at the Pig and Blanket proves that."

"It proves that Nancy Goff knew something, does it not? Something she didn't even realize was important until it was too late."

"Cat eyes and cloak? Maybe, but I can't make anything of that. I'm more suited to taking the lay of the land hereabouts."

My land. My gold. A spasm of possessiveness made Charlotte clench her fists. "Much luck to you,

Mr. Frost," she said with false lightness. "The land is a rock sponge. It's riddled with caverns and streams—the gold could be hidden anywhere."

"Do you have a different plan?"

She set her lips, mulish. Her silence told him enough.

"Ah, you really do think of yourself as my competitor." He sounded sorrowful. Sunset painted his face—not the color of a bruise, but that of a jewel. A ruby, warm and precious. A topaz, orange-golden. All a step away from gold, but only a step.

She released a deep breath, unknotting her hands. "It's for her, Mr. Frost." At a distance, Maggie called to Captain, two small shadows in the waning daylight. "With the reward, I could begin anew with her. We would live as aunt and niece, respectable in some small village. My parents could relax into peaceful retirement, and I . . ." She trailed off.

"Would be utterly bored?" He lifted his brows.

How did he know what she feared? "Maggie would be enough for me," she said firmly.

But what if she isn't? Is that fair to either of us?

This was her dream of perfection, but she might be too imperfect ever to make it succeed.

"I apologize," Frost said. "I spoke as a wanderer without a single root. But your dreams are your own business, and you know them best."

"There is nothing about business in a dream. That is what makes it such a pleasant diversion."

But here there was not diversion enough; Strawfield was quiet in all the wrong ways. Breeze and sleepy birdsong and the faint buzz of some twilight-hungry insect in place of London's hallooes and hoofbeats and carriages. How was one to avoid thought?

"I think," she said, "it must be time to go back inside. Captain will be getting tired, and Maggie, too, though she would never admit it. Mr. Frost, if you care to remain outdoors, I shall leave the door unlatched for you."

He rose to his feet, helping her up, and bent to gather her shawl and return it to her fumbling hands.

"I will stay a few minutes longer," he said, "and let the sun finish slipping away."

But you cannot see it, she almost said aloud. She could feel the darkening, though; and if *she* could, with her sense of touch grown lazy and subservient to sight, he certainly would, too.

She called Maggie and Captain to her, bundling them inside with a hurried good-night. Wanting to get away, to close a door between herself and the sunset, and Mr. Frost, as the night fell with the dread and promise of something new to come on the morrow.

Chapter Seven

The night seemed very short and far too long once dawn broke Charlotte's troubled sleep for good. Morning meant freedom to begin her search—as soon as she could slip from the vicarage.

She made certain she crossed paths with no one but the maid Barrett at breakfast time, a simple meal taken when one wished. Barrett took Charlotte's rough boots and lumpy-sleeved gown—knife in place—as a matter of course. She had learned when they were both no more than girls that one didn't ask questions of Charlotte, because one could not be sure of wanting to know the answer.

Silently as she could creep, now, Charlotte retrieved the horrible veiled bonnet from her shared bed-chamber and made for the staircase.

The second stair creaked beneath her weight; she bit her lip. She should have remembered that noise. She had sneaked down these stairs innumerable times during her teen years.

With a tiptoe, she tested the tread of the next stair.

"Off somewhere in secret, Miss Perry?"

She shouldn't have been surprised. She really shouldn't.

But she had hoped, all the same, that she wouldn't encounter him before leaving the vicarage. "Mr. Frost. Good morning to you. Of course there is no secret about my departure. I am an open book."

"Ah, well. You know I can't read such things. If you plan to leave the vicarage, a virtuous young lady such as yourself ought to have an escort."

Slowly, she turned and looked up at him through the film of her veiled bonnet. He stood outside the door of his bedchamber, wearing his naval uniform coat again, with clean linens. Arms folded; expression expectant.

Delicious collided with *damnation* in her thoughts. "I do not require an escort."

I am not a virtuous young lady.

She would have liked company on her errand, had it been any other sort. But she could not invite Frost along on this one. Could not bring herself even to speak the words of explanation. *You cannot come with me, because I need to check the places where Edward Selwyn once hid the contraband of our love affair, and where I fear he might again have hidden some clue. He is a man of great sentiment, you see, and great suggestibility.*

And he has eyes like a cat.

For my daughter's sake—not that she can ever know— I want to make sure he is not a thief.

Right. She was *not* going to say any of that—not to Benedict Frost, wry and waiting.

"You think you don't require an escort." He raised a brow.

Fine. Let him exercise his brow all he wished.

"That's correct. Farewell." She turned and descended one more stair before he spoke again.

"You have veiled your face."

She sighed. "It is so annoying how much you notice."

"A sighted man would notice far more," he said drily.

"I think not. A sighted man would notice different things." She had become familiar with the things such men noticed through the past decade, a long lesson in the pleasures to which they felt themselves entitled.

She hated the damned veil, but she needed its anonymity. Miss Perry had no reason to roam about the countryside. And in case someone recognized Charlotte Pearl—well, *La Perle* could not afford to be seen at present. Not while Randolph was still hunting for her.

If he was hunting for her. But she had the feeling he was. Randolph didn't like losing so much as a hand of *vingt-et-un,* and he had lost an entire courtesan.

Sleepy Strawfield had suddenly become too much like London: a few familiar faces surrounded by strangers. Each unknown face had an unknown story, made desperate by unknown motivation.

She knew little so far of Benedict Frost, though what she knew, she liked. But she would not allow anyone to accompany her. Not even him.

"I thought you would be speaking to the coroner with my father," she managed by way of excuse. "Surely you want to be prepared for the inquest this afternoon." Such events had to be held in a hurry, so the jury might view the body before it decayed. As the following day was a Sunday, all the events were to be squeezed in today.

"I have no need to prepare. I will hardly be called

as a witness." He leaned against the frame of the bedchamber door, as solid as though he were part of the house. "Your mother is giving Maggie her morning lessons. Your father will be gone all day, for after he speaks to the coroner, he'll be off performing virtuous works until the inquest."

Charlotte coughed. "Perhaps we'd better not use that phrase. Ever again."

A second roguish brow lifted to join the first. "Very well, hostess. But you must understand—it's just you and me for now. And I want to keep you company."

"That won't be possible. I'm sorry, Mr. Frost, but I really have to be go—"

"Ah, you are embarrassed to be seen with the rough, blind sailor."

"Indeed not." Piqued, she took a step back up. *Creak.* "I choose my company based on manners, not appearance."

"I have beautiful manners. The finest in all of Europe, with the possible exception of a few people in Paris."

"Is that so? The Parisians I have met have all been uncommonly rude." How did he always make her want to smile? "Mr. Frost, I have every confidence that a man who can explore foreign lands enough to write a book can occupy himself for a few hours."

"Oh, I've never lacked for occupation. I can always find a way to busy myself."

Something about the low swoop of his voice made her clench her toes within her boots. *Yes.*

"But it's you about whom I'm thinking." His expression turned serious. "Miss Perry, a young woman has been killed. Nance Goff had only the slight knowledge that came from a chance encounter with a stolen coin and the person who gave it to her. Someone in Strawfield is desperate. A woman walking alone might be in danger."

She was up again, mounting the top stair and facing him across the corridor. "But if I don't know anything, won't my ignorance keep me safe?"

"A fine question, though I wouldn't wager on the answer. Would you accept my escort if I place it on a personal level? If I would rather not trust to your supposed ignorance or to the logic of a killer, but to the presence of a brawny, well-mannered man at your side?"

Indeed he was, and her toes weren't the only body part clenching their interest at the moment. "You are very kind. Truly. But I always carry a knife."

A curl of a smile played on his lips. "Do you really? Where do you keep it?" He lifted his hands. "Never mind; I do not need to know. I only pray that I shall never encounter it."

"I cannot believe I would ever have to use it on you, Mr. Frost, though I'm willing to use it on your behalf."

The slow smile grew. "I find myself more convinced of your virtuous works by the minute."

"Ah, must I be virtuous?" On impulse, she flipped back her veil, and the world turned from gray to the color of life. Closing the distance between them— one step, then a small eager scoot of feet—she rose to her tiptoes and brushed her lips against his.

Mmm. Mint and starch, wool and shaving soap. The old copper tub had been pressed into service the night before, and each member of the household bathed in turn. Now they all smelled the same, like wintergreen soap. Breathing him in, Frost seemed already a part of her, each breath shared as her lips parted beneath his.

She slid her hands up his arms, feeling the hard muscles bunch within their sleeves. He unfolded his arms into a gentle embrace, cradling her shoulders in his broad hands. A gentleman, holding her steady, letting her lead. But my *Lord*, he kept pace with her every movement, eager and teasing at once. Learning the shape of her with soft brushes of lips, with a touch of tongue to tongue that made her sex wet.

When a kept woman permitted a kiss, she knew it inevitably led swiftly to the final act. A protector could not wait to shove his cock in, to be brought to pleasure. But she was no courtesan to Benedict Frost, and this—ah, this was a kiss for its own sake. And another, and another.

She was the one to draw him closer, body fully against body, filling her hands with the wool of his coat and spreading her palms across his back. So solid; so strong. Her eyes closed, she surrendered to the sensation of his touch. Against her belly, his erection thickened, but he did nothing more than kiss, and kiss. Lips, tongue, sending each small note of her trespass ringing through her body in vibrant pleasure.

"You are beautiful," he murmured. "Let me stay with you."

A false note, like the clang of a cracked bell. Her shoulders went stiff; her eyes popped open.

No. He didn't know her. He couldn't see her. With sweet words, he hoped to get what he wished—and she was letting it happen. She always let it happen.

She was such a fool.

"Mmm." She feigned a low moan of pleasure, raising herself up onto her toes to press fully against him. Clutching at him, turning his body so they were both within the doorway to his bedchamber.

And then she shoved him, hard, making him stumble back into the room. She slipped away from him and eased the door shut while he still reeled. *Yes.* The key was in the lock, and she turned it.

For a moment, she hesitated outside the closed door, hand outstretched toward the key.

She had kissed him first, and now she could not remember whether she had meant it as a distraction or whether she had simply not been able to help herself. It had not ended as a trick, though; Benedict Frost was far too intoxicating. He left her, as did all the best spirits, with a pounding head and a desire to act wanton.

Within the bedchamber, all was suspiciously silent. She clenched her fists, pulling them back from the key, and returned to the stairs. The first step, and this time she skipped the creaking second one. Silence, silence.

And then from behind her came the clunk of metal onto a wood floor, the creak of hinges as the locked bedchamber door swung open. She turned to see Frost in the doorway, shoulder against the frame, one booted foot planted toe-down in a pose of ultimate nonchalance.

"Ought I to have mentioned I carry a knife, too? Though I suppose it's more of a stiletto." He held up the small daggerlike blade in his right hand, gave it a little toss in the air, and caught it by its bone-colored hilt. "Just the right size for pushing a key from the lock."

The sleek movement of his hands as he tucked the neat blade back into his boot was enough to make her lick her lips. He felt about on the floor and scooped up the door key, then straightened.

"Now, Miss Perry. Are we to search for stolen coins together or shall we shove each other about some more first? I'm perfectly happy either way."

I might be, too, Charlotte thought. For what seemed the thousandth time, she remounted the few steps she'd managed to descend. "I intend to leave alone."

She faced him—looked up at him, really—expecting further protest. Instead, he caught her about the upper arms and swung her neatly about, like the step of a country dance.

And then he shut the bedchamber door with himself on the outside and her within.

She slapped the door hard with the flat of her hand. "Damn you, Frost. Let me out!"

His voice sounded through the wooden barrier, low and resonant. "Just because you locked the door doesn't mean I did. The only person keeping you in there is yourself."

Chastened, she pressed at the handle and let the door swing open. The vicarage was old and not quite level, and doors moved as they wanted to.

This one wanted to get out of the way, to let Charlotte look upon Benedict Frost.

Not at his eyes, where one usually looked for the seat of a person's true feelings. His were distant and blank, though they remained as dark and lovely as they had doubtless always been. No, instead, she had to pick out signs from about his person, just as he picked his way through the world. That crimp of his lip; the arch of his brow; a tightness in the strong line of his jaw. Again, too, he had folded his arms.

"You are angry," she realized. "You are quite good at not showing it, but you are angry indeed. Am I the cause?"

"It wouldn't be gracious of me to say so."

"In other words, yes."

The stern mouth relaxed just enough to allow the lips to curve. "Yes, then. I'm not sure why you won't agree to let me accompany you, Miss Perry, or what you think of me. Do you fear I'll steal your secrets, though I cannot see my hand before my face? Or are you simply certain I'll slow you down?"

She shook her head, not realizing until too late that this gesture would go unobserved. Each of his questions made her feel lower, until speech was impossible.

His arms relaxed, and he braced one hand against the white trim about the door. "Before I lost my sight, I saw a great deal of the world in His Majesty's Royal Navy. Some of it was lovely. War was terrible. And much of it was dull, days of nothing but sky and water and the same tasks over and over."

He turned the key in his fingers. "No matter the setting, I never met anyone who thought little of me once he really knew me. Maybe one day you'll be the same." Unerringly, he reached for her hand and pressed the key into it. "I'm fit to go where you do, Miss Perry. Don't forget that, please."

He turned to go downstairs, leaving her with those parting words.

"How *dare* you." The sentence issued from her throat like a growl.

He paused in the same spot where she had halted twice.

She muscled her voice under control—barely. "How dare you assume that I wish to leave alone because I think you unfit to walk out with me. How dare you assume that my reasons have anything to do with you at all, Mr. Frost. You and I met yesterday. I was born here. Derbyshire has claims on me you can never imagine."

He turned slowly, tilting his head. "I can imagine a great deal, Miss Perry."

"Imagine, then, that it is not your business where I search, or how. Imagine that I am a grown woman, and if I place myself in danger, that is my affair. I shall save myself and be all right, or I shall not, and I will be hurt or killed. And that is my affair, too."

As she spoke, her anger grew more powerful rather than dissipating. So long she had wanted to say these words, to so many people. "It is my affair," she said in a voice so thick with feeling, she almost choked on the words, "where I live, and with whom. It is my affair if I choose to have company or walk out alone."

It ought to have been true, all of it. But it was not for any woman, and certainly not for Charlotte Perry, who had never intended to become Charlotte Pearl. She had been born for a plain, everyday life in a Derbyshire vicarage. She had never intended to become notorious or infamous, but chance and fortune had made her both. Known for her caprice and frivolity, for the bare curves immortalized on canvas after canvas.

Her dress covered her too tightly, cutting at her breath. She had grown used to pale silks and red satins, the colors of elegance and lust. The plain blue serge gown she now wore, that she had worn again and again, was something she was not. But she could never again be what she'd been for so long.

She couldn't bear it. And she was afraid she wouldn't survive it.

At last, Frost spoke. "You are right. I am sorry. I should not have presumed. Since I lost my sight, I have often been dismissed or underestimated. I must be too ready to perceive a slight where none is intended."

"I know the feeling of being underestimated," said Charlotte. "But I do not know if such as we can ever be too ready to perceive a slight. We need our knives about us always."

"Perhaps we do." Patting the side of his boot where he'd sheathed the stiletto, he remounted the final step. "Though I'd be a fool to underestimate you, Miss Perry. Since you have kissed me senseless and locked me up, I consider you to be fully master of this situation."

"Mistress," she murmured.

"Right, yes. Mistress. I shall not impose upon you again. Of course you have the right to go forth without my company. Without *any* company, if you so choose." His smile was a rueful twist, somehow faraway even as he stood before her. "I suppose I just want you to be safe."

Reaching out, his fingertips brushed Charlotte's shoulder. He trailed them down from her shoulder to her elbow, where he found the edge of the shawl she had bunched and mangled in her tight-folded arms. "Wrap yourself in this, Miss Perry, and be warm. Though we each seek the same reward, I shan't be your foe."

She turned her head away, unwilling to look at him even though he could not read her expression. And he went downstairs—away—somewhere. Leaving her standing within the doorway of his bedchamber, pulling her bonnet's veil back over her face with hands that were not quite steady.

Maybe it was herself she couldn't quite face. For she knew, as soon as he tucked her shawl about her with sensitive hands, that she was going to take him to bed.

The only question in her mind now, as she descended the stairs and slipped away on her errand, was how long she would be able to wait.

Chapter Eight

Eyes like a cat.

As Charlotte's steps ate the distance between the vicarage and the stone wall, she could not stop thinking of those four words.

Eyes like a cat. Nancy Goff had said this as she swanned about the Pig and Blanket's common room, and she had said "cat eye" as her life slipped away.

Edward Selwyn's eyes were tawny green. And Charlotte knew from experience that he would do anything for a bit of notoriety. Wearing a cloak for the devil of it; paying a serving girl with a coin he knew to be stolen—that sounded like Edward, who treated life as a masquerade ball.

But arranging a theft from the Royal Mint? Shooting four guards? Stabbing a healthy young woman, who would surely have fought him? No. No, that did not sound like his way. He wanted to charm the world, not control it. He'd be more likely to stab a woman to the heart figuratively than with a knife.

Still. Charlotte would feel more at ease once she checked the hiding-holes she knew to hold meaning for Edward. Not only because he was the father of her child and the artist who had made her infamous, but because . . . well, she hated to think of someone she knew proving she did not know him at all.

For the next several hours, she searched every place in which Edward had once hidden secrets. First, the stone-covered crannies along the vicarage's side of the wall where she and her sister—and later, she and Edward—used to stash messages and treasures. She pried up rocks, cursing the softness of her hands, and confirmed that the spaces beneath were empty. Once, a brownish-yellow lizard, striated and spotted in black, put out a narrow tongue at her.

"Same to you," she murmured and covered its home back over. Better to find a lizard than a hidden note confessing a crime. Or a stash of stolen coins.

Where next to check, then? The great hollow tree just outside of the village proper had shielded many notes and packages. It might be large enough to hide some of the coins; its obviousness might divert suspicion.

But when Charlotte, skirting the rare figure she caught sight of, reached the spot where the tree had stood for generations, it was gone. Nothing remained but a stump, with its cut edge gray-brown with age. The tree must have rotted out and fallen at last.

For a long moment, she stared at the stump, almost dizzy. She knew it was illogical to expect the village would remain the same every time she returned, yet indeed she did. Strawfield was not the sort of place where one changed the color of one's shutters or converted a thatch roof to wooden shakes. It persisted unchanging—until it didn't. Change, when it came, was large and swift. A centuries-old tree felled. A lover wed.

A young woman's life ended, and all because of a bit of gold.

She turned away from the old stump, holding the hem of her veil down over her face. A breeze teased her, nipping her uncovered neck with a coolness that was not unpleasant.

Into her mind flashed Benedict Frost, stern but kind as he drew her shawl about her. Kissing her as deeply as a man drew breath, yet doing nothing Charlotte did not do to him first.

If she had met such a man ten years before, her life might have taken a very different path. But she hadn't. She'd met Edward instead.

She was careful as she slipped onto his lands, watching out for some member of the grand house's staff. She saw a man with a shovel once, but he was too far away for her to tell whether he was a gardener or whether he trespassed like Charlotte.

For a moment, she toyed with the notion of returning to the vicarage for a shovel of her own. There were several hiding spots on this side of the wall, too, and she must check them all. No; better to leave no trace or turned earth. She could pry free the stones with her hands. She always had in the past.

Empty. Empty. All of the nooks were empty. When she heaved the last stone back into place, her hands were raw, several fingers bruised.

This search had not set her mind at ease, though it was a necessary first step. As she had told Frost, there was an infinity of places to search in Strawfield and the surrounding land. No one would ever find the stolen sovereigns by chance.

This whole search had been ridiculous. Edward didn't need to steal money. Lady Helena Selwyn, eldest daughter of the Earl of Mackerley, had brought a rich dowry to their marriage eight years before and transformed Selwyn House into a showplace.

Eyes like a cat, Nance had said. But she had also said *demon eyes, red as fire. They glowed in the dark.* Even to the last, the barmaid had stuck to her unlikely story, talking of cat eyes and a cloaked figure. Comforting herself, maybe, that what had happened to her made sense. That it wasn't terrible and random and undeserved.

But it was terrible. And it made no sense.

Charlotte picked her way back to the vicarage, taking care no one should see her—not that she needed such caution today. That fellow with the shovel was the only possible reward seeker she'd seen. The formerly blithe visitors to Strawfield had retreated in the aftermath of Nance's death. Maybe some of them had decided the promise of riches was not worth the newfound risk. Or maybe they were lurking about the Pig and Blanket, hoping for a glimpse of the dead girl or a chance to be chosen for the coroner's jury.

She shuddered, wrapping her shawl more tightly about her with hands that were much less careful than Benedict Frost's had been.

When she let herself into the vicarage, she hung up her veiled bonnet on a hook by the door. After a second's thought, she added the shawl, too. Mrs. Perry's study door was still closed, and Maggie's voice could be heard through it faintly. *"Stin pragmatikótita, egó o ídios, me ta diká mou mátia, eída tin Sívylla stin Kými krémetai se éna boukáli . . ."*

So, Maggie was learning to speak Greek. Yet another thing about her that Charlotte had not known. The precious infant had become a fat child in leading strings, then a darling curious girl. Now she was a half-grown mystery. The only constant was Captain, now gray-muzzled and slow, curled outside the study door.

Charlotte bent to pet the old hound. Captain raised her head with a *whuff.*

"Does that mean you'll put in a good word for me with your young mistress?" She petted the graying brindled fur of the dog's head, until Captain lowered her head again and fell into a doze.

Charlotte would have returned more often if she could have, if she dared. But each letter to her parents was met either with silence or with a *not yet; maybe next year.* And it was wise, she knew, to give Strawfield time to forget her face between each visit. Wise to keep Maggie from growing too attached to her.

Her own attachment, she could not help.

"If you are quite done lurking outside the study, Miss Perry," came a low voice, "I should like your assistance sending a letter."

Frost stood in the doorway of the small parlor. Of course he had heard her enter; his scrupulous ears noted every footfall.

"I shall be glad to help." She straightened up, finding that she was not quite able to look at him. He was no longer just Mr. Frost, but someone she had kissed. Someone she had been unable to resist touching. Someone she had pushed, and who had pushed her right back.

Yet he called her *Miss Perry,* correct and proper as though she had never made him hard, as though he hadn't shoved her into his bedchamber. The memory made her blush; she, who had lived in the naked world of sex for years.

How little it had to do with her own desire.

Thank heaven he could not see her burning cheeks. "What is the letter, Mr. Frost? Do you need to seal it, or only to address it?"

"It is to my sister, Georgette, in London. I have written the direction, but need a seal or wafer. And then if it could be placed with the other correspondence—"

"Yes, certainly." She brushed past him, trusting him to follow her voice. "If you take your letter into Strawfield for posting when you attend the inquest, it ought to arrive in London the day after tomorrow. Oh—wait, tomorrow is Sunday. Well, perhaps two days from tomorrow, then. The mailing supplies are kept in the desk in the far corner of this parlor."

"The southeast corner or the southwest corner?" He slapped the folded letter against one palm, his smile puckish.

"Why don't you tell me?" Charlotte replied drily. "Five paces forward, and you'll knock right into it."

"Southwest, then." And with as much grace as Charlotte possessed on her most swanlike days, he wound around the long sofa and stood before the writing desk.

She moved to his side, handed him a gummed wafer, and took the sealed letter from him when he was finished. "It's past time I wrote to Georgette," he admitted. "She is . . . not aware of my present whereabouts."

"Is she usually? I thought you were busy poking your—"

"Miss *Perry*."

"—*nose* into any bit of the world you could."

"That's one way of putting the matter." He stepped around her, finding the back of the long sofa, and took up the noctograph he had laid upon the seat. "She usually doesn't know where I am, no. But at present she probably thinks I am sailing on the *Argent* again. I intended to be in England for only a few days. Long enough to turn my manuscript over to a publisher and arrange payment to Georgette."

Charlotte added his letter to the pile of outgoing post. "I presume nothing about your plan went as you expected, since you aren't sailing the seven seas."

"You are correct. Publishers are eager for accounts of travel abroad, but not those written by blind men. Not even if such a man pays the costs of publication."

Charlotte blinked, bewildered. "How could that not be of interest?"

"Oh, they thought it of interest. But not as a memoir. They think I made the whole damned thing up." His fingers clutched the wooden edges of the noctograph, the strength of his grip turning his knuckles bloodless white.

"How stupid of them. I am sorry."

"Do you believe me to be truthful, then?" His gaze was unfixed as ever, but his brows had furrowed, head turned toward her.

"It had not occurred to me *not* to believe you." She added, teasing, "Especially not with the illustrious Lord Hugo Starling vouching for you."

Though he murmured an epithet, a smile twisted his lips.

"Remember, Mr. Frost, I'm meant to have been abroad for almost ten years. But really, I've never left London save for a few brief trips home." She hadn't quite meant to admit that, but once she did, she was not sorry.

With great care, he set the noctograph down again. "So . . . you wish to write a fake memoir? I do not understand your meaning."

"So . . . it's difficult to keep a pack of lies straight in one's mind. Far too easy for them to get shuffled about. It is far easier to write the truth if one can."

"Is it just as easy to go somewhere as not when one is blind? That is the question to which George Pitman, publisher, says no."

"I am sure it was *not* as easy to travel as to stay home, but I believe you did it."

"Sometimes leaving is easier than staying." His smile was thin. "When one has no home to speak of. Though I don't suppose you know what that feels like, since you have ties to Derbyshire I could never presume to imagine." He spoke with lightness, but it hurt to hear her own words flung back at her.

"The ties of which I spoke are hardly the sort in which one would wish to be wrapped. I might understand better than you realize."

She had no home either, after years of dividing her heart. She had a house in Mayfair, but she could never return to it. How easy had been the decision to leave London at last, to cut ties with Randolph and the *ton* and the glittering world of fashion. The leaving itself had been difficult, with much to arrange, but the decision had taken no thought at all.

Coming to Maggie? No thought there either.

Where to go next? She hadn't a clue.

Gingerly, she perched on an arm of the sofa, hitching one leg up as though she were on a sidesaddle.

"Why do you want to claim the Royal Mint's reward, Mr. Frost?"

"I know you don't ask for an answer so simple as 'because I want the five thousand pounds.'" With a sigh, he flanked her, seating himself on the other arm of the sofa. "Yet I do want the five thousand pounds that will come to whomever finds the stolen coins. I want the money for my sister's dowry. As a Naval Knight—that is, an unmarried lieutenant of stellar character—I draw half pay and claim an additional pension from the Naval Knights' trust. But since our parents passed on, Georgette has nothing of her own."

Charlotte ought, perhaps, to have commented with sympathy on the loss of his parents, or on the difficult situation of his sister. But what struck her most was his financial dilemma. He received room and board, a half salary and a pension, but in exchange he had to remain a bachelor living in a room in Windsor Castle. The arrangement took as much freedom as it gave.

To a much less luxurious degree, this was not unlike the life of a courtesan. Since shaking free from Randolph, Charlotte had never been poorer; she had escaped with little, and her remaining wealth was unavailable, untouchable. But she also woke and slept when she wished, went where she liked, and kept the company she preferred.

This last part was the best of all.

And it would be for the unknown Georgette, too, Charlotte thought. "What if you claim the reward, but she doesn't wish to marry? Will you turn the money over to her and allow her to live as an independent spinster?"

"Would she like that?" He tipped his head, considering.

"I cannot imagine she would mind having the choice, but you know her better than I. Maybe there's already some young man she's decided to wed, and her lack of a dowry is the only thing preventing their marriage."

"If there is such a man, she's never revealed his existence in her letters." He felt along the side of his boot, reassuring himself, probably, of the presence of the blade within. How elder brotherly.

"Where does she live now?"

"Where she always has." He sighed, as if this were a dreadful thing. "My parents owned a bookshop, with living quarters above. I was raised there until the age of twelve, when my wish to go to sea was granted. As their eldest, the bookshop came to me upon their deaths three years ago."

"You own a bookshop." Charlotte considered. "How intriguing. I was not aware you were a man of property."

"Ah, are you going to start flirting with me now? I'd be delighted by it, but I mustn't let you throw yourself at me under false pretenses. I have sold the bookshop to cousins with the understanding that they were to house Georgette until she turned twenty-one."

"I understand. A man can hardly run a bookshop when he is sliding down one of the Alps, or whatever it is you plan to do next."

"Right," he said drily. "Sliding down a mountain

does have appeal, but there is also the fact that blind men are poor readers."

This she had to grant. "This is none of my affair, of course, but you *could* give your sister the money you received from selling the shop."

"And I may yet do that." A humorless laugh. "It was meant to finance publication of my book—which would, of course, become the latest fashion and would sell in the thousands. I intended that the proceeds from the sales would go to Georgette while I continued to travel."

Charlotte mulled this over. Publishers either bought the copyright of a book outright, ending the author's chance to profit from it, or the author paid publication costs and granted the publisher a commission on each copy sold. Frost had evidently preferred the latter method, though it might never earn the author a shilling. "It was not a bad plan, though trading your inheritance for publication of a book would be a gamble."

"It proved a gamble I couldn't win on my own terms, so I chose not to make the bet." He shrugged. "Perhaps one day I'll write a novel based on my travels. Perhaps not. At present, though, Georgette is almost twenty-one." He shook his head. "How odd that is to realize. I suppose she might have a beau after all."

"I did when I was twenty-one."

"I have no doubt of it. I imagine you had all of London at your feet."

"Not precisely *all* of London." She coughed. "I was cultivating a . . . close acquaintance with one of the royal dukes."

To her surprise, Benedict laughed. "Was it Clarence, that old salt?"

"It was not. The Duke of Clarence was devoted to Mrs. Jordan and their children." An actress who had never been any sort of *Mrs.* as far as Charlotte knew. Kept women required their fictions.

"Not to sound like an overprotective older brother, but I do hope Georgette doesn't come in the way of any of the royal dukes."

"I heartily wish her the same," said Charlotte. "Does she like living with your cousins at the bookshop?"

"She has never told me she does not. But she *has* told me she cannot stay beyond her birthday. I shall send her the inheritance if I must, and she can use it to pay room and board, but . . ."

"The arrangement could only be temporary," Charlotte replied. "Until she sorts out what comes next."

Yes. That was how she felt about her stay here. *Family* did not equate to *home,* or even to *welcome.* Her parents never chastised her for the choices she had made; they simply ignored them. When she returned to their house, she was Miss Perry. Maggie's aunt.

The door across the corridor opened, spilling forth a final *"Méchri ávrio"* from Mrs. Perry.

"Entáxei," said Maggie, followed by "Captain! You waited for me! Good girl."

Mrs. Perry called for the capable Barrett, ordered a light luncheon, then poked her head into the parlor. "Lessons done at last. That girl of ours hasn't my head for Greek, but she's not entirely without talent. She'll make a fair translator one day."

That girl of ours.

Of hers and the reverend's, of course. "Mama, what if she does not want to be a translator of ancient Greek?"

"Then she can translate modern Greek instead." Mrs. Perry frowned. "Why the sudden questions, Charlotte?"

A good question. She couldn't put the feeling into words; she only knew that she felt some duty to Maggie—and even to the unknown Georgette Frost—to claim freedoms for them.

"They wanted asking," she replied simply.

Her mother, sturdy and ruddy-faced and pragmatic a creature as had ever been made, shrugged and moved on. "Mr. Frost, do you intend to go to the inquest? The vicar should be able to walk over with you after luncheon. I expect him home anytime."

"I think I will, yes. It might give him comfort not to go alone."

"You can keep him from being worn to a thread. Always finding someone else to talk to or someone else's house to go visit."

"Well, he *is* the vicar," said Charlotte. "People look to him for comfort. It's not as though he's playing cards at all hours."

"And who's to comfort his family if he's never here?"

Who was to comfort him if his family was always in London or ancient Greece? "That wants asking, too," Charlotte said.

"Asking. *Eureka*. We ought to work on interrogatives next." Mrs. Perry disappeared from the doorway, saying something else in Greek to Maggie, then mounted the creaking stairs.

Maggie was next to peek in. "Why are you sitting like that on the arms of the sofa?" Before either Charlotte or Frost could answer, she added, "I am going to take Captain outside. She missed the fresh air during my morning of lessons."

"Captain missed the fresh air, did she? What about her mistress?" Charlotte slid to the seat of the sofa, mindful of the noctograph at her side.

"I did, too. This is the only time of year when I can be outdoors without wearing an itchy cloak or getting itchy with sweat."

With her light brown curls and green eyes, Maggie really was the image of the late, lovely Margaret. Charlotte could almost wish the family's lies were true, and that her sister had birthed this child. Her life would be easier, she knew, if Maggie had no claim on her heart.

But then there would be no reason for it to keep beating at all. "Give dear Captain a pat for me, Maggie, and mind you stay off the Selwyn lands."

"*Entáxei.*" Maggie smiled, her nose wrinkling. "That means 'all right.' Grandmama says my accent is terrible."

"It's much better than mine," said Frost.

Maggie laughed, and she was off.

Frost slid to the sofa seat as well, then cleared his throat. "Look, Miss Perry, I think we ought to speak about—"

She pressed his hand, quick, hard. *Silence.* She had got in the habit of caution, of speaking her mind only behind a closed door.

This morning, at the top of the stairs, had been a rare exception—but then, she had been provoked.

"About the inquest," she said smoothly. "Yes, I

agree that we should speak of it. And how kind of you to wonder if I wish to go with you. I think not, though. Not many other women will be there. It doesn't seem quite the thing to do."

As though she gave a damn about that.

No. Rather than that, she did not wish to hear Nance spoken of in the past tense when she had so recently been present to so many. The jury would look at her, laid out, and look at where she had died, then where she had lived. Her plain chamber in the attic of the Pig and Blanket, with the scraps of her dreams around her. Maybe a silk ribbon from an admirer, or a book or two, or a family miniature. An inquest was just another way of leering, with no justice to be had at the end of it.

Charlotte had been the subject of inquests, time after time. Her naked body on canvas, draped only in jewels, stilled in paint by Edward before the stares of many men. The courtesan and the artist; they made one another famous. And Edward knew every inch of her.

On the outside.

"If you could go," she said through a tight throat, "and listen to everything quite well with your marvelous noticing ears, there might be clues as to what Nance knew. And that might have something to do with where the coins are, and—"

"Why, Miss Perry, are you suggesting I share information with you?" Somehow his hand had found hers again; they rested together atop the ruled surface of the noctograph. "That sounds suspiciously like cooperation."

When one of his fingers began to stroke the back

of her hand, her heart began to beat faster. "You swore you should not be my foe."

"Nor shall I. I shall be the ears where you cannot go, and you can spend the time in . . . virtuous works."

She choked back a laugh that trembled a bit.

"And in return," he stated, rising to his feet and pulling her up to face him, "will you be the eyes for us both?"

"That sounds as though we would be one flesh." Still, he held her hand, and her fingers could not seem to release his much thicker ones.

"Perhaps later," he murmured. "In the meantime, I rather think we shall be unconquerable. Don't you?"

Without waiting for her reply, he eased his hand free, then took up his noctograph and the cane he'd laid next to the doorway. *"Méchri ávrio,"* he said. "'Until tomorrow.' Just as your mother told Maggie."

"You speak Greek, too?" She raised her eyes to heaven. "I am outnumbered."

"Only a few words of it. I picked up bits when sailing about the Peloponnesus." He winked, the gesture looking oddly shy over his unfocused gaze. "Marvelous noticing ears, you know."

He sketched a small bow, then left her with a smile that was reflected on her own features.

Unconquerable, he said they would be. Though she suspected, as she gave a little shiver of longing, that she was already beginning to surrender.

Chapter Nine

"Last call, Frost. Another pint for you before we close for the night?" Mrs. Potter, the innkeeper's wife, spoke to Benedict in a tone of considerably more cheer than the one with which she had begun the evening.

After the inquest, the atmosphere in the Pig and Blanket had turned convivial, desperately so. As the odors of tobacco smoke and ale thickened, toast after toast ensued. A young woman had died, the living had heard the verdict issued—*murder by person or persons unknown*—and now they wanted to drink away the knowledge.

So followed hours of raucous, determined cheer, as strange voices overlapped and thickened with drink. Toasts to Nance, toasts to success in the hunt for the stolen sovereigns. Toasts to Mr. and Mrs. Potter; to the Bow Street Runner, Stephen Lilac, sent by the Royal Mint; to the coroner; to the vicar's blind guest, even.

No amount of liquor could have made Benedict

raise a glass to this last toast. "The vicar's guest is a writer," he protested. "A lieutenant. A physician."

But he wasn't really any of those things; all were half-tried or abandoned. And so he had to accept the claps on the back, the slurred *welcome*s and *I don't know how you manage it*s. It had been rather horrible, smiling and laughing through such an evening. But it had been necessary for him to seem as though he belonged.

He stored such thoughts away for later, though. At the moment, he only took up his hickory cane and replied to Mrs. Potter, "Nothing more for me, good lady. A fellow such as I can't afford to get too fuddled during his walk home."

He felt fuddled already, head aching with the strain of trying to tease one strange voice from another, to recall everything said about him. The inquest had been much easier, with one person speaking at a time, each identified. In a public room? He was half-drowned in sound.

He rummaged in his pockets for coins, feeling each one carefully, then added a shilling above his shot. An exorbitant gratuity that would make Mrs. Potter think him either generous or drunk. Maybe both. He gave an intentional sway as he bade the publican's wife a good night; then he left, leaning heavily on his stick.

No self-respecting sailor, with his daily ration of a half pint of rum or a gallon of beer, would become tipsy in a village pub. But it wouldn't hurt for Mrs. Potter and the last few souls lingering in the common room to think so. He didn't want anyone to suspect how closely he'd been listening all afternoon, all evening, and into the night.

As soon as he passed through the outer door of the Pig and Blanket, his strides straightened out. He pulled in a deep breath, the air of late May pleasant and fresh in his lungs. It smelled like nothing at all, and the streets held all the quiet of a village gone to sleep. The respite was welcome, the ache in his head lifting almost at once.

And now back to the vicarage. It was true enough that he couldn't afford to become fuddled. Though it mattered little to him whether he walked under a new moon or a noon sun, he could not drift idly, lost in thought and counting on rote memory to bring him to his destination. He had to count steps, carefully, to remember his turning.

Here was the scent of the baker's shop, bready and sweet even during these sleepy hours. Next came three other shops to his left, the village green to the right. *To the west,* he would tell Charlotte, just to imagine her expression of disgruntled amusement. Maybe to make her laugh. What was the shape of her smile? He knew only what her lips felt like when being kissed, but what would they feel like when . . .

Damnation. He was getting fuddled, and no mistake.

He halted, and his final footfall echoed in a crunch of gravel. To straighten out his thoughts, he pulled forth the watch from his waistcoat pocket and felt the raised numbers on its face. Near midnight.

He snapped the case shut again—and froze.

There had been no echo for that sound. Which meant that had been no echo to his footfall either. Someone was following him.

To be certain, he took another step, and another, then stopped.

There came the same echo that wasn't truly an echo: a footstep planted a bare instant after his.

All right. He was being followed. So? He'd been followed before. Not only by cutpurses, but by jealous husbands and lovers. The streets about ports weren't known for the virtue of those practicing, well, virtuous works.

Of course, those encounters had been when he was still possessed of his sight. But no matter. He had a metal-tipped walking stick in one hand and a hidden blade in his boot.

Stowing his watch again, he bent and drew forth the stiletto from its sheath. He turned, holding the hilt between thumb and the breadth of his hand, tilting it slightly so any moonlight would wink from the blade. "Greetings, person following in my steps. Would you like to chat, or have you some other purpose in mind?"

A slight indrawn breath. Benedict estimated it at perhaps twenty feet away.

"Truly," he added in a bland tone. "Let us chat if you've a mind to. I'm quite ready. I've beautiful manners. What do you want to talk of? My money? You may try to take it, though I doubt you'll succeed."

Two footsteps, another breath. This one sounded closer on the night-silent street. There seemed no one else about, no one else awake in the world.

"You must be shy." Benedict flexed his fingers on the bone hilt of the stiletto. "Fortunately for you, I am not. Maybe you want to talk about the inquest, but you can't quite summon the courage to broach the subject. Were you there today?" In his other hand, he held the head of his cane lightly, ready to swing it.

"Did you play a part in it? Or in the death of Nancy Goff?"

"What do you want?" The voice was closer still; male, hoarse, and rasping. Obviously disguised.

"I might ask you the same, shadow."

But the figure following Benedict said nothing.

After a moment, he took a step back. And another. The figure did not follow.

And then in a rush, it came at him, a flurry of footsteps for which he was ready but somehow still unprepared. Dropping his knife, he laid both hands on his cane, top and midpoint, making of it a bar before him.

The man rattled into him at full speed, jarring his bones and making his teeth clack together. A grunt and wheeze told Benedict that the cane had caught the assailant across the midsection, but he wasn't slowed for long. *Snick* came a clean sound, and then a pressure and a rip of cloth. Cool air touched Benedict's arm before a hot liquid flowed down it.

His arm had been slashed, he realized dimly.

"You," growled Benedict, "just ruined the undress uniform coat of a lieutenant of the Royal Navy. Bad decision." He swung the cane, its tip connecting with the long resistance of a limb bone.

The knife came again, but off target; it hacked into the cane. Benedict cursed, and in the moment the assailant took to pry the blade free of the precious hickory staff, he freed one hand and drove a fist into whatever he could reach. Midsection again, but the fellow must have guts of iron. He absorbed the blow and gave the same back, making Benedict gag. He sucked in air, eyes watering, not allowing his body to bend and shield itself. If he bent, if he fell, he was certain he would never rise again.

Staggering a little as he planted his feet, he held the cane lightly at his side. The crunch of gravel sounded from his right—now from right before him, and without thought, he drove the solid metal tip forward, hard as he could.

He hit something.

There came a whimper and a curse, and the knife-wielding shadow fell to his knees with a gritty thump. He'd caught the man in the belly, then, or the groin.

Had the attacker dropped the knife? Could Benedict find his own stiletto? Heart in a thunder, he allowed himself three seconds to feel about on the ground for whatever he could grasp.

One. Nothing but mud and something sticky—his own blood? It made his fingers slippery.

Two. Grass, another clump of grass, pebbles, pebbles, pebbles.

Three. Nothing . . . nothing . . . a tip of something that he knocked away with his clumsy fumbling.

Three and a half, then. He patted for it with a flat palm, then closed his hand gently about a thin blade. He slipped it into the customary spot in his boot, then straightened, tucking his cane solidly under his arm.

And he sprinted for the vicarage as if he were being chased by the devil himself.

Breathing hard, he shut the door behind him. "Charlotte," he whispered. "Charlotte. I need you."

"I am here," came the answer after a second, from the direction of the parlor. "Papa returned hours ago, but I waited up for—my God, you are bleeding."

"I'm all right. Lock the door." He tucked his hickory cane in the corner, within easy reach of the doorway. "And then let us put something heavy against it, and against any other way in or out of the house you can think of. I may not be the only person in Strawfield who knows his way through a locked door."

"I—yes, all right." Then followed the sounds of scraping metal, of a key turning and a bolt being thrown. "One moment. Your cut—it looks very bad." A cloth was wrapped about the cut on his arm, then tied off snug. At once, a burning pain was eased that he had not realized he felt.

After helping him muscle a chest from the parlor and stand it on end before the door—"where it will make a god-awful crash if anyone tries to break through," she noted—she walked Benedict to the rear of the vicarage so he could do the same before the servants' entrance. While he shoved furniture, she checked window latches, then crept down to the servants' quarters, presumably to secure those windows or alert the servants.

When she met him again in the corridor outside the dining room, both agreed that no one would be getting into the house without being heard at once.

"By you or me, that is," Charlotte said. "My father was ill at ease after the inquest, so my mother gave him a sedative. His sleep looked so peaceful that she and Maggie took one as well. They have both taken upon themselves some of his worry."

"He has worry enough for several people," Benedict agreed. *But it still might not be enough.* He flexed the fingers of his left hand; they tingled, a little numb from the pressure of the cloth about his biceps.

"Let me get a lamp and a few items for treating your wound"—Charlotte's footsteps receded, then returned after a minute or two—"and now to your bedchamber."

"Well, well. You certainly know how to comfort a man." His wry tone fell flat; it was too shaky for humor. God, his arm was beginning to hurt again, and the blow to his belly made him ache straight through.

"I certainly do." She preceded him up the eighteen narrow stairs. "In this case, I'll clean your arm and give you a fresh shirt while you tell me what happened."

He made his way to the bed and sat on its edge, letting her close them into the bedchamber and bustle about as he briefly described the attack. The timing; the surprise of it. "It was as though someone was waiting for me. I think it must have something to do with the inquest."

"Perhaps, though there could be another reason. The fact that you are a guest at the vicarage? A friend to Lord Hugo Starling? The owner of a noctograph? Simply a man walking alone whose purse might be taken?"

He shook his head. "I do not think I was targeted because of who I am, but because of something I know. Which, unfortunately, I do not know I know— *damn it.* Er, sorry about that. I didn't know you were about to untie the cloth about my arm." His numb fingers were easier to move now, but the cut began to ooze again.

"He curses," she murmured. "What a surprise for a sailor. I thought they were meant to be so elegant." She plucked at the torn edges of his coat sleeve. "You will have to take off your coat and shirt. Would you like my aid?"

"I'd be a fool to say no." Though he tried to sound roguish, in truth, he wasn't sure he could shrug free from his garments without opening the wound wide again.

He planted his boots on the floor, set his teeth, and gave Charlotte a nod. She stepped into the cradle of his legs, a figure lightly scented of wintergreen, bracing and calm. "Shrug your good shoulder so we can slip this off of you—"

"They are *both* good shoulders."

"Right. That's what I meant to say. Shrug your brawny and handsome right shoulder, and we'll get your coat free on that side—there. Now I can ease this sleeve over the arm that was hurt. Quickly, lift up your arm—and press at the wound with this cloth while you hold your arm in the air." She stepped back, taking away the faint prickle of heat her nearness imparted. The coat fell to the floor before the bed, heavy as a sack of potatoes.

"Careful with that, please." He began to lower his upraised arm until Charlotte exclaimed. "It is the mark of my rank. I earned that coat through years of effort."

"Doubtless you did, but I am sorry to say that it was the work of a moment to ruin it. The rend in the sleeve could be sewed, but the white piping will never be the same."

Briefly, he considered stitching up the slashed fabric. Wearing the bloodstained coat as a sign of pride and achievement, as other men did after serving in battle.

He discarded the idea at once. It would be just another way to make a spectacle of himself. The uniform coat had become a way to dress without thought or expense, but maybe it was time to leave it behind. To take his chances with fashion, to wear the clothes of the everyday man he had become.

"Set it aside, then," he said. "I shall decide later what is to be done with it."

Buttons scraped and jingled as Charlotte picked up the coat. "I am hanging it over the chair at the writing desk." Her footsteps returned, and she stood again before him. "May I take the rest of your ruined clothing, Mr. Frost?"

"Call me Benedict." His voice seemed not to be working properly as she undid the buttons of his waistcoat. Fingers pressing, tugging at his clothing, traveling down, down. The skin of his abdomen shivered, and not because it was bruised and sore.

He squeezed his eyes shut, a meaningless gesture—but it was enough to remind him to keep control of himself. *Don't get fuddled. Again.* An unwilling smile touched his lips. If he let his injured arm sink down, it would rest on Charlotte's back and pull her into an embrace.

"Benedict," she repeated, undoing the bottom button of his waistcoat. "All right, then." Closer, she leaned, slipping the doubtless-bloodstained white waistcoat from his right side. He lowered his injured arm to shrug free on the left—and he encountered a curve, soft and strong.

"That's what the Greeks call a *derrière*," she said wryly. "You've got one yourself. Move your hand, please; we've got to get that shirt off before I can clean the wound."

"I'm not sure that's Greek," he replied. "I know most of the interesting words, and what I had hold of deserved an interesting word indeed."

"I am honored that you find my *derrière* worth resting your injured arm upon. Last layer, now."

Linen was whisked over his face, faintly smelling of soap and starch, of perspiration and the metallic odor of wet blood. When the sleeve slid over the wound on his arm, the injured skin burned. The shirt was tossed aside, landing with a light flutter on the floor several feet away.

Though a low fire burned in the grate, casting warmth through the night-cool room, his nipples pulled flat and tight. She would see him now, half-bare, and he had no idea what he would look like in her eyes. He was naked from needing help, not begging for seduction.

But if he had been a begging man, his every fiber would have been crying out for her touch.

When it came, it was the cooling touch of a damp cloth on his cut skin. "Your mysterious friend left you with a narrow wound," she observed, "but a deep one. It ought to be stitched, but I'd get sick if I tried."

"What will happen if it's not stitched?"

"It will heal if you keep it bound and don't move your arm much. I think. Though you might be left with a scar." She dabbed at the wound. "I'm sorry, I don't know much about this sort of thing. I've far more experience driving men to madness than cleaning their wounds afterward. It *is* clean, though, or as clean as it can get with water and—"

"Damnation! What was that, acid?"

"—brandy." She wiped his hands too, lightly abraded by his scrabble on the ground.

As she wrapped bandages about his biceps and tied them off snug, a lock of hair brushed his bare skin.

Was her hair unpinned and tumbling down, ready for sleep? Was she undressed? Ready to be taken to bed?

He clenched his free hand and tried not to think about the fact that they were here, *right here by a bed.* Again, he planted his boots, trying to ground his thoughts.

When he shifted his right foot, the boot felt odd.

He wiggled his foot as much as one could within the stiff leather bounds of a tall boot. It was the sheath for his stiletto causing the problem; it wasn't flat against his calf as it ought to be.

He jerked, realizing at once what had happened. "My knife—Charlotte. The knife in my boot. It's not my knife."

A flurry of tiny noises as she set down everything she was holding; then the mattress sank as she sat to his right on the bed. "It's your attacker's knife? You escaped with the knife that cut you?"

"The particular gift of a blind man under attack. Do not tell The *Times* or I shall have to fight every notable in the country." He tried to smile, but he wanted the thing out of his boot. Now. Giving the handle a tug, it slid free, heavy and sleek as a snake.

Repulsed, he stretched down to set it on the floor next to the bed. "What does it look like?"

She shifted closer to him, her sleeve against his bare arm. "It's a dagger. A thin one, with a straight blade and a tarnished silver guard. The handle is pearl and . . . some sort of stone, though I cannot tell what. The light of the lamp isn't sufficient."

And apparently she didn't want to touch it, to examine it more closely. Nor did he. "It is a rich man's toy, then."

"And it might be the knife that killed Nance." Her voice was low and tinged with sorrow.

"Yes, I am afraid of that, too."

What do you want? the assailant had asked. Not *why are you here,* or *leave off the search.*

What do you want? It was the question of a man fearing blackmail or exposure. The question of a desperate man, afraid of something Benedict knew.

Whatever that might be. He knew only what everyone at the inquest knew, no more. Surely not everyone would be attacked. No, there had been traffic to and from the public room for much of the evening. If anyone else had been hurt, a cry would have been raised at once.

So. Almost certainly, the other inhabitants of Strawfield were not in danger from this assailant. That was a balm for Benedict's ragged emotions.

Another was Charlotte, pressing against his side, sliding an arm about the bare skin of his waist.

How quickly a pain could be forgotten; how quickly a body could wake. "Intriguing," he said thickly. "Is this part of the treatment for my wound?"

"For mine, if you do not mind." She rested her head on his shoulder; long hair fell in a ticklish waterfall over his arm, his back. "I . . . I don't want to hear about the inquest. Not yet. She reminds me of me, you see. So quickly, everything changed."

"All right. That's all right. We won't talk of it." Charlotte might never have been hurt with a knife, but something had nevertheless cut her to the heart. He did not ask what, or when. He only put an arm around her, and they were in darkness together.

For a minute, no more, her chest hitched with

tears that were completely silent. Then she hooked a leg across his lap.

Benedict sucked in a sharp breath, heart thudding at the unexpected touch. "Miss Perry . . ."

"You called me Charlotte downstairs."

"I should not have done so until you gave me permission." In his rush to the vicarage, his worry to secure it, he had called her the name by which he'd thought of her since she first revealed it.

"You have it." Again, she tucked her head into the hollow beneath his jaw, resting on his shoulder. "Please. Say my name again."

"Charlotte." He cradled her in his unhurt arm as he said her name slowly, tasting each sound. The secretive beginning, the saucy flip at the end. Now, on his lips, it was as erotic as a kiss. "Charlotte."

Her response was a hand trailing down his abdomen, coming to rest on the fall of his breeches. "Benedict."

His body responded at once, cock growing thick and hard as his hickory cane. *Don't get fuddled.*

But she kept touching him, slow and unmistakable, and he had to ask before he was fuddled beyond all reason. "Do you really want this, or are you using me to forget something?"

"Must it be all of one or all of the other?"

Her nails teased the sensitive flesh about his navel until he could have groaned. "It is a bit of both, then? I can live with that."

And he sank to one elbow, rolling her over him onto the bed. He was all ready to ravish her—but then she spoke.

"Before you touch me, there are a few things I ought to tell you."

Chapter Ten

"You are lying atop me," Benedict groaned, "and you want to *talk*? How many secrets have you?" It would have been funny had she not removed her hand from the fall of his breeches.

"More than my share. But somehow you've learned the biggest of them—that Maggie is my child. This is . . . the second biggest."

"If it is a secret smaller than the existence of a human being, I am quite sure I can accept it." Benedict could hardly think with a solid, sweet, wintergreen-and-seduction bundle of woman atop him on the bed. "I can't imagine what it could be. Last time you told me there was something I ought to know, you revealed a secret identity."

She raised herself up onto her forearms, which had the interesting effect of pressing their hips together. She still wore her gown from the day, and he took the opportunity to undo a few buttons at the back of her bodice before realizing what her silence meant. "Oh, God. You *do* have another secret identity? Please tell me your name is at least Charlotte. I've already got used to calling you that."

She laughed, as he hoped she would. And then, in a rush, she blurted, "I was a courtesan in London for ten years."

"All right." He raised his head to kiss her. "That makes sense. I didn't *really* think you'd been a traveling missionary."

She permitted a quick press of lips, then pulled her face back. "That's . . . does that not matter to you?"

"Does it matter to me that you are intelligent and intriguing enough to earn a living by fascinating men?" He let his head fall heavily to the mattress. "I admit, it does. I think it is rather wonderful."

"It isn't. Wasn't." She let out a deep breath. "It's over now. I've left that life behind me."

"For Maggie?"

"For many reasons. A life of pleasure is really nothing of the sort." She slid down his body, the buttons at her bodice abrading the bare skin of his chest. "I can tell you that I never took a protector who had a problem with . . . who had any sort of . . ."

"Shy girl. Are you reassuring me you don't have the pox? I don't either."

"Always to be preferred." She nuzzled at the taut muscle of his abdomen. "You don't mind that I've been with other men?"

"Charlotte, you are mere inches from my cock. You could stab me in the other arm and I wouldn't mind."

"All right," she said. "All right, then. I wanted honesty between us."

"You have it. Now, could there be fewer clothes

between us? You've been ogling me for the past half hour and I haven't so much as touched your breast."

"Ogling! Honestly." He could tell she was smiling. "You probably got yourself slashed just so I'd take off your clothing."

"It is a benefit I never foresaw." And then a thought occurred to him—of something he wanted as much as he craved her intimate touch. "Will you let me feel your face?"

"Does it matter to you what I look like?"

"It's only fair for me to know, is it not? You know what I look like. Think of it as my turn to ogle you."

"If you feel my face, I ought to feel out your short-comings."

"Charlotte, your face is as the Creator made it, just as would be my shortcomings—if there were any, which there are not."

"None?"

"Not of the sort that are relevant in a bed."

"All right," she said again. He was beginning to love that phrase.

She crawled back up his body, arms and knees straddling him, the loosened front of her gown teasing the hairs of his chest. And then she tucked herself against his left side, her face and unbound hair pillowed against his shoulder.

With the forefinger of his right hand, then, he reached across to touch her. The moment felt trembling and slight, like the first raindrop to fall into a pond—but at the brush of his skin against hers, something much larger rippled between them. And at last, he learned the shape of her.

There was one of her brows, with a wicked arch, and there was the other. This was the shape of the eyes she had surely rolled at him more than once, the lips that spoke and smiled and had welcomed his kiss. Her nose was—well, it was a nose, straight and seeming a fine size for the rest of her face. He felt the line of her jaw, the column of her neck. Passed a thumb about the curve of her ear. Stroked her cheeks, one of which bore a puckered scar just below the cheekbone.

"There you are, then, Charlotte," he murmured. "I knew you were beautiful from the first time you spoke to me."

She swallowed heavily. He cupped her cheek, and wet lashes blinked against his rough thumb. "Here I am."

Since she was within such easy reach, he found the laces of her stays. No sailor had tied these knots; his fingers had them undone in a moment. "How were you going to get out of these clothes if I hadn't been so obliging as to remove them?"

"I've slept in my stays before. But I would far rather have them off."

"I would prefer that, too." Keeping her in his embrace, he eased down her sleeves and stays. "If you don't like what I do, only tell me to stop."

"Do not stop," she said.

So he kissed her again. Sweetly at first, as light and teasing as the touches on her face. Coaxing her to take her pleasure of him instead of the reverse. Just kisses, to taste and breathe her in. To learn not the shape of her body, but of her will.

Did she want comfort? He would comfort her. A thrill? Yes, she might have that, too. He would kiss her until her tears were dry, or until desire poured from her like a fine wine uncorked.

For a few minutes, the world was all hot mouth and gentle tongue. And then her fingers clutched in his hair as she shifted, moving closer on the bed. "We must be perfectly silent," she murmured. "No one must hear." Her hips shifted, riding the line of his thigh, and she took his hand to her breast.

Finally.

"If you want silence, you will have to work for it." He helped her to sit so he might further untangle her from her bodice and stays—pushing down the former, pulling away the latter. Then he faced her and explored her body as gently as he had learned her face. Her shoulders, flexing under his warm touch; her arms, about which he had once wrapped a shawl. He trailed light fingertips down her ribs, across her belly. He dipped lower to toy with the hair about her sex, a slight pressure that made her squirm.

"Silence," he reminded her. He drew his fingers up her back, holding her steady with his broad palms. Bending his head, he nuzzled at one soft breast. The curve was soap-scented and warm and delicious. He nibbled the skin until her breathing came more quickly and she wrenched his head to her nipple.

He took it between his lips, drawing on the tenderness until it grew tight. "Yes," she moaned. "Just like that." Ah, he could have groaned; he wanted to stroke himself in rhythm with her every passion-caught breath.

But this was for her. Cupping one breast, he teased the other; then he switched mouth and hands. Again and again, alternating pressure and play, until her legs began to shudder, her hips to twitch and shake the mattress. She was eager; she wanted release. She had come to him for pleasure, and he would see that she got it.

"Slide down the bed," he said. "Seat yourself atop my traveling trunk." He stood, lending her a hand, and helped her to the foot of the bed where his sea chest kept pride of place.

"You want me to sit on the trunk," she said, half-amused, half-questioning. "Are you going to tell me a story?"

"Hmm. Let's say I'm going to act it out. I think you'll like it—especially the ending."

"All right," she said yet again, and he grinned.

When she perched on the flat lid of the chest, he sat before her on the floor. Drawing up her skirts and bundling them at her knees, he spread her legs with his free hand. "May I?"

She knew what he meant. "Yes," she said faintly. The bed creaked as she rested her weight against the footboard and opened wider to his touch.

Whether her skin was rosy or pale, whether her private hair was brown or black, he didn't care. Sight mattered least at moments like this, when one could breathe in the intimate scent of desire. When he could touch her folds, slick and ready, and slide a finger within her; when he could bend to taste, pulling at her bud of pleasure, and feast his ears on the sound of her gasp, her quickly covered moan. Fingers, lips, tongue, he drew on her until she tightened about him, quaking her pleasure.

She started to fall from the height, but he would not let her land. "Silence," he murmured again, just to be wicked. Pressing a kiss to her thigh, he thrust a second finger into her core, then spread them. Somewhere was a mysterious little spot that could send her to the peak. *There.* He knew he had found it when she went tight about him, muscles clenched, calves bunched, as though she could strain her way to another climax.

He would help her with that. Fingers still working the inner spot, he again found her bud with a gentle nibble of lips. Then he licked it with force. *Come now.* She did, shuddering as if caught in a storm—and *ha,* she cried out, too, clapping a hand over her mouth to cover the sound.

"How . . . Benedict . . . my *God.*"

He withdrew his fingers, kissed each thigh in turn, and sat back as he eased her knees together. "Wicked Charlotte. You weren't silent."

"Not even a saint could have been entirely silent while performing such virtuous works." She shoved her skirts back into place in a rustling bundle, then flopped from her seat on the trunk right onto him.

Oof. He hadn't been prepared for that, and he fell back, rolling prone to the floor with her atop him.

At this angle, half-naked and with Charlotte on his lap, the faint remains of a fire kissing him with warmth, he didn't notice the bare floor. He didn't remember why he had been hurt, or what existed outside this room. All that mattered was that Charlotte had wanted something of him, and he had given it to her, and she had liked it.

He felt like a god-damned king.

Later that night, he sat before the trunk again, trailing his fingers over the lock. Charlotte had gone to bed in her chamber, and he was alone, and the fire was out.

After a few minutes in their puddled embrace on the floor, she had offered to pleasure him. He declined—rather heroically, he thought. "Too much of a risk of being heard," was his excuse. "I couldn't possibly be quiet once you put your hands on me."

"Oh, no, you misunderstand," she said with false innocence. "It wouldn't be my hands on you. It would be my mouth."

His will almost collapsed. "Cruel temptress. But I think—best not. For now."

Stubborn of him to refuse, maybe, but he had wanted her to receive pleasure with no obligation to return it. She probably hadn't had such an experience for ten years, if ever.

She seemed to understand his meaning, for she kissed him, gentle and slow, on the plane of his cheek. "You are kindness itself, Benedict Frost. Another time, then, shall I?"

"If there is *another time* of any sort, I should be the luckiest man in existence."

When she kissed him farewell for the night, he wondered if she could taste herself on his lips.

Once he was alone, he brought himself off with a few strokes, spending with a smothered groan. Ever since Charlotte had kissed him ragged that morning and shoved him into the bedchamber, lust had soaked the edge of his every thought.

With it slaked, at least temporarily, he removed his boots and cleaned his hands.

And now he sat before the trunk again. Flat-topped and battered, it was constructed of camphorwood, and a faint fresh smell issued from the wood itself. The small lock had long since corroded too much for the key to turn easily, and Benedict was in the habit of opening the chest with his stiletto.

Not possible right now. Fortunately, he still carried the key about with him, and he eased it into the lock. The iron had grown fragile and stubborn from sea salt and the clumsy cuts of the stiletto blade, but eventually he got it open.

Within the neat drawers and compartments of this chest were all of his possessions in the world. It seemed a paltry collection: breeches, stockings, linen shirts, a spare waistcoat. A hat. All the money he had from his pension and the sale of the family bookshop, heavy in the form of silver and guinea-gold. Since losing his sight, he had always insisted on being paid in specie. Paper currency meant nothing to a blind man.

And here, wrapped in brown paper and string, was his manuscript. He hefted it, the weight pleasing in his hands.

Even more than the chronicle of his travels, it was a record of his mastery of the written word. Throughout his sighted years, letters—whether scribbled with a pen or printed in a book—had wiggled and shifted into incomprehensible jumbles. Every volume in his parents' bookshop was a silent witness to their disappointment: that they loved this world of words, and that he was too stubborn or imbecilic to join them.

At sea, literacy was almost irrelevant. All that mattered was doing one's work well. Following orders. Making up part of a crew that worked together like the beating heart of a ship.

He sometimes thought the Royal Navy had saved his life.

Writing was different with the noctograph, though;

the stylus seemed to pin words in place. Working with hand and mind, without the trickery of his eyes, sentences came forth in careful order. He felt each letter's shape and etched it with his pen. Though he could never reread his own work, he knew: he could write. Finally. An unexpected gift granted by blindness.

And maybe the writing of it was all the good he needed. It had fastened memory in place as well, making him reflect on what he'd done. After years of war, he'd crossed the Channel and freely strode the streets of Paris. He'd been snow-whipped on Mount Blanc, teetered in a gondola through the murky canals of Venice. He had been pleasured by a French widow who could do amazing things with her tongue, and he had passed along his newfound knowledge to a *signora* of Venice who declared him her finest lover ever.

Some things were too private to be set to paper, but they made part of the past years' arc nonetheless.

He could not publish it as a fiction, as though these things had not truly happened to him. But if it were never to be published at all, and it could not be reread, the manuscript had no value. Why should he bother holding fast to it?

He hefted the parcel in one hand. It took up the space in his trunk of a pair of dancing pumps, or a few satin waistcoats. Men of fashion needed such things more than they needed a bundle of worthless paper.

Why should he bother traveling again, for that matter? Often he disliked it—the discomfort, the rootlessness. The absence of anyone to trust as he attempted to exchange money or learn his way about a new city. Always hearing *There's the blind traveler.*

Sometimes it would be nice to walk without smacking his cane at every step to feel his way through the world. To stride, instead, through a town whose streets he knew as well as the angles of his own face. To hear *There is my friend, Benedict.*

Or even, since he was dreaming, to hear *There is my husband.*

Welcome home, darling.

Papa! I missed you!

Sailors didn't have those dreams. Blind men didn't either. Naval Knights weren't permitted to marry. Men who roamed the world never expected to find a home.

But he was all these things, and more. Benedict's dreams, like his travel, were a gesture of defiance to a world that looked at him with seeing eyes and said *You can't.*

He could.

Rising to his knees, he shuffled his possessions about in their tidy stacks and nestled the manuscript into the chest again. Another *he could*: he could afford to let it lie cocooned a while longer.

So. What ought he to do next? It was a much larger question than tonight—though for tonight, he would start by wrapping the mysterious dagger in the discarded cloth Charlotte had wrapped around his wounded arm. Tomorrow they would decide what to do with it. Turn it over to the Bow Street Runner, maybe.

He felt around on the floor until he found it, a trailing pile of fabric.

Of brocaded fabric, with—he felt the edge—yes,

with a tasseled edge. It was her shawl. The shawl he had tucked about her arms, the shawl on which they had sat and talked, when he had pried into her life because he couldn't seem not to. She had bound his wound with her shawl.

"Hell," he muttered, but he might have meant the opposite.

The theft from the Royal Mint had brought death and danger, but Benedict feared neither. Charlotte Perry, though—she was a hazard of an entirely different sort. Around her, he was in danger of forgetting the royal reward, the quest, the need to care for his sister's future.

He was in danger of shutting away the man he had become over laborious years, and of planning a new start.

Chapter Eleven

"She won't get up! She won't get up!"

Charlotte jerked awake to the sound of her child's cry for the first time in more than ten years. The sharp odor of animal urine wrinkled her nose. Blinking bleary eyes, she lifted her head from the pillow. "Maggie? Are you all—"

"It's Captain! Aunt Charlotte, she did a puddle and now she won't get up." Maggie's voice teetered between fear and despair.

Feet tangled in the bedcovers, Charlotte took a moment to extricate herself before stumbling to the tableau before the hearth. On her favorite rug, Captain lay soiled and prone. The labored rise and fall of her side, the blink of her puzzled dark eyes at Maggie, proclaimed her mute distress.

"She's never done this before." Maggie petted the brindled head. "She's such a good dog. She knows to go outside."

"She did it plenty of times when she was a puppy." Rise, fall, rise, fall. Each breath the dog took was a reprieve. "Let me fetch a cloth, all right? We'll clean her up."

"All right." Maggie's voice was thick with worry.

Charlotte tied a wrapper about her shift and opened the bedchamber door—only to walk into her parents and Benedict, all crowded into the corridor. "Good morning . . . everyone in the world. Were you all awoken by Maggie?"

"Nonsense. It's quarter to seven. Past time for the household to be awake," commented Mrs. Perry. "Church in little more than two hours, and here we are a bunch of slugabeds." Indeed, she was dressed. The vicar and Frost were unshaven, but they, too, had pulled on trousers and shirts.

"Right," said Charlotte. "Well, sorry I'm such a slattern. I need some sort of cloth for cleaning up after Captain. She forgot herself a bit during the night."

"You can use my shirt," said Benedict. Charlotte's parents stared at him. Somehow, he must have felt their gazes, for he added, "The ruined one, I mean. I'll get it." He disappeared into his chamber.

"What ruined shirt?" Mrs. Perry looked suspicious, as though certain Charlotte had been ripping the clothes off their guest.

Charlotte coughed. "Ah—that is Mr. Frost's tale to tell."

Having experienced the attack firsthand, he'd do a better job than she describing the events of the previous night. Minus, of course, the part about how he'd tongued her to ecstasy. Twice. After she had *not* ripped off his clothing, but had removed it with great care and concern.

The stairs creaked as someone climbed them, and Barrett's white-capped head poked into the corridor next. "Does Mr. Frost's tale have anything to do with the furniture piled against the doors? Cook is in a fidget about getting the breakfast ready."

Benedict reappeared, handing his worn, torn, blood-spattered shirt to Charlotte. "I'm sure it's a sight, but Captain won't mind that."

"Why is there furniture piled against the doors?" said Charlotte's father, bewildered. "Is that a . . . sailor sort of thing, Mr. Frost?"

"It is a safety sort of thing," said Charlotte. "Mr. Frost, perhaps you'll tell them what happened while I tend to Captain."

As Frost, rubbing at his left biceps, agreed, Charlotte left them in the corridor. She returned to the sniffling Maggie, crouching next to her and the dog. "Would you like to clean Captain, or shall I?"

"I'll do it," said Maggie. "Once she is clean, will she be all right?"

Unwilling to say no, unwilling to lie, Charlotte considered her reply. Finally she said, "She is not young anymore, dearest. She needs more rest than when she was a pup."

Maggie turned her face away, silently sopping up the mess with what had once been a man's linen shirt.

"I never did plait your hair with ribbons." Charlotte said, as she tried to change the subject. "Shall I do that for church?"

"No. I don't want to go to church today."

Charlotte almost laughed. How often had she said the same to her parents as a girl. She never wanted to sit indoors, listening, when she could be wading through the stream at the base of the Kinder Downfall or fashioning a twist of rare wildflowers for her hair to try to impress that Selwyn boy.

That wiped the smile from her face quickly enough.

"—a cutpurse, I presume," she heard Benedict explaining from outside the bedchamber door. "Your daughter bandaged my arm, and in the interest of security we barricaded the doors."

"What has this village come to," bemoaned the vicar. "Ever since that serving girl was given a gold sovereign, it's been strange faces and theft and . . ."

"Reverend!" His wife cut off this recital.

Maggie let out a strangled sob.

"How quickly a place can become unfamiliar, can't it?" Charlotte said, hardly knowing to whom she was speaking.

"Cook is still fair fit to pull out her hair," reminded Barrett. "Because of the doors being blocked and all."

"Right, yes," said Charlotte's father. "Now, now, please. This is all very—I'm sure it was nothing, and Mr. Frost is quite all right—my sermon. I shall speak of charity, and . . . and not lusting for money. Yes, if I could find my notes . . ."

The clamor outside the door faded away, leaving Charlotte and girl and dog in a quiet that was far too heavy.

"Well." Charlotte broke it inanely. "Let's get dressed, shall we? And then we can go down to breakfast."

"I won't breakfast today. Captain cannot come down the stairs. Look how tired she is. I'm staying with her." Maggie set aside the ruined shirt and petted the dog's front paws, gently over the small bones and clawed toes. Captain's tail gave a slow thump as she squeezed closed her eyes.

What would a parent say? "You need to eat," Charlotte said. "Then you can come back to her."

"But I can't leave her alone!"

"Dearest," Charlotte began in a tone that might as well have said *Stop all this fuss over a dog*.

She drew in a deep breath, halting words that were sure to be sharp. Trying to argue Maggie out of her distress would only add to it.

Did Maggie have any human friends? Such marvelous creatures had been in short supply for Charlotte and her sister. As the daughters of the vicar, they were too respectable to mingle with the servants and too shabby for the fine families of Strawfield. Not in trade but too poor for gentility, they were left alone.

The same must be true for Maggie, who kept company with an ancient dog and the ancient Greeks. She ought to have a half-dozen brothers and sisters and cousins; she ought to be mingling with the children of merchants and soldiers and sailors and . . . and, well, maybe amateur explorers, too.

Charlotte swallowed. "All right. Let's see if we can carry her down with us."

A rap at the frame about the door made her look up. "Frost."

Benedict stood a polite distance outside the doorway of the bedchamber. "I have moved all the furniture away from the doors. Will you now allow me to be of service to my Captain?"

"Mr. Frost, you're not dressed," Maggie chided.

Without the slashed and bloodied lieutenant's coat, he wore only shirtsleeves and a waistcoat on his upper half. His fit form was outlined and displayed, the snug breeches and tall boots completing the picture of capable masculinity.

Shamelessly, Charlotte caressed him with her eyes.

"I am as dressed as I can be," he said with a comical pull of his features. "My coat met with a misadventure last night. Did you not hear me telling your grandparents about it? Come, let me carry Captain down for you and I shall tell you the scary parts."

Maggie hopped to her feet, in instant agreement.

"She is before the hearth. On the braided rug." Which would now need to be cleaned or discarded, like Benedict's shirt.

Benedict murmured something, too softly to overhear, as he stepped closer to the dog and crouched before her. It was a croon of sorts. She leaned closer, hoping to pick out a few words that would help her to identify the song.

"Hmm hmm hmmmmm . . . Don't listen, Miss Perryyyyy . . . ." he half sung, "because it's a sailor's song, and it's not fit for the ears of human women . . . hmm hmmmm."

The song had Captain thumping her tail again, and Benedict eased the bony bundle into his arms. "Miss Maggie, would you walk ahead of us and open the front door? I think this good sir could do with a little time in the sun."

They made a queue that slowly creaked down the stairs, and then Maggie opened the front door without another protest about wanting Captain with her at breakfast. They piled out onto the stoop, half-dressed all, and Benedict laid the dog on the dewy ground. With a rustle and *whuff*, she stretched out her legs and rolled onto her belly.

"There, she feels the sun to be as welcome as I do," he said.

"You're nice to her." Maggie folded her arms tightly, the thin linen of her nightdress little shield from the morning breeze. "Did you ever have a pet?"

Benedict frowned in thought. "No, I never did. I lived in London until I went to sea at twelve, and there's no room on shipboard for dogs and cats."

"What about rats? Or parrots?"

"Er . . . a sailor's relationship with rats isn't really a friendly one. And isn't it pirates who are meant to have parrots?"

"Or privateers," said Charlotte.

He snorted. "Alas, I was neither. But if I ever settle down, I'll have to get a pet."

"It ought to be a dog," said Maggie. "They can sniff out anything you like, and a dog can learn your way around and guide you safely if you don't know where you're going."

"How would the dog know where I was going?"

This gave her pause.

"Shall we allow Captain to rest and play while we ready ourselves?" Charlotte asked.

Miraculously, Maggie agreed, and she marched back into the house.

Charlotte caught Benedict's sleeve before he could follow. "Thank you," she whispered. "I didn't know what to do."

"You were with her. That was all she needed." He grinned. "Besides, I couldn't have carried the dog if you hadn't bandaged my arm so well."

After he went inside, Charlotte remained outside for a moment alone. Benedict said he could feel the sun, and she wondered if she could, too. It arose early with the late spring, but it was distant and watery. She shut her eyes, extending her hands palms out to catch any fallen drop of warmth. Listening for a bird, or for some movement of the world around her.

She thought she heard a step, far away. A skitter of something hard across the stone wall, like pebbles.

Captain sneezed, then rolled over with a rustle of grass. Charlotte's eyes popped open.

"So much for my attempt to understand the world." The hound was standing on spindly legs, head cocked. "I can't even understand you. Was this whole dramatic fuss intended to get Benedict Frost to carry you about?"

The tail beat a slow tattoo through the air.

"Well done, then. I can't fault you for that. Roll around in the dew some more and get yourself clean, all right? I'm afraid you'll have to stay outside for a while." And with a curious glance around—she saw nothing, of course, nothing important at all—she returned to the house.

The capable maid Barrett saw to the tidying of the bedchamber and helped Charlotte lace her stays, diplomatically not asking how they'd got unlaced the day before. Eventually everyone was clean and tidy and ready for breakfast: Papa, Mama, Charlotte. Maggie. Benedict Frost. They collected about the table in the dining room, a simple meal of porridge and tea before them.

It felt oddly like a family gathering such as . . . well, such as they had never had. Margaret had married when Charlotte was seventeen, and she went away. Never had a suitor dined with the family.

Not that Benedict was a suitor. He knew what she

was, and what she'd been. They understood each other. That was . . . a comfort.

She did not even mind that he was more at ease with her family than she was.

"I realize," he said, spooning up a bit of porridge, "that you must be nearly ready to set off in the direction of the church. I don't mean to be shallow or worldly, but I find myself without a coat to wear."

The reverend dropped his spoon with a clatter. "I should not have permitted you to walk home alone!"

"Indeed you should have, Vicar. It was my decision to remain late in the taproom of the Pig and Blanket. Therefore any risk was mine to accept, too."

"Passive voice," commented Mrs. Perry. "Very difficult to translate."

But Charlotte's heart gave a quick thump of recognition. "Your words are so sensible, Mr. Frost. Someone wise must have said something like that to you not long ago."

"There is something wise indeed about pleading one's right to do unwise things." He winked at her, oddly charming over his unfocused gaze.

"My father's things are up in the attic," said Maggie. "Maybe you could wear one of his coats, Mr. Frost."

Charlotte was glad, suddenly, that Benedict was not capable of shooting her a sharp glance. "What an excellent idea, Maggie. I'll ask one of the maids to retrieve something later for Mr. Frost."

The man Maggie called her father was, of course, nothing of the sort. He had been Margaret Perry Catlett's husband; Charlotte had met him only once, at her elder sister's wedding. A respectable tradesman of no family, he had predeceased his wife by several months.

"You can't come to church like that, Mr. Frost," decided Mrs. Perry. "You'll have to stay back just this once."

"Then you can take care of Captain while we're gone!" cried Maggie.

"Your aunt," said Benedict gravely, "has already asked me to do so." A lie, but Charlotte was pleased by it when Maggie beamed at her.

"Did I—I think I did not ask Barrett to get the baskets ready for this afternoon," said the vicar. "I need to pay some calls to—"

"Reverend, this is meant to be a day of rest." Charlotte's mother had set aside her spoon. "The calls can wait until tomorrow."

"They cannot." Twist, twist went his hands. "I meant to take these items about yesterday, but—"

"You spent the time in the inquest instead." She sighed. "There's always something, Perry."

"Indeed, Mrs. Perry." The following silence was not a taut one, but rather exhausted. "No peace for the wicked, or from them. And I have grown so tired that I do not know in which company I belong."

While Charlotte and her father made the rounds of the village that afternoon, Benedict remained at the vicarage.

No one had expected anything of him since he'd carried Captain downstairs this morning, which was both freeing and distressing. Maggie had her dog; Charlotte was playing the good vicar's daughter—and helping to muscle the armful of baskets packed by Barrett, he could tell by her breathless good-bye.

What was he to do, then? He had already written to Georgette. He had nothing in particular about which he needed to write Lord Hugo, and his other correspondents were far too casual on which to use costly paper without cause.

He wandered into the kitchen and passed a pleasant, idle hour with the cook and the maid Colleen, who helped in the kitchen and occasionally about the house. They refused to allow him to peel vegetables— "not on account of you bein' blind, Mr. Frost, but because you're a gentleman and the reverend's guest"—so he simply soaked in the scents of roasting fowl and sweet stewed fruit and listened to the comfortable arguments between the pair of women.

Cook had the wheeze and stomp of a woman of great bulk, and she was exacting in her instructions to the slight young Colleen. When their conversation turned from a pleasurable discussion of who might have gutted Nance Goff to a far more contentious row over the proper color for a gravy made from drippings, he excused himself.

Passing through the dining room and into the ground floor's corridor, he encountered his hostess. "Hello, Mrs. Perry. Taking a break from the Trojans?"

"Tut, Mr. Frost. The Trojans are the enemy. I am expert in ancient Greek."

"What are you translating now?"

She didn't reply for a long moment; Benedict began to wonder if he had offended her with the question. "No one ever asks me that."

"Surely Lord Hugo does."

"Not my correspondents. I mean, the people with whom I live." Another pause. "Would you like to explore my study? You can smack your cane about on the floor as long as you do not disturb the papers."

He recognized this as a generous offer and fetched his hickory cane from its spot next to the front door. A few blows, their echoes, the vibrations that assembled his world into sense, told him that the space was small and deadened around the edges by shelves of books and papers. There were—he felt about—a desk and two chairs. "Sit, sit," offered Mrs. Perry, and he did so.

"You asked what I'm working on," she said. "It's *The Odyssey*. Just a bit of fun, really. It's been done before, time and time again. I made a translation of it myself when I was just learning Greek in the early days of my marriage."

"Oh, I thought you had known it much longer." He knew little about this friend of Lord Hugo's besides her fondness for the language, despite living under her roof for several days.

"No, I took it up when Perry got the Strawfield living. It's my calling, I suppose you'd say. A vicar's wife must have something to do while her husband is gone at all hours, caring for his flock of sheep." With a sigh, she shuffled a stack of papers. "I like the idea of *The Odyssey*. A family split apart that comes back together in the end."

"The story takes years, doesn't it?"

"It does, at that. I believe I've been waiting longer than Penelope."

The silence drew out long and soft, a woolen yarn of quiet. "I shan't keep you from the work that gives you comfort," Benedict said.

But he wasn't sure now if it did.

* * *

After a few minutes in the first household she and
her father visited, Charlotte remembered why she
had given up *virtuous work*.

Mrs. Fancot, the laundress who had so infuriated
Barrett, lived behind a shop in a rented set of rooms.
The scents of her trade, astringent soaps and lyes,
stung the nose as soon as one walked in. A stringy
widow with several grown children, she began wailing
as soon as the vicar crossed the threshold.

"Oh, Reverend! If someone would only find them
gold coins." She dabbed at faded eyes. "My little
grandson Jack has the scrofula, and him no more'n
three years old. Gold rubbed on the sores will take
them right away!"

No, it won't. The only way gold would help a child
with scrofula was by lining his physician's pocket.

"There, there." The vicar bent his gray head to
rummage through a basket. "I came to pray with you,
and I have brought you a length of felt."

"What good is felt to a little boy with scrofula?"
Mrs. Fancot blew her nose on her sleeve.

The vicar looked nonplussed. "None, I—well,
that is—last time I visited you mentioned needing
cloth for—"

"Oh, vicar! I need *gold!*" A fresh wail succeeded,
and the widow buried her face in her apron.

"You are not the only one," muttered Charlotte.
More loudly, she added, "God bless you and all that.
I'm sure you're grateful for the fabric. Well, good-
bye." She took her father by the elbow and hurried
him out.

"Why, Charlotte . . ." He shook his head, blinking

dimly into the afternoon sunlight. A ghost of a smile hovered on his thin features. "I have never finished an errand at Mrs. Fancot's house so quickly."

"You're welcome," she said. "Where next?"

The next several calls were less tearful and slightly more pleasant, as Charlotte bore the curious stares of families who had never met the vicar's sole surviving child, or who had not seen the virtuous—*ha*—Miss Perry for some years. As her father dispensed prayers, comfort, a few more bolts of cloth, and a jar of calves'-foot jelly, she allowed herself to be looked at and even tried soothing a fussy baby.

The baby bit her.

"Why don't the Selwyns see to the needs of these people?" she asked as her father led them to the final visit. "They are the squires hereabouts, and they ought to—"

"They see to their tenants." And that was all he said.

But that was all he needed to say. Charlotte understood: Lady Helena, the earl's daughter who had married Edward eight years before, was as ungenerous as she was rich. The people of Strawfield who did not live on her land were of no concern to her.

"I'm glad you gave away that calves'-foot jelly," Charlotte said. *I'm glad you give your time like this.*

"No one in the vicarage likes it," he replied. And she wondered if he, too, meant more than what he said. By this point in the afternoon, the sun was hot on the crown of Charlotte's bonnet—*not* the one with the veil—and her father's shoulders drooped.

"Let me carry the basket, Papa. You are tired." She took it from him and knocked at the final door, in a lodging-house at the far end of the village's main street.

This was the residence of Miss Day, an invalid who had once served as governess to the Selwyn children. Miss Day's maid-of-all-work let Charlotte and the reverend into a single room with bedstead, table, and a hearth full of ashes. Everything was poor but clean, yet the room stank of the smoke and grease from the other chambers in the house.

"Oh, what a comfort to see you." Miss Day tried to push herself upright. "You have brought my medicine?"

Charlotte looked questioningly at her father.

"Yes, Miss Day. Exactly what your doctor ordered. One spoonful three times daily."

Rummaging through the odds and ends left in the basket, Charlotte found the stoppered bottle. She handed it to the maid, who curtsied her thanks and began to prepare a dose.

"And how much do I owe the doctor? I am afraid it must be very dear." Miss Day's thin hands picked at the stitches on her quilt—which, Charlotte noticed, was much better pieced than her own work on the quilts at the vicarage.

"Not so much as a farthing," said Charlotte's father. "He did not want you to go to any worry, but just to recover your health."

If this was the same doctor who had seen to Charlotte when she was a child, he was not the sort to bother himself about a patient's feelings. She thought she knew who, instead, had paid for the treatment.

"How kind," said the invalid, and she swallowed a dutiful dose of the medicine. "Will you convey him my thanks?"

"I will."

She coughed feebly. "Lady Helena—at the great house, you know—she had promised to send some arrowroot and beef tea. So kind and generous ever since I had to leave her service. Although I suppose she forgot to send it over. The distraction of her husband's return home." *Cough cough.*

Cold raced over Charlotte's scalp. "Lady Helena's husband is returned?"

"Oh, yes. Last night, maybe, or today. He traveled in a crested carriage. It was before the house this morning, and you know how quickly word travels through the village." Another feeble cough. "Reverend, you mustn't be angry at him if he traveled on a Sunday. Who could resist returning to those little dear lambs sooner?"

By this, Charlotte assumed, Miss Day referred to her former charges. Edward's children. Edward's *other* children.

She wondered if they looked anything like Maggie. She supposed she'd rather not know.

Dimly, she stood by and tried to look proper and dull as her father said a few prayers with the bed-bound Miss Day and then bade her farewell.

And then came the walk back to the vicarage, long and thirsty, the basket heavy in the crook of her arm. Footsteps made ridges in the mud at the edges of the road. Here there was no pavement such as in London.

Her father was the first to break the silence. "Thank you for coming along today, Charlotte. It—it was good to have your help."

This seemed not to be quite how he'd meant to finish, but he fell silent again.

"I should have helped more," she said. "Not today, but for the past years. Papa. I had no idea all that you—" Her throat caught, and for a moment she was trapped between silence and sound.

"I should have helped more," she said again.

Her father looked down at her with eyes that were green like her own, and somehow sad. "I should have allowed you to," he said.

Chapter Twelve

The next morning, the weather was fine, and Charlotte wanted to feel pretty—a woman's best armor, even if she were a spinster vicar's daughter, against social trespass.

Which she and Benedict were going to commit.

They had agreed upon this at breakfast, which they ate at a lazy hour of the morning. She told him of her plan. "We cannot hunt the gold. We've got to hunt the person who knows where it's hidden."

"I notice a lot of 'we' about this business. Not a foe anymore, am I?"

"You were never that." She swallowed tea, black and overbrewed, and choked a little. Ever since she had taken her pleasure of him—or since he had given her pleasure?—she had developed a strange softness about the heart where he was concerned. "Yes, we. I know you want to find the sovereigns, too, and I've come to think we need each other to do so."

"Tell me more." He clunked one elbow onto the table, rested his chin on it, and raised one brow.

"Well . . . someone always knows something. A

driver took trunks into his carriage. A servant loaded coins into trunks. A person at the mint looked aside while an unfamiliar driver took a shipment into his carriage."

He lifted his head, frowning. "Where are these people? Dead or paid for their silence, if they're in London."

"But they aren't all in London—or they weren't the night before last." The night Edward Selwyn had returned to his grand house. Maybe. She really needed to find out when he'd arrived.

"I understand," said Benedict. "The person who attacked me is one of those people who knows something."

"I think so."

"And you think the person who stabbed Nance was—"

"The same person who paid her the coin. I do not know whether he meant to, or why. But she must have noticed something—or heard him say something— he never intended to."

"Now I must have, too." Benedict's mouth was a stern slash. "Or so he thinks."

"This is why I want to keep you about," said Charlotte. "You might be a target."

"Or bait." He sounded cheerful about the prospect. "You still carry your knife, don't you?"

"I'll find a way to do so," she had promised, then went upstairs to finish dressing for their outing.

Rather than the long-sleeved blue serge, she wore a lighter day dress of pale blue printed all over with black flowers and vines. A week after removing to Seven Dials, she had purchased this gown ready-made from a hopeful dressmaker. The fit was nothing like the bespoke silks Charlotte had sold off in secret, but the cloth was pretty, and she had become starved for prettiness almost as soon as she'd left Mayfair.

One problem: the gown had short sleeves. Where was she to stow her knife? Remembering Benedict's trick, she wiggled a small folding blade into her boot. It was not easy to reach, but it was better than being defenseless.

At her throat, she fastened an old family cameo, then she pinned a lace cap over her coiled hair and covered it with a plain bonnet. Last of all, she plucked up the dagger Benedict had retrieved from his attacker and slipped it into her reticule. The little piecework bag bulged oddly, true, but who would assume the bulge was due to a knife? "You're a spinster vicar's daughter," she told herself in the glass. "You spend your time in virtuous works."

Her cheeks were pink as she danced down the stairs.

"You are ready to conquer the world today," commented Benedict. "I can tell by the bounce in your step. I shan't be elegant enough to accompany you, but I plan to take your arm all the same."

To replace his ruined lieutenant's coat, he was wearing an ill-fitting coat that had belonged to Margaret's husband. Ezrah Catlett had been shorter, though just as broad, and the sleeves hit Benedict several inches above his wrists. The blue of the coat was faded with age, the buttons tarnished.

Her heart gave a squeeze. "You are as handsome as any fashion plate I ever saw," she said, and meant it.

He arched one of those wicked brows. "I like this mood of yours. I shall have to do my best to sustain it."

Before exiting the vicarage, he took up his hickory

cane. He had not used it around the house since his arrival, and she had forgotten what a stern air it lent him. He seemed again the large stranger from the inn, one who had caught a roomful of people in a mystified web.

Until he grinned at her and offered his free arm. And just as she had when he smiled at her for the first time across a table, when she could hardly see his features for her veil, she melted.

Only this time she was far more melty than before.

As they walked, they talked of everything and nothing, a lightness that belied their errand. Charlotte wondered if Benedict's brain hummed as hers did beneath the light chatter. When they turned into Strawfield proper, she studied every face. The familiar ones—the miller's wife and eldest daughter, now married and with a baby; the stationer; the poulterer, reeking of blood—they greeted her as Miss Perry and she provoked them into conversation.

Each time, when they passed on, Benedict said, "Not the voice of the attacker."

"I hardly thought Mrs. Burton's one-year-old had slashed you with a knife," she said. "But I'm glad you remember the voice clearly enough to absolve the little fellow of wrongdoing."

"Stop. Just here." He planted his feet and looked about. Or rather listened about, or took deeply of the air; Charlotte made herself as still and silent as she could.

After a few breaths, he nodded. "This. This is nearly where it happened."

"This is the place where you were attacked?" At his affirmation, she asked, "How do you know? I do not doubt; I am simply curious."

"The emptiness of the village green compared to the shops that wall one in at other points on the street. The distant smell of the bakery. And here the road gets soft and dips downward, probably because puddles form every time there is rain. What do you see hereabouts? Anything unusual? Anything that might give us a clue?"

As she skimmed over the scrubby grass, the gravel, the mud, and hard-packed dirt, she wished for some modicum of his focus, his ability to hone in on what was helpful. "I see trampled mud. There are prints of boots."

"What are their sizes? Or the direction? Are there prints going off like . . ." He made some complicated motion.

"I am sorry. I cannot tell one set from another. So many feet have walked here since that the prints overlay one another."

"Any bloodstains?"

"Good God, do you think you bled that much?" She strained her eyes for anything, anything that would make her useful. "If there were any, they have been trod into the mud. But let me look about for your stiletto."

He described how he had tossed it aside, desperate to hold fast to his cane as a barrier, and she toed aside every clump of grass in the way. To keep an innocent appearance for curious passersby, she maintained a steady stream of chatter about Strawfield, as though Frost were a tourist.

At last her search came to an end. "I did not turn up your stiletto. But I found a penny, some hazelnut shells, and a horseshoe nail."

"Clearly the remnants of some diabolical scheme."

"Maybe you and your assailant traded blades. Or maybe it was picked up by someone walking along the road."

"Or eaten by a goat."

"Doubtful, though possible. I am sorry. I wish I could have found it for you."

"It's all right. My boot is more comfortable without a knife in it."

She chuckled. "You're trying to make me feel better."

"No, I'm trying to make myself feel better."

"Is it working?"

He stepped closer and drew her hand onto his arm again. "Yes."

Before they had proceeded more than a dozen yards, Charlotte caught sight of the Bow Street Runner who had been hanging about in Strawfield ever since Nance received the gold sovereign. "I am going to hail Mr. Lilac," she told Benedict. "I think we ought to give him your attacker's dagger."

"Taking sensitive information to the proper authorities? Tosh, Miss Perry. One would think you'd never read a gothic novel. You ought to hold on to it and play at detection yourself."

"Thus putting myself into unnecessary danger? I think not. I *am* playing detective, but only for money. I will not play about with your life, Benedict."

"It was only a cut about the arm," he murmured, but he smiled nonetheless as she called out to the Bow Street Runner.

A slight man with plain clothing and a neatly trimmed beard, Lilac threaded his way between a bonneted woman carrying a basket of eggs and a portly man attempting to light a pipe, then greeted the pair.

Charlotte realized too late that she had met Lilac only as the veiled stranger, not as herself. Benedict must have realized the same, for he thanked Miss Perry for summoning Lilac. "I was fortunate enough to meet the Bow Street Runner at Miss Goff's inquest."

"Officer of the Police, if it pleases you," replied Lilac in a lilting brogue at odds with the shrewdness of his hazel eyes. "And how can I help you this late morning?"

"Mr. Lilac." Charlotte hesitated. "Are you seeking Nancy Goff's killer or the stolen gold sovereigns?"

"Well, now that's a good question. I wonder why you're asking it."

"Typical," murmured Benedict. "An answer that gives no information at all. Lilac, I don't know how you do it."

"Practice, Frost, practice. 'Tis my line of work, the way learning new swear words over the waves is yours."

"That is *not* all that sailors do. Although the point is well taken. And the reason for the question is that we might be able to help you with one investigation, but probably not the other."

"Ah, now." Lilac laid a finger aside of his nose. "I wouldn't be too certain of that. What is it that you'd like to tell me?"

"It's something to show you, rather," said Charlotte. "But—not in the street. Here, let us go to the bakery."

A few little tables had been squeezed in front of the bakery counter when Charlotte was about fifteen years of age, transforming the small, warm building into Strawfield's first tea-shop.

As soon as she stepped through the doorway and breathed the sweet, bready smell, she recalled how badly her younger self had wanted to sit at one of those tables. Had wanted to be asked to share a plate of cakes with a friend.

"I'm not meant to pop in for cakes while I'm in the midst of an investigation, Miss Perry," mumbled Lilac.

"Then we won't order cakes," she decided. She was past that stage of wanting, surely. "Have you tried the tart, Mr. Lilac? One can always think better when one is full of cake and jam."

"If that's so, the Officers will have to change their diet."

The three of them each ordered a slice of tart, and Charlotte arranged a pot of tea for the trio and directed Benedict to a small table. They squeezed into the tiny chairs around it, the only customers in the shop for the moment. After the baker's daughter brought by their confections on little white plates, she then disappeared into the rear of the bakery, leaving the three entirely alone.

"Tart before business," said Benedict.

"That's not the way I've usually conducted my affairs," Charlotte murmured in his ear. It was always so gratifying to make someone choke on unexpected laughter. More loudly, she added, "This is a local specialty, Mr. Lilac. The tart shell is filled with jam and almond sponge-cake."

"Jam?" Lilac sounded dubious, but he cut free a slab with the side of his fork and shoveled it into his mouth. "Mawwaghhha." An incoherent sound of delight issued from his lips; his eyes bugged open wide.

"Fwuhhhhuhhh," agreed Benedict.

Charlotte bit into her own slice. "Mmmmmm." *Perfection.* The almonds crunching, the cake soft and heavy, the jam a pop of plum-tartness. When Charlotte was a child, she'd received it as a rare treat—on her birthday each year, and once when she had correctly held fifty Bible verses in memory for as long as it took to recite them for her father.

She had tried to guide her cook in London through the recipe, but it was nothing but guesswork on both sides. "You asked me what I liked about this part of the world, Mr. Frost," she mumbled around a mouthful of tart. "This. I should have said this."

Heedless of her poor manners, the men were already scraping up the final crumbs of their sweet.

"All right," said Lilac with a satisfied sigh. "You've fed me, Miss Perry, and I do thank you. That was a real treat. Now, shall we get to the heart of why you've asked me to meet with you?"

Charlotte slung her reticule onto the table with a metallic *clunk*.

"That's no common lady's gewgaw inside, I'm guessing," noted the Runner. "Mind if I take a look?"

"Please do, but carefully."

Lilac teased open the drawstring of the piecework bag, peered inside—and whistled. "That's a pretty little toy you've got there, Miss Perry."

"It's not hers," said Benedict. "Though it's not mine either." Briefly, he told the officer about the attack upon his person after the inquest, the way he'd fought off the attacker and accidentally switched blades.

"And have you any evidence of this attack other than your own word?" Lilac asked.

"I saw him arrive at the vicarage in a panic, and I saw the bleeding wound," said Charlotte. The Runner studied her closely, and she lifted her chin and tried to remember what it was like to look innocent.

"I was not in a *panic*," grumbled Benedict. "I was moving with an understandable amount of speed, considering the circumstances."

"I also saw Mr. Frost's stiletto," Charlotte said, setting Benedict to choking again. "This is not the blade he was accustomed to keeping about his person."

"I should say not," he murmured, and she had to elbow him and hide her smile.

As Lilac pulled free the dagger, though, the trio became entirely sober. It was a pretty weapon, she supposed, looking at it for the first time in daylight. She described its detail for Benedict. The pearl handle held an emerald, the stone's color split in two with an inclusion. The blade was slanted and sharp and unpleasantly speckled dark.

"Good God." Her fingers went clammy. "Benedict, it's got blood on the blade."

She realized at once she had blundered. "Mr. Frost, I mean." She shook her head. "Forgive my informality. I was—I think I may swoon."

"Rrright," said Lilac. "Well, I wouldn't stop a lady from swooning if she needed to. Mr. Frost, is it your opinion this is your blood on the blade?"

"I don't know who else's it could be."

"But you think it might be someone else's?"

Benedict was unbothered by the cold scrutiny of the hazel eyes. "Yes. I think it might be. Or might have been." He tipped his head toward Charlotte and said, "Look—Miss Perry, this would be a good time for you to find a friend to chat with. Somewhere other than right here at this table."

"You're going to talk about gruesome things, aren't you? That's all right. I won't really swoon." She straightened in her chair. "But, Mr. Lilac, please, stow the dagger before someone else enters the shop. You may take it in my reticule, if you like."

"I don't need to be carrying a lady's purse around," he scoffed. Wrapping the blade in a handkerchief, he tucked it into a pocket of his coat. "What's on your mind, Frost?"

"I have some medical training," he began. "I heard the evidence at the inquest, though of course I couldn't study Nancy Goff's wound with my own eyes. But from the description, it was caused by a thin yet planed blade like this."

"That's so." The Runner stroked his scanty beard. "Though there must be many thin, planed blades in the world."

"But how many in Strawfield, carried by people who cannot resist using them?" Charlotte asked.

"I don't think Miss Goff was meant to die," Benedict said. "A single stab wound would usually cause bleeding, perhaps infection. But for all the fragility of the human body, the rib cage is a marvelous shield for our . . . ah, softer bits."

"It's all right," Charlotte assured him. "I really will not swoon."

As Benedict went on to explain to Lilac how he thought Nance had died—something about an unlucky slip through the ribs, a punctured lung or a nicked some-part-of-the-heart—Charlotte wondered.

Maybe there was no conspiracy to Nance's death. Maybe it was a crime of passion. A jealous lover.

Her fingers drifted to the scar on her cheek, rubbing at the still-unfamiliar pucker.

"You've thought about this a great deal," Lilac said when Benedict finished his explanation. "Coroner should have called you as a witness."

Benedict laughed, a dry, harsh bark. "What good would a blind man be as a witness?"

Lilac picked up a last crumb of tart on his forefinger and consumed it with great relish. "Any that don't want to learn the answer to that question are nothing but fools."

Charlotte decided the Runner would be a worthwhile person with whom to share a plate of cakes, if the opportunity ever arose. "Mr. Lilac, do you think Mr. Frost's attack and the attack on Nance are connected?"

"I don't say what I think until a case is closed. But one thing I wonder about is how come a sleepy little hamlet like Strawfield plays host to a murder right after a stolen coin is found."

Again, Charlotte rubbed at the scar on her face. Lilac, of course, noted this, and Charlotte at once folded her hands in her lap. "Do you not think—ah, beg pardon. Do you *wonder* whether Nance's death was unrelated to the coin about which she told so many people?"

He regarded her steadily. "No, Miss Perry. That's not something I wonder about at all."

* * *

Charlotte and Benedict agreed that their interview—with Mrs. Potter, wife of the publican who kept the Pig and Blanket—might be kept brief.

Not that Charlotte was in danger of swooning, for truly, she was not. But the conversation with Stephen Lilac, Officer of the Police, had shaken her up a bit more than she wanted to admit.

If Nance hadn't been meant to die, but she did all the same, then Benedict could have been marked for death and only lived by chance.

"That makes no sense," he chided Charlotte gently. "That makes the *opposite* of sense." But that softness about her heart where he was concerned—well, it wasn't so quick to stop worrying.

Mrs. Potter was stout and red-faced, with a knob of thick blond hair she patted often. "I don't have time to talk wi' gossipmongers," she huffed when she met Charlotte and Benedict in the entryway of the Pig and Blanket. "Nance Goff left me shorthanded, and the Piggie's busier'n ever."

Charlotte swallowed a sharp reply. She must remember, she was a prudish spinster. "How dreadful for you." She did not state whether the dreadful part was Nance's death or the fact that Mrs. Potter was doing so well out of the matter. "I would *never* gossip. My father asked me to offer you comfort."

Two fat lies in two sentences. Efficient.

But the soothing words relaxed the angry crimp about Mrs. Potter's mouth. "That's right kind of the vicar. I could tell as it troubled him to come to the inquest. In sympathy, he must have been, for the trouble as I went through wi' Nance."

"I have no doubt of that," Charlotte cheerfully perjured herself.

Benedict folded his hands, and his voice poured out slow and soothing as morning chocolate. "Might we speak to you in the private parlor?" When he opened his hands, a shilling winked silver.

"Mr. Frost is a friend of my father's," Charlotte explained. "As well as a dear friend of *Lord Hugo Starling*."

"A lord?" The magical name had its usual effect. "Oh, yes. Mr. Frost. I didn't recognize you at once without your lovely coat, but of course I remember you. A proper sense of what good service is worth. And what good ale ought to cost."

"I believe I do have that," said Benedict.

Mrs. Potter gave her hair a luxuriant pat that was entirely wasted on Benedict. "I suppose I can spare a few minutes."

She led them upstairs to a plank box of a chamber directly over the common room. Noise, smoke, the scents of sweat and ale all filtered upward and pervaded the little parlor. Charlotte motioned for Mrs. Potter to sit in the only comfortable-looking chair; then she and Benedict crammed themselves into the others.

"Ah, it's good to rest my feet," Mrs. Potter said. "One of the kitchen maids has been serving today, but she's worthless wi' customers. They need the gentle touch. A bit o' flirtation, too, if you don't mind my saying so, Miss Perry."

Charlotte tried to look shocked.

She must have done well enough, because the older woman leaned forward with not a little glee.

"I shouldn't tell you this, not wi' you being the vicar's daughter and all, but Nance was no better than she should be. I'd decided to let her go. Charging whatever she liked, even as she met her young man in the stables every time she could slip away—"

"She had a young man?" Benedict's head shot up.

"Don't they all?" sighed Mrs. Potter. *Pat pat pat* on her hair.

"I never did," Charlotte lied primly, and for the first time the innkeeper's wife's ill-used expression was sprinkled with pity.

"He wasn't a nice Strawfield boy. Never seen him until recently. He turned up a little before the other treasure hunters." Mrs. Potter sniffed, as though these people she dismissed weren't filling her purse. She didn't need to hunt the royal reward to heap up gold. "Haven't seen him about since the day Nance died."

Charlotte had a thought. "Did he wear a cloak?"

"A—how now?"

She tried to look pious. "If one could identify him, one could give him spiritual comfort about his loss. I believe Miss Goff mentioned in her final words that he wore a cloak."

"She talked about cloaks and eyes like a demon and eyes like a cat ever since she got that coin," said Mrs. Potter. "Probably just raving with guilt in her final moments, knowing she didn't ought to have been away from her work."

"Her final words." Benedict's brows were knit. "Miss Perry, your father said they were 'cat eye' and 'cloak.'"

"You see there. Full of talk about 'eyes of a cat,' like I said." *Pat. Pat. Pat.*

"Not really," Benedict said drily. "She said 'cat eye.' Just one."

"Out of her head." *Pat. Pat.*

"You must be right. Why, she could not even repeat the prayers through which my father tried to lead her in her final moments." Charlotte made her tone reproving, though her throat wanted to close off the words.

"Would you know the young man if you saw him again?" Benedict asked.

"I might," granted Mrs. Potter. "Never got much of a look at him. Oh—but here's news! That talk of young men reminded me. Mr. Selwyn is back in Strawfield!" She turned to Benedict with a lofty smile. "You won't be knowing him, of course, Mr. Frost, but he's as famous as can be."

"A painter of portraits," Charlotte hurried to explain. *And other subjects.*

"Oh, I don't know anything about that. But he married an earl's daughter! The finest brood of children they have. Three little boys."

And a Pudel dog.

She shifted against the rigid, spindly back of the chair. She disliked hearing her first lover spoken of in the presence of her last.

Her most recent, she corrected herself.

"Mr. Selwyn has no daughters?" asked Benedict. Charlotte looked at him sharply—not that the gesture had any effect on him.

Mrs. Potter patted at her knob of unlikely blond hair. "What would he be wanting a daughter for?"

"Girls lend civilization to a house," Benedict said

solemnly. "Were it not for the steadying influence of my younger sister, I'd be a heathen."

"Mr. Frost, you must have met Miss Maggie, staying at the vicarage. She's a nice little thing, now."

"My niece. Of course." Charlotte forced a smile. "I am relieved my parents are raising her well. As my sister would have wished."

"Your sister was a good lass," granted Mrs. Potter. "Sorry I was to see her move away when she married, and sorrier when she passed. But at least she left you her babe to remember her by."

Benedict scooted his foot forward, touching the toe of his boot to Charlotte's. All he could do by way of sympathy or support at present. It was enough to help her adopt the proper misty expression.

Ten years after her sister's death, Charlotte still wondered—*what would Margaret think of this? What would my sister do?* Her sister had always been so kind and sure. So perfect. Older, first, most dutiful. Going before, doing things best.

With the softness of time, this was something to be admired rather than resented. Margaret had given their family a lifelong gift. She had lost her husband to illness, then had fallen ill herself. Charlotte went to tend her and formulated the idea after that: that her own unborn baby should become her sister's child. Margaret agreed, lingered long enough to see her niece baptized as her daughter, then handed the baby to a wet nurse for care.

And released her gentle hold on life.

The misty expression wasn't feigned anymore, and Charlotte left it to Benedict to make their farewells. Dimly, she noticed another shilling changing hands, then Mrs. Potter gave her hair a final prideful pat and squeezed from the tiny parlor.

Leaving Charlotte and Benedict alone.

Charlotte had drifted so far from the expected life of a vicar's daughter that the role felt awkward on her. She wanted to shed her troubled, trailing memories, to be clean of the close, tobacco-stinking room.

"I think we have paid enough calls for today," she said. "You asked me what I loved about this part of England. If you don't mind, Benedict, I should like to take you to my favorite bit of it."

Chapter Thirteen

Even when it slowed to a drought-starved trickle, Charlotte always paused to listen for the Kinder Downfall before she saw it. At this point in late spring, warm and rainy and muddy, it had grown to a great rush of water.

Charlotte approached it from the base, where the water poured into cracked and fallen stones. Benedict planted his cane and tilted his head. "At first I thought it was a great wind, only because the truth seemed impossible. How did you arrange a waterfall in flat moorland?"

Charlotte laughed. "How dearly I would love to take the credit for everything that impresses you. But I did not make the Kinder Downfall—and in fact, it isn't flat here at all. Shall I tell you about it, or would you rather find your way around?"

"Each in turn." He had tucked his cane beneath his arm, finding it of little use on the spongy, yielding ground outside the village. Any more rain, Charlotte knew, and they'd have been ankle-deep in muddy moors, but for now the ground held its place.

Here, though, there was rock underfoot. Broken at first, a piece here and there, and then in larger and larger slabs. Benedict was scaling one of them now, hat and cane laid aside on one of the patches of misted grass. Clearly impatient with his too-short coat, he tossed it to join the cane, felt his way up the side of a cracked block.

"Come sit by me, Charlotte," he called down the yards separating them, "and tell me everything you see."

She untied the strings of her bonnet, flung it atop his borrowed coat, and clambered up after him.

"I like all of this stone. This is a more solid place to find one's way about than any other in Strawfield," he said as she tucked herself in place beside him on the gray slab of rock.

"I've always thought so." She squinted into the distance. "If I could have lived here instead of at the vicarage, I'd have been a happy child. At least until a mealtime or two trailed past and I grew hungry."

For a moment they sat together, warm under an endless sky.

"Tell me about this waterfall," Benedict then said. "I feel the spray in flecks on my skin, so I know it's not a huge fall. It tumbles slowly, doesn't it?"

"Yes, though more quickly with every rain. Over time it has washed away the earth and found the stone beneath and cracked it. The stone is gray, like . . . like an elephant's back."

"I have never seen an elephant's back," Benedict said wryly. "But the color gray I am familiar with."

"This is my thanks for trying to be poetic and descriptive. Next time I shall describe for you only in the plainest, barest terms."

His fingers found hers, just a touch of warm fingertips atop cold stone. "Describe for me however you like. I want to see it as you do."

"No one ought to see the world as I do. You know what I've done, what I've been."

"I am learning," he said, "what you *are*."

As he blinked into the distance he could not see, she found herself, too, blinking through lashes that were wet.

"Then here is what I see." She drew in a deep, clean breath, damp from the Downfall's mist. "The ground is covered in green and yellow and brown, with grass and—and whatever plants grow on the moors, some growing, some dying, some yet dormant. The land rolls so gently you cannot feel it as you walk, but when you look back, you see how far you have climbed."

"I can feel it," he said softly. "When you tell me about it, I can feel it around me. What else? What is the sky?"

"The sky is so light that it looks almost white, and the clouds blend into it. Sometimes the clouds are low and glum, but right now they are high and wispy like great tufts of cotton. And the farther away one looks, the more everything is washed with blue, until the land and the sky look like the sea."

She laced her fingers into his. "Or how I imagine the sea. I have never seen it. I have only seen the Thames."

His thumb ran over the back of her hand, sending

a sweet prickle up her arm. "Listen to you. You should write a memoir."

She laughed, a little breathless. "Tosh. What would I have to say that anyone would want to read?"

"As a former courtesan? I think *everything* you had to say would be something people would want to read." He grinned. "I know I would, if I had the ability. But since I don't, I suppose I'd have to ask you to read it aloud."

"You would want to hear of my dealings with other men?" This struck her as . . . odd.

He lay back on the flatness of the cracked slab of stone, freeing his fingers from hers and folding his arms behind his head. "Not for the sake of the tales themselves, no. But I want to hear of you, taking the polite world by storm. And I'd be curious to hear of anything related that you wanted to tell me."

As always, he left it up to her to say *no*.

She drew up her legs, folding her arms around them in her favorite posture. Making of herself a sturdy ball. "There is no great mystery about the matter. It happened out of necessity and determination, one day at a time."

"How did it begin?"

She tipped her face up to catch the wind. "With a painting of me more than ten years ago, when I was only eighteen. I liked being told I was pretty enough to be painted in oils. I liked it so much that I didn't balk at taking off my clothes."

"Lucky painter." Benedict stretched his legs out long, then crossed one booted ankle over the other. "Was it a Londoner who painted you?"

"No, it was"—she swallowed—"Edward Selwyn."

Because of the timing, he must surely guess that

Edward was Maggie's father. But all he said was, "Oh. That neighbor of yours."

"Maybe he once thought of himself thus. Now he thinks of himself as London's most underappreciated painter."

"How can that be possible when he painted you? The subject alone should have made him a king in artistic circles."

"Flatterer. Might I remind you that you have no idea what I look like in oils."

"No, but I've run my hands over the most famous statues in Paris, and they do not come close to the beauty of your form."

She scrubbed an impatient hand across her blurring eyes, then wrapped her arm about her legs again. "When you say such ridiculous, kind, flirtatious things to me, I cannot think what to tell you next."

"So don't tell me anything." One of his folded arms must have, well, unfolded—because his hand stroked her back, up and down, slow and gentle. "I'll tell you more of the—what did you call them? 'Ridiculous and kind' . . . no, I really can't allow that, Miss Perry. 'Truthful and truthful,' maybe."

"The last thing I said was 'flirtatious.'"

"Ah, well. There you have me."

He stroked her back some more, silent and *there*. Replacing the sore bits with tenderness, the lostness with the anchor of his body, with the stone beneath them and the slow sounds of water at their side. The scent of damp earth and a sky that was new over the old, old ground.

"It's all right," she said. "You can ask me whatever you want to know."

"I admit, there is one thing about which I wondered."

"Anything."

"I know a courtesan is an entertainer and hostess, above all. But when you took a protector, your role must sometimes have taken you to the bedchamber."

"It did." Lord. She was such a hussy. Her face burned, yes, but her sex grew damp. *Bedchamber,* he said, and his hand kept up that slow trail over her back. He had taken her to his bedchamber—or she had taken him.

"How is it possible . . . ah, I shouldn't ask."

"Now you have to. You have me afire with curiosity."

"Um." She glanced at his face. Beneath his tan, his face had gone a bit red, too. "All right. How can one have intercourse with someone to whom one is . . . not attracted?" He asked it as a curiosity, a secret, forbidden question to which he had allowed his mind to turn in private moments.

She squeezed her thighs together. "If the occasion required . . . that . . . then I had to find a way in which that person attracted me, and I clung fast to it. Perhaps a man smelled nice, or perhaps he had a lovely speaking voice. Perhaps he was generous or kind. There is something to like about almost everyone."

"Almost?" The slow, stroking hand paused.

"One time I changed my mind. The better I got to know that person, the more it became clear that there was nothing to like about him." *Randolph.* His wealth and handsome face were but the means to an end: the growth of control.

Benedict was again stroking her back; now using a bit of raking nail that she could feel through her thin gown and light stays. "You are very clever," he said. "To tease out the best way to be successful."

"A necessity. When an unmarried woman lets a

man put a part of his body into hers, she becomes worth less as a human being. Under the guise of being proper, people are obsessed with the intimate behavior of young women. Does that not seem remarkably vulgar?"

"Both vulgar and unfair." He sighed. "I had not thought much about the matter, I admit. I grew from boyhood to manhood on a ship, and dainty *ton* ladies were never spoken of. A few officers were married, but most sailors thundered to port whenever they had the chance for"—he coughed—"virtuous works. And the women took as much benefit as the men, or so I thought."

Ah, he made her smile at the most unexpected times. "And did you do the same?"

"I was a paragon of virtue, shall we say."

Now she laughed. "As long as you left the ladies with as much benefit as you took."

He stopped stroking her back. "I believe I did. Sometimes twice as much."

She shot him a quick look; he was grinning, arms again folded carelessly behind his head. Her sex was wet now as she remembered . . . *Yes. Twice.* Those broad hands splaying her wide, that wicked tongue . . . oh, so wicked. Giving her pleasure after pleasure, asking nothing in return.

"I took my benefit, too," she said. "Of a material sort, since the world had decided I was now worth less than when I had been proper. I remade myself as Charlotte Pearl—*La Perle,* but not the pure, driven-snow sort."

"So dull and cold, the driven snow," Benedict said. "I cannot blame you for wanting to be something entirely different. Did you get many jewels?"

"Sometimes."

"A house?"

"Oh, above all a house."

"Servants?"

"The finest. A household full. A lady's maid just for my clothing and another just for my hair."

"Will you ever return to them?"

"No." The syllable came out faint, so she tried again, more loudly. "No. I let the servants go, and the house—for a multitude of reasons, I can't go back there. I've a fortune I cannot touch."

Besides her memories and her house, Charlotte had one other item left from her years of luxury and captivity: a necklace. Edward had given it to her to wear for that first nude sitting—and when art turned to an affair, he gave it to her for always. Again and again, she had posed for him while wearing it. Naked but for gems, a shackle about her neck worked in emeralds and diamonds.

She would eagerly have sold it, but it had appeared on canvas so many times that it was instantly recognizable as the necklace of *La Perle*. She couldn't allow herself to be traced by Randolph, so she stuffed it into her trunk. Hid it within cheap woolen stockings.

Maybe if she'd broken it up, crushing the gold and ripping the stones free, she could have sold it.

Maybe she still would.

The breeze grew arrogant, teasing the wisps of hair about her face—and then it snatched off her lace cap.

"Oh!" She grasped for the scrap of lace, but the laughing wind carried it away—and Charlotte let it go and sat back down.

"Something amiss?"

"The wind took my cap. I must have loosened the pins when I took off my hat."

"Do you want to chase it?"

"No. I don't feel like dressing as a spinster right now." She settled back, hoping his hand would again begin its slow comforting path up and down her spine. "I cannot sell my house," she finished explaining, "without an intermediary. And any person involved in my affairs is a weak link. Too vulnerable. I cannot afford to keep the house, but even less can I afford to sell it."

"Being a courtesan is not the sort of employment one can just walk away from, it seems."

"No, it is not," she agreed. "Nor is it the sort for which one can claim half pay."

"Or a small stipend for being invalided and respectable?"

"Definitely not that." She plucked a pin from her uncovered hair, then another. "No, it's the sort in which many people think they have a claim on . . . everything."

"Then maybe it's not so bad to be Miss Perry. Or a mysterious treasure seeker with a veiled hat."

Inside her boots, her toes curled. "It's not so bad to be with you."

He tutted. "Silver-tongued witch."

She laughed. "I like you, Benedict. Everything I know about you, I like."

Like was such a watery word for what she was beginning to feel.

But the Kinder Downfall poured by, endless and pure. Strong and lasting enough to crack stone and reshape the earth.

Maybe a watery word wasn't so inadequate after all.

* * *

Benedict knew he ought to say something roguish and wry in reply, but he could think of nothing that would fit around the great lump in his throat.

Only a week ago, he had not known her. Now he could not imagine not knowing her.

Did she like him because he was here, and she was lonely? Or because he was himself, and she was falling for him?

As he was for her. As he never had allowed himself to fall before.

There was no room for a lasting romance in the future of a Naval Knight, who lived within the narrow strictures required for his pension. No romance at all for a pretended spinster aunt raising her niece.

One day, probably soon, they would have to part ways. He knew this.

He also knew that parting would hurt like the devil.

"The feeling is mutual," he said. "Entirely, completely."

He felt a little shy, adding these last words. He was accustomed to quick affairs of pleasure, then to moving along.

These conversations were different. *Wanting* to have them was different.

Not knowing when he'd leave—that was different, too.

She was taking her hair down; the long strands tickled his face, touching him with the faint scent of wintergreen. It was soft, whipping about and tickling his skin. He unfolded his arms and caught a few strands like a silk-spun spiderweb between his fingers.

He liked touching it, and being permitted to touch it.

The roughness of the air about gentle slopes reminded him of the land surrounding Edinburgh. Those rolling lowlands of Scotland, friendlier than the moors that stretched nearby.

"Tell me about this stone on which we've made ourselves comfortable," he said. "Is it part of the ground, or did it fall?"

Charlotte lay down, tucking herself against his side just as she had, so briefly, in his borrowed bed in the vicarage. "I think it must have fallen as the Downfall wore it away. Great stones lie about here like a dropped tray of pastries."

"I must get my similes from someone who has led a less luxurious life for the past decade."

She laughed against the curve of his neck. "Very well, they are like fallen ice. They break in great cubes, and they shatter into shards."

"You know ice well."

"I *have* performed virtuous works in an icehouse."

"A chilling thought—ouch! No hitting," he protested. "That was a wonderful joke."

"No joking," she said, and climbed atop him. "Not now."

He had been half-hard since lying down on this stone; now he was surely harder than it. "Not now," he agreed, hips rolling up to meet hers.

He caught her about the waist, keeping her steady as she did . . . things. Wonderful things. First she undid the fall of his breeches and palmed him. Rolling his stones gently. Working his length with her hand until a hot drop leaked, eager, and trickled down the head of his cock.

"Back in a moment." She lifted his hands from her waist and slid down—and she licked that hot little drop off of him and took him into her mouth.

Shite. Every muscle in his body clenched: toes curling, calves bunching, thighs tight. Even his scalp prickled. And she kept right on, her tongue a hot delicious sin, a sweet promise fulfilled. She pressed at a little spot below the base of his stones, and his hips jerked up with the shock of it.

"Sorry," he groaned. He must have just jabbed her in the throat with his cock. "I can't hold on—I— Charlotte, *please.* It's too much. Let me love you."

She stopped moving, though that marvelous mouth covered him. Taut. Tight. The moment vibrated; his breath came hard and ragged.

When she lifted her head, she blew cool air over the head of his cock, sending him into a shudder. "You want to . . . love me."

He realized how it sounded—this dance that people did about the word *sex.* It was confusing when one's feelings became involved, too.

And he realized what he wanted to say.

"Yes."

With a soft sigh that left him wishing he could see every flicker of expression across her face, she slid up his body in a sweet abrasion. Rustlings told him she was bundling her skirts; then her knees were on either side of his hips, and she was guiding him within her slickness. It was a prayer and a blasphemy at once—*God, God*—to feel welcomed and wanted like that.

He struggled for words. "Do you need me to withdraw when I—"

"It's all right," she said. "I know what to do." She

ground her hips on him, linking them as tightly as two could be.

Again, he cradled her waist, pushing up into her hard and fast, sinking together. She rocked on his length, working herself into a wet fervor. Hard and fast, they clashed and loved and, yes, *fucked,* and he bore on relentlessly until her breath turned to moans and the moans shattered and she cried out her release atop him.

He came into her with a groan of pleasure, pumping slowly now as the final shudders rocked them and ebbed. Then he eased her down to lie on his chest, still joined below.

He was lying on a rock with a waterfall flinging chill mist on his face, and he cared nothing for any of that. "Good Lord," he groaned after a long and luscious silence. "This is my favorite place in Derbyshire, too."

He could feel the curve of her smile against his neck. How sweetly her head fit there, against his shoulder. How easy it was to hold her.

Too soon it was time for them to draw apart, to right their clothing and clamber down from the rock that had become Benedict's anchor. He found his coat and hat and cane—but left them where they lay. He wasn't ready to leave this precious space yet.

So he found his way to the edge of the stream created by the small falls—a step too close in his fuddled state, as he splashed one boot before drawing back. Crouching, he trailed his fingers in the shifting coolness. Some of the pebbles at the edge were sharp and new; some smooth and sleek with age.

His fingertips encountered one that was pleasantly solid, a tiny version of the slab on which he and

Charlotte had lain. He held it up. "Charlotte, is this pretty?"

She had been struggling with her bonnet; he heard her toss it aside and tread toward him across grass and stone. "It's pretty if it is nice to hold."

As a matter of fact, it *was* nice to hold. Hefty and smooth despite its irregular sides. "Come now, have I found you a diamond? If I have, we can stop hunting for stolen gold sovereigns and live like kings. Or a king and a queen, to be more accurate."

"I'm not sure I'd recognize a diamond uncut." She crouched beside him, hair trailing long over his hand and kissing his wind-smacked cheek. "Ah, no. There goes our fortune. There cannot be diamonds of such size in England. Besides which, this is brown, though it's got some lovely green streaks in it. Like a beryl."

"What is a beryl?"

"A . . . sort of streaky stone. A cat eye, it's sometimes called."

She drew in a sharp breath.

"Ouch!" The stone had fallen from her fingers onto the tender space between his knuckles. "A— wait. What? It's called a—oh, holy—"

"Shite," she finished. "Exactly. Cat eye."

"It's a stone?" Benedict palmed the rock, clenching its contours as though this would help him understand. "A cat eye is a stone? 'Cat eye'—what Nance said . . . I never thought of it being a *thing*."

"You think Nance meant that the person who stabbed her had a beryl?"

"Would she know one when she saw it?"

Charlotte's hand covered his clenched fist. "By the name 'cat eye,' maybe. She didn't even know a guinea from a gold sovereign."

He understood. "She'd be describing what she thought something looked like, not what it was truly called."

"Like the dagger," she said. "The one we gave to Lilac. Its handle held an emerald split down the middle." Charlotte released his hand, then stood.

"It doesn't make sense." Benedict shoved himself upright in the slipping gravel at the chill water's edge. "Why wouldn't she have said the name of the person who stabbed her, if she knew it? If it was her lover?"

"The person was cloaked," said Charlotte. "All she saw was the cat eye and the cloak."

Benedict rubbed at his sightless eyes, then extended the stone in his palm to Charlotte.

"I don't want it," she said.

"I don't either." With a sideways whip of his wrist, he tossed it back into the stream. "If only everyone listened to voices as well as I do. We'd have all the problems of this village sorted out and a fortune at our fingertips."

"If only everyone did many things as well as you do," said Charlotte. She stepped closer, laying her hand on his chest. "But right now, you're the only one I'm thinking of."

"Am I, now?" His heart thumped heavily. "Have you a problem you'd like me to sort out for you?"

"I was hoping you would. Twice, even." And she brought his hand to her breast.

Chapter Fourteen

Charlotte and Benedict returned hand in hand to the vicarage, a laughing triumph of sore limbs and pleasure-soaked senses. Soon, she knew, she would need to treat herself with vinegar and brew some pennyroyal tea—a daily requirement for women in her profession.

But for now, she let herself *feel*. To feel what it was like to hold the hand of Benedict Frost, even knowing that holding him could not keep him with her.

Such a feeling hurt, like the skin that grew fragile beneath a scab. She felt thin and new and raw.

But it was not unwelcome after feeling so long calloused. So surfeited and lonely at once that nothing could give pleasure. Now as she walked, everything rubbed at her senses: the drift of her long skirts about her legs; her boots, heavy, the knife never yet slipped from its spot beside her ankle. Her breasts, her sex, touched as though they were wondrous. As though she were of infinite value.

Let me love you, he had said, and she had been startled into wishing he meant it literally.

Maybe Maggie didn't have to be cared for, someday, by her spinster aunt. Maybe she could have an aunt and an uncle.

Maybe. Maybe. As she walked, Charlotte's hair flicked long and unbound, dark and straight. Just as it had when she was a girl, and she lived on dreams of *maybe* and the vivid corners of the world that she wanted to see.

But she was not a girl now, and she knew better than to live on dreams. Silks and satins, jewels and mansions—dreams never turned out quite the way one expected. There was always a catch, even if one didn't perceive it right away.

Sometimes it didn't make itself known for years.

And then, one day, when one dared to let heart-pattering emotion guide one's steps, the catch would make itself known. And one would be caught.

That day was today, when Charlotte and Benedict returned to the vicarage and the first sight that greeted her, held in her father's shaking hand, was a sealed letter addressed not to Miss Charlotte Perry, but to Charlotte Pearl.

In hindsight, Charlotte thought her father could have handled the matter with a great deal more subtlety.

"This—this—I did not know what to—well. Charlotte, you must take it!"

Charlotte's mother and Maggie poked their heads out of Mrs. Perry's study. "What has happened?" asked Maggie. "Did Captain come back into the house?"

Mrs. Perry snapped the letter from her husband's

quivering hand, skimmed the address, then tossed it aside. "No such person here. Send it right back where it came from."

Twist, twist, went the vicar's hands. "This cannot be. I knew if we allowed—but there, it is done. But it should never have been done!"

"What's done?" Maggie picked up the fallen letter. "Who is Charlotte Pearl? Did they spell Aunt Charlotte's name incorrectly?"

"I am sure it's an accident," Charlotte said in a careful voice. "The names are not so dissimilar. Someone must have written my name ill, that is all."

But she knew this was not the case. No one knew Charlotte Perry was also Charlotte Pearl except for her parents and Edward Selwyn. And Edward was pompous, but he did not have a bad heart. He was not cruel enough to expose her secret.

"Who brought this letter into the house?" she asked.

"Barrett fetched the post," quaked the reverend. "As usual. It was . . . there. As though it belonged."

"It doesn't belong," Charlotte murmured. She had more questions: *Was it handled in the village? Did anyone there know of the London courtesan, gone missing a month ago?* But the more she asked, the more attention she would draw. Maggie studied it still, brow creased, hair unruly about her face.

I never yet plaited it with silk ribbons, Charlotte realized.

She felt distant, unreal, as though she were watching a theatrical performance. *The Secretive Courtesan's Most Secret of Family Secrets.* With an epilogue of more secrets.

She pressed a hand over her mouth, forcing back a wild giggle.

Benedict leaned in and whispered in her ear, "Some letter, I gather. Is it bad? Ought I to do something, or just stand here like a statue?"

"A statue . . . please. Please don't leave." She couldn't hold his hand now, but she liked having him near.

"Let me see it, dearest," she said, and Maggie handed it over readily enough. Charlotte turned it over to check the seal. The origin from which it had been posted.

"It's franked," she realized. The letter had required no postage, meaning it was sent by a member of Parliament or a peer.

And then she knew who it was from.

The Marquess of Randolph, whose heart was as shriveled as a walnut.

"I'm sure it's nothing," she said again, though this time she knew it was a lie. "Excuse me, Papa. I'm sorry that your lessons were interrupted, Mama. Maggie."

"*Lypámai.*" Maggie looked pleased with herself. "That's the way people apologize in Greek."

"That might be how *some* people get out of a difficult situation," Benedict said. "But not the people who hang about the ports."

"You must teach me some of their vocabulary," said Mrs. Perry. The vicar closed his eyes.

Charlotte began to sidle past them all, making her way through the corridor. She hardly knew where. The first empty room she encountered. She would open the letter and see what it said. She did not want to open the letter. She had to open the letter.

With a light touch on her shoulder, Benedict

caught up to her. "Would you like me to bear you company while you read your post?"

There was so little he did not know about her now. "Yes. Yes, I would. It is addressed to my"—she lowered her voice—"London name."

He cursed. "All right. The dining room. Anyone in there?"

No, the small chamber was empty. She leaned against the wall in the far corner, wishing she could disappear into the paper. A heavy maze of vines and acanthus that looked like nothing anywhere in England.

Benedict stood next to her, seeming relaxed, but with a coiled awareness that made his body hum in harmony with hers. "I would read it for you if I could."

"I know. I thank you." With a deep breath, she added, "Best done at once."

She cracked the seal—and almost laughed at the brevity of the message.

Pearl,
   I do not excuse you from our arrangement. If you return to your quarters in London before the end of the week, all will be forgiven.

Randolph

"A man of few words, in or out of the bedchamber," she muttered, refolding the letter and stuffing it into a pocket of her dress.

She told Benedict what it said. "He is mistaken, though. All will not be forgiven."

"By him, maybe, but it takes two to forgive. And who is Randolph?"

How best to sum up the man? Handsome at first glance. Dark and cutting. Wealthy, of course, and so she had agreed to take him as a protector.

She had not known then that he was a slave to his desire to triumph at any cost. Or that he was cruel, liking to cause pain—but only if it was not wanted or welcomed.

"Randolph is a marquess. And the reason I fled London."

Benedict stretched out a hand, finding the wall beside Charlotte. He made of himself a cradle about her, arm and body like the sweep of a shell. "And he wrote to you here. Damn."

"You felt the scar on my face," she said. "It is—not an old wound. Randolph cut me. When I told him I no longer wanted him as a protector, he slashed my face. He said he'd never let me go, and that he'd make me unfit for anyone else."

"Well, he failed spectacularly. But this is the reason you carry a knife? Good God. I am sorry."

"Do not pity me. I got away from him, at least for a while. Besides which, you carry a knife, too. Or did."

"Yes, well. I'm a big strong man who also happens to be blind. I have to protect myself in case anyone decides I'd be a good person to fight with." Somehow he always knew the right thing to say. The right place to touch—right there, on the line of her scar, before his hand dropped again. "Where did the letter come from? London?"

She checked the post stamp. "Cheshire. One of his estates."

His mouth screwed up in calculation. "Three, four dozen miles? He is less than a day away, then."

"He might be here." Had not Miss Day mentioned Edward arriving in a crested carriage? Such as was owned by a nobleman? *Oh, Edward, you fool.*

Benedict reached back, found the corner of the table, and boosted himself up onto its top as a seat. "Let's solve this, then. Who knows you are Charlotte Pearl and Charlotte Perry?"

"My parents. You. Me. Edward Selwyn."

"Edward Selwyn." He swung his feet, knocking them into the leg of the table. "I keep hearing that name."

"One does, in Strawfield."

The silence lingered, the only sound the hollow *conk* of Benedict's boot heel against the dining room table's leg.

He didn't ask for more information, which was why she could tell him. Always, he left it up to her. "He is Maggie's father. He painted me, and . . . well, things happened."

"I should have been a painter." Benedict sighed. "I suppose it's too late now."

She choked. "You do well enough without a paint-brush in your hands."

He gave a modest shrug, then asked, "Does Selwyn know the truth about Maggie's parentage?"

"Yes. But he has said nothing of it publicly, and I hope he never will. Maggie's life now is as a legitimate child. If it were to become known that she was a bastard . . ."

Not unless one were fathered by a royal duke could one hope for a place in society. Other illegitimate children could look forward only to the most blighted of futures.

"This damned country," he said. "Right. I know. So after things happened—including Maggie—you went to London and he kept right on painting you."

"That's the shape of it, yes. Save for the moment when I told him I was with child and he declined to marry me. He had higher aspirations than a vicar's daughter."

Benedict's curse was both calm and eloquent.

"Well put. That marked the end of our affair, too."

"I imagine it has a chilling effect on the passions, being told one is not good enough to wed."

"Indeed." She ran a forefinger along the wallpaper, tracing the winding lines of a curling vine. As a girl, she had always thought this paper oppressive and old-fashioned. "Though as it turned out, he was correct that he could do better for himself. His fame as a painter won him the eye of an earl's daughter."

"*You* won him the eye of an earl's daughter." Benedict slid from his seat atop the table. "The world is a strange place sometimes, Charlotte Perry Pearl. I have only this to say: he might have won the hand of a richer woman than you, but it would not be possible for her to be a better one."

All she could say, in a small voice, was *oh*.

"If Edward Selwyn knew your two names, it seems he's been telling tales. And he's due an interview. Wouldn't you say?"

His confidence was contagious. She lifted her chin. "*Interview* sounds so polite compared to what I would like to do to him."

"True. But you are elegant and refined, despite the fact that you are a knife-wielding terror, and so you shall call tomorrow during proper hours. Er . . . whatever those are."

"I could visit just after luncheon." The hours before then seemed endless, yet too short.

"Good. There is your plan." He placed a steadying hand on her shoulder. "Now. I always find that when I receive an unexpected and vaguely threatening note from a rejected former lover, I need some comfort. Are you the same way?"

"I . . ." She shook her head, a smile beginning to tug at her lips.

"I thought so. Let us visit the kitchen."

"I don't go to the kitchen," she said, bewildered.

"Why not?"

"Because it isn't done by daughters of the house."

"Ah. And you never do anything but what's precisely proper." His hand slid from her shoulder. "How silly of me. I should have recalled that about you, since it is a defining characteristic of your personality."

She caught his fingers, tightening hers around them—and then she laughed and let his hand go. "You are right. Take me to the kitchen, Benedict Frost, and show me some comfort."

If Benedict had not gotten into the habit of escaping from his parents' bookshop to the kitchen, he would certainly have developed a love for it after losing his sight. A kitchen was far more sound and smell than a place of wondrous things to see.

This one bubbled with savory, spicy, meaty smells. Then the clang of the iron oven door against brick, and out wafted the hot scent of fresh bread. Even if he had just eaten a full meal, the smell would be enough to make Benedict's stomach growl.

Colleen, the kitchen maid, greeted him cheerily, then gasped. "Oh. Cook! Is the butter supposed to look like that?"

Cook began a scold, the housemaid Barrett stepped through with quick strides and a set of instructions for dinner, and during the whisk of voices, Benedict eased Charlotte into a chair next to the worktable.

"Nice and calm," he said. "Breathe it in. *Ah*. Food. Warm things."

She brushed him with the back of her hand, which was, he thought, the gestural equivalent of a smile.

"Miss Perry!" Barrett was the first to notice her. "Is everything all right?"

"Everything's fine," Benedict assured her. "I told Miss Perry what a fine time I had visiting you all in the kitchen, and she wanted to see if she could wheedle a few biscuits from you."

"No, indeed," Charlotte said, the edge of a laugh in her voice. "Mr. Frost is teasing you all. The truth is far more sober." She paused. "I was actually hoping for a slab of bread."

Cook clucked. "Meals put back to all hours, first for the vicar to pay his calls, then the missus, lost in her work! I don't wonder you're hungry, Miss Perry. Colleen, fetch the butter."

"But it's . . ."

"Right, right." Cook cut her off. "Jam, then."

A pot clunked onto the wide worktable, and Colleen brought over a breadboard and knife. "Sit with us," said Benedict. "Have a slice. It smells good enough to make a sailor give up his rum ration."

"Oh, I can't," said the maid in her soft brogue. "You can't imagine what I've done to the butter, and I've got to try to fix it."

She crossed the kitchen again, footsteps echoing more quietly.

"What did she do to the butter?" he whispered to Charlotte.

"I really *can't* imagine," she said just as quietly. "But it's gone a sort of orange color."

"All settled?" Barrett paused in her click-click movements about the kitchen. "I'll take some of that bread for the reverend's tea, now."

When she left the kitchen, Benedict smiled. "Accent thick as a Yorkshire pudding, isn't it?"

"That's how I always thought of it, too." Charlotte scraped a knife across the top of the jam pot. "We see her the same way. Or . . . that is . . ."

"It's all right. I know what you mean." He placed his hands atop the smooth-worn wood of the worktable. "In my dreams sometimes I can see. Then when I open my eyes, ready for morning light, and there is nothing but blank, I wish I had not awoken. I wish it had never happened, that my life had never taken such a turn."

She took one of his hands—then flipped it over and placed a slice of warm bread on his palm. "What do you do, then?"

"I get up and try to make my life take another turn. The alternative is passing time; wasting it. Waiting for death." He lifted the bread to his lips. "That seems a terrible waste of such a handsome man who has learned so much."

"Indeed it does," she agreed. "And so modest! A true paragon."

He took a huge bite. Hot, fresh bread, dense and satisfying, slathered with plum jam that was both tart and sweet at once.

"If I hadn't lost my sight," he said after he swallowed that blessed bite, "I wouldn't be here in this kitchen, eating this bread. So some turns are quite nice."

"Would you have kept your commission if you had never fallen ill?"

"*What if* is a poor exchange for certainty." He smiled. "Which doesn't keep me from wondering. I think I'd have liked to keep sailing—but it's possible I would have been purged in peacetime, unable to sell my commission. Without a pension or half pay."

Her hands were moving over the table, tiny vibrations as though she were rolling crumbs about. "Would you have wanted to marry?"

What if. What if. "What I've wanted has never changed. But I can't marry or I lose my post as a Naval Knight—and if I lose that, I lose my half pay, too."

"They really have you tied up in a box," she mused.

"They really do," he said. "But I'm used to it. What is a ship but a box that floats around?"

"What is a mansion in Mayfair but a large and elegant box?"

He had not thought of that, but—as he took another huge bite of bread—he decided it made sense. Any place could be a cage. And maybe, with the right person, any place could be a home.

He had blamed all of England for the trapped gloom he felt upon returning—but really, it wasn't England's fault. It was the bookshop that should have been a home, but was nothing but a cage for him. A place where love was conditional and disappointment eternal. Benedict, the wayward son, who could read if he just tried harder. If he loved them enough to try harder.

Outside of the bookshop, though, there were ports and streets and parks. London stretched outside of it, great and unknown. He didn't have to sail the world to find somewhere new to lay his head.

He'd been too used to leaving. Leaving his family, his country. Once he became blind, he allowed the Naval Knights to support him, but he left them, too. They asked him to live in another cage, this one in Windsor Castle.

But they granted him a leave of absence to travel. They didn't make him stay, day in and day out.

At the moment, he was where he wanted to be, and he could think of no better company. And the only *what if* on his mind was: "What if I accompany you tomorrow when you call on Edward Selwyn?"

The first post of the day came early to Frost's Bookshop, Paternoster Row. Cousin Mary tried to put down baby Johnny to fetch it, but he cried. Just as he had cried all night, sobs bleeding through the thin walls and waking Georgette along with his parents.

"Teething, poor mite." Cousin Mary looked exhausted, her dark hair straggling from its pins. "Georgette, go pay the postman, and keep note of what it cost."

Georgette would have met the night-soil man if it meant escaping the wailing baby for a few minutes. She darted downstairs, grabbed a few coins from the till, and paid the amounts due. Some post was local:

a catalog about an auction of the Earl of Wendover's library; Cousin Harry would like that. A few books bound up in brown paper.

And a letter for Georgette, her name written ruler-straight. The lines were flattened at the bottom, the *t*'s left uncrossed. She knew this hand, reshaped by the noctograph on which the missive had been written.

"Benedict. Finally." She hadn't received so much as a word from her brother since he'd been traveling in France.

After relocking the bookshop door, she slipped the letter into her pocket and mounted the stairs. "New books and a catalog, Cousin Mary. Where would you like them?"

"Me open it!" The two-year-old, Eliza, loved to tear open parcels.

Mary tucked another lank lock of hair behind her ear, bouncing the crying Johnny on her hip. "I don't know. I haven't time to look at them before the shop opens in half an hour."

"I'll set the catalog on the table for Cousin Harry." To do so, Georgette had to clear the remains of breakfast. Likely the housemaid was changing a nappy, or washing one, or performing some chore to do with some substance that had come out of some small person's body.

The main living room above stairs was small and cramped, as full of books as the shop below. Adding to the clutter were the unmistakable signs of a house full of children: wet nappies drying before a fire, a few well-loved toys, some chewed-on books. Mary and Harry Fundament had four children aged four years and under. Privately, Georgette was not surprised

Cousin Harry spent so much time traveling away from London to buy books from country house libraries. The place of neglectful peace in which Georgette had been raised was now full of sobs and chatter.

But the bookshop, at least, was thriving. Benedict had sold the shop to their cousins for a fair price, and for a few more weeks, Georgette would help them to run the business. And during that time, she had a place to live, and—well, that was how the world worked. It wasn't as though an unmarried woman could be trusted to run a bookshop herself. Georgette knew that. And her cousins needed Georgette's bedchamber more than they needed her help, which would soon be done by a day clerk for a few pounds a year.

Georgette set the parcels down before little Eliza, a red-cheeked cherub with curling dark hair. "Mind the bindings, all right? Gentle on the books."

"'Liza gentle."

Georgette smiled, then turned to her harried cousin. "I received a letter from my brother. Shall I pay the postage?"

"Oh." Cousin Mary shut her eyes, swaying as much with fatigue as to soothe the baby. "Maybe. From where was it sent? Not France again, I hope?"

Georgette pulled out the letter to see. Since recipients paid for their post, she'd had to lay out a great many coins for Benedict's letters over the years. When he'd been studying medicine in Edinburgh, at least he'd got a frank from Lord Hugo so Georgette didn't have to pay postage.

She almost dropped the letter when she saw where it had come from. "From Derbyshire. But I thought—"

She'd thought he was sailing with the *Argent* again. How lowering to realize she was not kept apprised of which continent her brother was on.

"That's all right, then. We'll cover the postage. Lord knows you do enough around here to help." Mary managed a smile. "It's nice that he wrote to you. Maybe he has a place for you to come and live with him."

"Maybe he does."

Georgette knew he didn't, of course. She and her brother were all but strangers. He had never liked books and had begged to go to sea, taking a post as a cabin boy at the age of twelve. She'd been only three years old then. For almost eighteen years, they hadn't shared a home. Not even when he went blind and almost died had he returned to London. Nor did he come back when their parents grew ill and *did* die the following year.

Part of Benedict's condition of sale to Cousins Mary and Harry was that Georgette must be allowed to live with them until she was twenty-one.

Which was less than a month away. And then what would become of her? She was a colorless girl to look at, all pale blond hair and pale skin and pale eyes. Just the shade of a book's pages; she faded into the bookshop as though she were part of it. There was no hope a customer would enter and be bowled over with love at the sight of her.

Well, there was always hope. A faint sliver. But such a hope had gone unfulfilled year upon year, as Georgette read novels and fairy tales and minded the shop. Through its windows she watched the *ton* eddy by, passing and changing each Season.

"I'm going to read my letter, Cousin, and then I'll open the bookshop."

"That would be lovely. Once Mr. Fundament returns"—Mary and Harry were formal before their spinster cousin—"I'd love to catch a bit of sleep."

"'Liza all done."

The proud two-year-old had opened the parcels, which contained unbound books. Seeing more paper, she had kept right on "opening" them, shifting pages from one pile to another.

Georgette could have groaned. "And I'll take these down with me and sort them out."

The housemaid, Polly, came from the larger bedchamber with a one-year-old and a pile of stinking cloths. "We'll need the laundress today and no mistake."

Mary's face fell. "I haven't time to go for her. Polly, could you—"

"I'll go for her," said Georgette.

"Be quick, then. I'll open the shop if you're not back in time." A nervous glance at the clock. "But of course you want to read your letter first. I forgot."

Mary wasn't unkind, just stretched beyond her limit. Georgette worried sometimes that the slightest thing could break her, and she didn't want to be that thing.

It had been different when Mama and Papa were alive, though not in the warm family manner some might imagine. No, it was different because the business was *theirs*. Because Georgette was the only child at home, and they trusted her to help, and the harder she worked, the better her family prospered.

This won the distant fondness of her parents, both scholarly types who had surely met and mated between the pages of a book. They were too distracted to pursue anything but knowledge; it was left to Georgette to pursue business. Now that the typhus had taken them, any gains were to the benefit of Mary and Harry.

Georgette had had the benefit of a haphazard but broad education. She knew plenty. Enough that she would never throw in her lot with a scholar again.

She carried her letter into her bedchamber, a cubby of a space containing a desk, a trunk, and a narrow bed. Seating herself at her desk, she pushed aside a litter of newspapers and books and skimmed the tidy lines from her brother.

And then she slapped the paper down, furious. "That . . . that *rat.*" She wished she knew more curses. She wished she knew a word bad enough for a brother who visited London to sell a manuscript but who had not visited the bookshop in which he was raised.

He had not even come to say hello to her.

Instead, he had hared off to Derbyshire for a pressing errand . . . what errand? Lord Hugo was in London, and Benedict's other friends were scattered about the world.

Honestly, she got more news of Benedict from Hugo than she did from her brother himself. Lord Hugo Starling called on her irregularly and perfunctorily. It was clear he'd rather be anywhere else but interacting with a dull human creature such as she.

At least he bought a lot of books whenever he visited the shop.

She picked up the letter again, skimming the lines. *Derbyshire . . . do not worry about anything . . . I will write again soon.*

Ha. Right. She'd just spend the leisure she didn't command relaxing into the pile of money she didn't possess.

The only bit she could put any faith in was that he was in Derbyshire.

She rubbed at her temples, then fumbled through her papers for a quill and a sheet of foolscap. As she shifted them, a newspaper shouted at her:

DERBYSHIRE INQUEST ON MAIDEN IN ROYAL REWARD CASE: MURDER BY PERSON OR PERSONS UNKNOWN

Derbyshire.

She hadn't given much mind to the hunt or the murder case, but the word caught her eye.

Strawfield, Derbyshire, was the location of this case. And it was—she checked the post stamp on his letters—yes, it was where Benedict was, too.

That pirate. He wanted to find the royal reward.

He probably thought he'd find it for her, and then she'd be all squared away and he could go back to pretending he had no sister and his family's bookshop hadn't passed out of their line and Georgette hadn't been evicted.

Damn Benedict. Damn damn damn. He did the most horrid things for noble reasons.

Sort of noble reasons.

Well, she thought, as an idea swirled into form. *I could do the same.* Or maybe this was more of a noble thing for a horrid reason.

Either way, it began with a lie.

Poking her head out of her bedchamber, she

called, "Cousin Mary! I have been invited to visit my brother and his friend Lord Hugo Starling in the country. Is that not marvelous?"

"How grand for you," Mary called back. She barely managed to hesitate before asking, "Shall we keep your room, or will you be gone more than three weeks?"

Don't come back once you're twenty-one was implied.

"You needn't keep it," decided Georgette. "I think I shall be able to fit all my things into my trunk."

She was a Frost, was she not? And she was going to pack her life away and prepare for a journey.

As soon as she fetched the laundress to deal with a pile of filthy nappies.

Chapter Fifteen

"If they're good to you," Benedict had promised Charlotte, "I'll behave myself."

But as they stood before the massive wooden doors of Selwyn House—doors that were, he could tell, more than an ordinary story high—he doubted that he would be required to come up with proper manners. Already they had been kept waiting for ten minutes.

He was glad he had worn his ripped and bloodied lieutenant's coat. "Let's be honest," he told Charlotte. "It will serve you better to have a companion who appears a violent lunatic than a companion who does not even possess a coat that fits."

This wrung from her the only laugh of the day. Now, her fingertips were tight on his free arm. The other arm held his cane.

Which he knocked against the door, making a pleasing *thump*.

At last, a servant swung the door open, and Charlotte handed over a card.

"Miss Perry," came a pursed-up reply like pickled cabbage. "From the vicarage. And . . ."

"Lieutenant Frost. From Windsor Castle." He shot the unseen servant a dazzling grin.

After a moment's hesitation, the servant—a butler, from the fussy tone of him—allowed them inside. "I shall see if Lady Helena is at home to callers."

"And her husband," said Benedict. "I'm here for—you know. Man talk."

Charlotte's fingers did something quivery on his arm.

"Man . . . talk," repeated the butler. "I shall . . . yes . . . wait here, please."

Footsteps clicked away across a floor of hard stone. Marble, no doubt, polished to a sheen like glass. The house was all luxury in sound and even smell; a faint odor of lemon, maybe from furniture polish, and the rotting-sweet scent of a vase of hothouse blooms.

"Man talk," murmured Charlotte. "What *do* you have in mind?"

"Nothing at all," he confessed. "But if there's something you need to say to Edward Selwyn, he ought to be in the room, don't you think?"

Lady Helena was the first to descend to the entryway, her feet as delicately placed on each step as a cat's would be. From the height of her voice, she was not a small woman; from the tone of it, not a patient one. "Friends of my husband's from the country. How quaint."

"I'm not a friend of your husband at all," Benedict said.

"I see." She mustered a few manners, enough to invite them to sit in the Blue Parlor. His cane rang pleasingly on the marble floor, echoing off a ceiling

high enough to belong to a church—and then it
knocked on the carpet of the parlor, and the world
closed to a tiny padded cell. Draperies and puffy
furniture and carpets, all drinking in the sounds that
made a picture in his mind. There was a strong smell
of mummified flowers—what was it called? Potpourri.

He shuddered.

Somehow they all found their way to seats. Lady
Helena did not ring for tea. "I do not have much
leisure at present for callers, though I suppose I can
grant you a few minutes. The Marquess of Randolph
is visiting, you see."

He could imagine what was running through
Charlotte's mind. *Shite.* But all she said was, "How
unexpected."

"Oh, no." Lady Helena's voice was all cool pride.
"He is a great friend of my husband's. Mr. Selwyn was
recently visiting Lord Randolph in Cheshire. One of
the marquess's many estates, you know. Or perhaps
you did not."

If her voice had held the slightest question,
Benedict would have retained his manners. "I did
not. How edifying! Thank you for the information.
I've been traveling Europe writing a memoir and am
only familiar with the locations of my friend Lord
Hugo Starling's estates. The son of the Duke of
Willingham, you know." He paused for a dangerous
moment. "Or perhaps you don't."

"Is your husband home at the moment, Lady
Helena?" Charlotte broke in.

"He and the marquess were riding, but they have
recently returned. I do not believe they are at home
to callers at present."

"Ah! They're covered in road dirt and manure,

I expect." Benedict gave a knowing smile. "It happens to men who aren't good on horseback. Nothing to be ashamed of."

Charlotte muffled a cough.

The sounds issuing from Lady Helena's throat made him dearly wish to see her expression. He kept his own features placid and composed.

A new set of footsteps entered the parlor just then, the heavy tread of a stocky man wearing boots. "Why, Charlotte! Matterhorn said you'd called. How marvelous to see you. Oh—ah—Miss Perry, I mean."

Benedict's shoulders tensed. The fellow's tone was all self-congratulation, the smirking preen of an aren't-I-bad rogue who had never quite grown up.

"Look at you, though!" Selwyn moved to Charlotte's chair, tutting with dismay. "This scar—quite ruins the effect of your features. How ever did you get it?"

"I received it in the course of my work. Trying to protect a child." Her tone was crisp.

Protecting Maggie, she meant; indirectly, from Randolph. The response dovetailed nicely with her identity as a virtuous-work-performing spinster, too.

"How noble!" Benedict said. "You are very brave. Anyone who would endanger a child is surely the worst sort of scum."

Selwyn shifted his weight. "Friend of yours, Char—ah, Miss Perry?"

Lady Helena had gone completely still and silent upon her husband's entry into the room, but now she spoke. "He *says* he is a friend of Lord Hugo Starling."

"Not that that's relevant at the moment," Benedict said cheerfully, turning his cane between flat palms. "I'm happy to be known as a friend to Miss Perry. And

I'm glad you regard yourself as one too, Mr. Selwyn. One would never want to hurt a friend."

"Of course not," he agreed jovially.

"Or betray a friend's confidence," added Benedict. "For example."

"Did . . . you call for a reason?"

"Purely a social call. Upon friends," added Charlotte. Benedict was pleased to hear the arch lift in her voice, as though they were all in on the same joke.

If only it were not such a serious matter, having a man she feared here in her home village.

"Tell me, Mr. Selwyn," Benedict said. "When did you and your illustrious guest arrive? Saturday night, was it?" When he had been attacked.

"Sunday morning, rather. You mustn't tell your father, Miss Perry! I know vicars hate knowing that someone has traveled on Sunday." Again, that tone Selwyn was *sure* was charming.

"I don't think it would make a difference to him, Mr. Selwyn," she said. "It's a person's heart he's concerned with, not the rote following of a rule."

"Right, right." Selwyn seemed to be casting about for some jaunty reply. "Well! Heard we missed a bit of excitement. Murder and inquest and all that, eh? Pity I wasn't here to enjoy the show."

"It was a lot of nonsense about a barmaid, Selwyn," murmured Lady Helena. "No better than she should be, clearly. I did not see fit to attend."

Benedict was too polite—barely—to knock their heads together. In her own chair, Charlotte was perfectly composed, but he thought her breathing came a little faster.

No better than she should be. Who the devil were they

to judge? Especially Selwyn here, who took whatever he liked of the world.

Sailors became either callous or tender as they saw loss and fighting. Benedict had become the latter— a boy of twelve, surrounded by cannon fire; a midshipman of sixteen who tied off his shipmates' gory wounds; a lieutenant of twenty-five who could not protect his men from the tropical ailment that took their lives and took his sight.

"Do you see fit," he said at last, "to acknowledge the fact that her death was related to coins stolen from the Royal Mint, and not to any fault of hers?"

Four guards had died at the Royal Mint; Nance made a fifth loss. Would any more fall before the glow of the stolen gold? Fifty thousand pounds. There were many to whom lives were cheap, far cheaper than the promise of fortune or reward.

He felt a little ill, being part of the hustle to find it. Sitting in this pompous palace, the pursuit of wealth for its own sake seemed tawdry.

Georgette. He must remember, he was in Strawfield for her.

And he was in Selwyn House for Charlotte, who spoke up in that daughter-of-a-vicar tone that could not be gainsaid, the one she'd used to such great effect with Mrs. Potter. "As the first family of the area, I'd have thought you'd be involved. Not in a bad way. In a noble way."

"Of course, it's our responsibility to—"

"I have instructed the groundskeepers to warn reward seekers off our lands, Selwyn," cut in Lady Helena. "We are not concerned with the carnival atmosphere cultivated by the villagers."

"No, no. Right, right." Selwyn fell silent, but his feet tapped against the carpeted floor.

Lady Helena stood in a rustle of silk skirts. "I thank you for calling, but I must see you out now. Lord Randolph—"

"Talk of the devil, and he is presently at your elbow," came a lazy voice.

And as Lady Helena took her seat again, the Marquess of Randolph joined the group.

"Randolph!" Edward stood, bowed, and sat again in an obsequious flurry. "Randolph and I are planning a little exhibition of my work—the portraiture, of course. He has taken an interest."

This explanation was likely for Charlotte's benefit, but she hardly listened. She only studied Randolph, trying to decide how she felt about seeing him again.

The last time, she had been alone with him at night, and he had a knife in one hand and a switch in the other. He'd refused to listen; he had slashed her with a cool fury that terrified her.

Now the flight was over. In the daylight of Selwyn House's Blue Parlor—an overstuffed horror of horsehair furniture and velvet drapery—Randolph regarded her with the same possession, the same cold anger. His lean jaw was set, his eyes appraising. He had changed from riding clothes into a bespoke coat of superfine, a satin waistcoat, a pair of buckskin breeches too immaculate ever to have seen use. His dark hair was sleek and groomed.

But none of this made of him a gentleman—and at that thought, Charlotte found, she could look him in the eye and pretend that she did not tremble.

"Well, well," said Benedict in a hearty voice. "The devil! What an honor for me to meet you at last. I can't tell you how many times I've been told to go to you, sir."

"Did you not hear, Mr. Frost?" asked Lady Helena. "This is the *Marquess* of *Randolph*."

Benedict thumped the end of his cane against the floor. "*Oh.* My mistake. Blind, you know. I thought— well, he *did* introduce himself as—hmm."

His feigned confusion was generating real confusion on Edward's face, which Charlotte didn't mind in the slightest. Edward Selwyn was the sort of man precisely calculated to appear handsome to a vicar's daughter who hadn't met many men. Because he was exactly that: calculated. Everything from the angle at which he tilted his head to the arrangement of the fobs in his waistcoat. The lilac of his cravat, tied in intricate but not ridiculous folds and pierced by a diamond stickpin that probably cost as much as her father's annual stipend.

The light brown hair, just the shade of Maggie's, coaxed into cherubic curls. The smile that showed a scoop of a dimple in one cheek, disarmingly youthful.

He *was* young, really. Only three years older than Charlotte herself. Only twenty when their affair had begun; far too young, he said, to think of marriage. Barely of age when Maggie was born. The youngest artist ever *almost* to have paintings accepted to the British Institution, he was fond of saying. His fame had been won by his startling portraits of the woman who became known as *La Perle,* though he cemented it with more traditional portraiture. He had a gift for seeing what he wished to in people.

Charlotte had always looked, in his paintings, like

a woman in love, just tumbled or just about to be. Only in the first portrait had this been accurate. To Edward, the world was full of things that might be taken. The fact that something might be destroyed in the taking seemed never to have occurred to him.

Since Maggie's birth, Charlotte's arrangement with Edward had been a cordial use-and-use-alike. The notoriety that had been thrust upon her alongside his fame could be made to benefit them both.

Until Randolph, when Charlotte began to feel all used up.

Next to Edward, Benedict appeared rough and dark. But not ill at ease; never that. She wondered if he had been so comfortable in his large, blunt body before he went blind, or if his enforced habit of listening, of taking note of his place in the world at all times, had put him at ease in his own skin.

Right now, he appeared to be enjoying himself, going on and on about what an honor it was to meet the Marquess of Randolph even if he *wasn't* the devil.

"How charming," murmured Randolph, extending a finger of greeting that, of course, Benedict did not see.

His hand bore a cabochon-polished emerald ring. It winked, first tawny yellow, then green. Like the eye of a cat.

A cat-eye ring. A cat-eye dagger. A man with cat eyes—Edward—who now looked ashamed that he had led Randolph to Charlotte. Yet none of this present meeting had anything to do with the Royal Mint's sovereigns. Charlotte had stolen herself away, and Randolph was determined to reward himself for locating his lost property.

"You have been busy traveling of late, Miss . . .

Perry, should I call you?" Randolph's voice was lazy, but his gaze missed nothing.

She must give it nothing, then, on which to latch. Affixing a cordial yet poisonous smile to her lips, she said, "So have you been, my lord."

Lady Helena, a buxom Teutonic giant stuffed into wispy silk, knit her blond brows. "You are acquainted?" She sounded affronted. "How does a marquess come to be acquainted with a country vicar's daughter?"

"His lordship"—Benedict swung his cane in a little arc before him—"must be interested in virtuous works. Miss Perry is a notable performer of selfless deeds."

If he had looked at her, Charlotte would have burst into hysterical laughter. Even Edward's smile grew a little strained.

"Miss . . . Perry." Randolph's pause grew more conspicuous each time. "Do you intend to leave the vicarage anytime soon?"

Do you plan to return to my keeping?

"I don't foresee that," she replied. "Especially not within the next week."

Hell. No.

"I see." His tone was considering as his gaze flicked over her. Taking in the straitened state of her gown and boots, no doubt. Comparing them to the silks in which he'd last seen her and thinking how far she'd fallen.

But thanks to him, those silks had been torn, and they had got blood on them. This gown—the pretty one with vines and flowers on it—suited her much better.

"If you plan to remain in Strawfield for more than a week, then," said Randolph, "you'll be present for an exhibition of Edward Selwyn's artwork. We'll hold it in the—what is the name of that inn?"

"The Pig and Blanket?" Edward looked bewildered, but he managed a laugh. "Surely not here, Randolph. Surely? The Royal Academy, after all—the most notable people will still be in London for the Season, and—"

"What matters is who sees the exhibition. Not where it is held." Randolph's words were for Edward, though his gaze never left Charlotte. "And in a week, Selwyn, you shall have as many illustrious guests admiring your work as you could possibly wish."

Edward shot a glance at Charlotte. "The, ah, portraits, right? Randolph? We agreed to focus on my portraiture?"

"Oh, yes. Portraits. Most assuredly." The marquess smiled.

She'd once found the expression intriguing, hinting at secrets and hidden depths. And she'd realized she was right about that. Just—none of them were pleasant.

He had dropped no veiled hints about Maggie, thank heaven. Edward must have kept her parentage a secret. And perhaps he always would. Lady Helena would make his life a misery if she knew he had sired a child with someone as lowly as a vicar's daughter.

"Delightful." Benedict clapped his hands about his cane. "An art exhibition. Any sculpture?"

"N-no," Edward said with some doubt. "I do not sculpt."

Benedict looked reproachful. "A pity. Well, I'll try to enjoy myself all the same. And now, Miss Perry, ought we to be going?"

She was fronted by two Selwyns and a Randolph, and suddenly she wanted to burst from the room in a run. "I think," she said with tight control, "we ought."

"Not wanting to overstay one's welcome?" Randolph's voice was a torn silk. "No question of that, I assure you."

"It's not that." Benedict stood with a thump of his cane. "I know Miss Perry has old and dear friends here who wish her the best. But you see, her dog is quite ill. It was her sister's hound. The last memory she has of her departed sister."

"You seem to know a lot about the family." Randolph again.

Benedict shrugged. "Only what courtesy has permitted as their household guest."

"You would leave us for a dog?" Edward seemed able to manage nothing but questions.

Charlotte recovered her voice. "For Margaret's dog. You must remember, Mr. Selwyn, how important my sister was to me."

"R—right," he stammered, but she dared not look at him closely to see if her warning was received.

They managed farewells that were close to polite, with Randolph reminding her that she had promised to remain for Selwyn's exhibition. "But perhaps," he said lazily, "I will call on you before then. At the vicarage—yes, I recall. I know where to find you."

When they exited the house, the sun was warm on her forearms, but she could not stop trembling.

As they descended the front steps, Benedict gave her his arm on which to lean. "Steady, now," he murmured. "In case they are peeking through their windows. Lead the way off these illustrious lands, please."

"You were terrible," she said in a shaky voice. "By which I mean you were perfect. Thank you."

"Me?" He lifted his brows. "Did I do anything so unusual? Anyone would have been honored to meet the devil. Or, barring that, the next best thing."

He kept up a flow of pleasant talk as they strolled across the Selwyn lands, his words calm and cheerful, asking nothing of her. She was caught between the scent of the hothouse flowers that seemed trapped inside the house and those rare blooms outdoors, so thin that one stumbled into their sweetness unexpected.

All the while the trembling came from deep within her, untouched by sunlight.

But there was one thing that warmed her. In a room with a man who had ruined her and a man who wanted revenge on her, there had also been a man who took her part. Now he had drawn her hand within the crook of his arm, and she knew he would hold it as long as she wanted him to.

She still shook, but less so with someone to hold. And so she stopped walking, raised herself onto her tiptoes, and kissed him on the cheek.

He blinked. "Why, thank you. What was that for?"

"For being you."

"It's the thing I'm best at," he granted, though he looked puzzled still. "I'm sorry you had to meet with Randolph. Did you get anything useful from that conversation?"

"I don't know." She began walking again, and Benedict fell into step with her. "The exhibition— there's something to that. Randolph wouldn't go out of his way to do Edward a kindness."

His biceps tensed. "Not even as thanks for directing him to you?"

"No. It's not enough. Randolph wants to hurt me. He . . . likes hurting." The sun was far away again.

"How can portraits of a bunch of society nobs hurt you?"

"I don't know," she said again, though she thought she might have an inkling. If Randolph found paintings of Charlotte . . .

But no; Edward had insisted. Portraiture. If he were supplying the paintings for the exhibition, he would see to that.

The stone wall was before them at last, and Charlotte clambered over it. Benedict handed her his cane, then sprang over the wall himself.

When they passed by the stable, Captain picked up her head from her usual tired huddle and gave a bark of greeting.

"Still banished to the outdoors, is she?" Benedict asked.

"Indefinitely," said Charlotte. "Mama's decree since Captain's mess indoors. Here, let me pet her a bit, since she gave us an excuse to depart." Caring for Captain was almost like caring for Maggie. It was showing the girl love without being too intense, too smothering for someone who ought to be an aunt.

An aunt. Her knees went watery, and she collapsed onto the ground beside the dog. "Benedict. Randolph can't be allowed to see Maggie; he'll understand right away. Her coloring is too much like Edward's. Randolph—he is shrewd, and he'll put together the pieces. He'll know she's mine." The trembling again. This time it shook her into action: she stumbled to her feet, boots and skirts in a desperate tangle. "I have to—I have to leave with her. Right away."

He stepped closer. "If you run with her, it will show Randolph how precious she is to you."

Oh, she could have *shrieked* with impotent anger. She smacked a fist against the door of the stable, setting the rusty old lock to rattling. "I could not go anyway. I have no money on hand, nothing I could sell in time. My penknife—maybe I could get a few pennies. This cameo was my grandmother's. My trunk itself . . . perhaps, and I could use bandboxes instead . . ."

"Charlotte. Stop. You shall not beggar yourself to stay safe." His hand found hers, brushed it, then fell to his side. "If you wish to leave Strawfield, I will lend you the money you need."

"No!"

"Because . . . ?"

Because I don't want you to help me leave you. She stopped herself. That was not a rational protest. She had to think about his offer. She drew in a deep breath. Another, until the desperate edge of her feeling was blunted.

He had money from the sale of the family bookshop, and no one would expect him to give it to Miss Perry of Strawfield.

"But your sister," she said. "You were going to send the money to her."

"We can spare the costs of your travel. She will be fine." He smiled, lashes a dark shadow over dark eyes. "Besides. It's only a loan. You'll have to pay it back sometime, which means even if you leave, I'll get to see you again."

How easily he hopped on board an adventure—and yet reassured her. It was like being held.

"I think," he continued, "you might go to Edinburgh. I could give you my letter from Lord Hugo, which would be like a letter of reference for finding lodging. Even a post, if you decide to stay up there. Maybe you could stay in his house—did I mention he has a house there? Dukes, you know; they have so many houses, they like to strew them about a bit and give them to random relatives. Even their younger sons."

Edinburgh. How far could Randolph reach? Certainly across the border, though the shield of the Duke of Willingham's name might provide some protection.

Benedict's calm recital had helped to ease the trembling within her. She had choices. She had a—friend, for lack of a better word.

If she fled now, she would never stop running. And she would be farther, always farther, from Maggie. From everyone she knew.

From Benedict Frost, who must know they would never meet again if she left him now.

What was the point of being safe if one must be always alone?

She mulled over his suggestion, remolding bits of it in her mind. "I have a different idea, one that will not separate me from Maggie for long. But we will have to talk to my parents' whole household about it. I want to . . ." Another deep breath. "I want to ask for help."

Letting more people into her life, telling more about the vulnerable bits of it. This was the opposite of how she had lived for a decade.

But fleeing alone hadn't worked before. She was ready—sort of, almost, maybe—to try something different.

Benedict offered her his arm again. "Then come inside the vicarage and ask."

Anyone watching the mail coach's evening arrival at the Pig and Blanket would have seen Miss Perry, garbed and capped plainly, board in the company of her heavily swaddled maid. "My servant is recovering from influenza," she said loudly. "Will you give her room inside, please?"

Squeamish passengers rearranged themselves, and the vicar's daughter presented the coachman with her trunk. Stephen Lilac, the Bow Street Runner, searched the belongings of every traveler that departed Strawfield, and he gave his nod of approval for Miss Perry and her maid to embark.

Mr. Potter liked to watch the passengers come and go, and he noted this departure with some interest through the front windows of the inn. "That Barrett from the vicarage looks poorly. Never seen her wrapped up so tightly."

Mrs. Potter was in a genial mood due to the day's high receipts and only commented that folks who treated their servants as skinflinty as the vicar mustn't be surprised when they took ill. "They'll be lucky if she comes back a-tall from wherever she's accompanying Miss Perry. Can't imagine a life of good works being worse abroad than it is here."

Privately, Mr. Potter thought the vicar did kindly by his few servants. But he only shook his head and emptied the till. "She'll be back. Been in service here since she were a mite of a girl."

His prediction proved right, for Barrett did return the next day on the mail coach—still swaddled, and with a muffler about her face.

Potter stepped out and hallooed her from the doorway of the Pig and Blanket. "Back without yer missus?" He never missed a chance to collect a little gossip. It was lifeblood to an inn, as much as the ale that flowed from the taps.

She bobbed her head. "Havin' chills," she murmured in her thick Yorkshire accent. "ha' to coom back 'efore Miss Perry was ready, but she met a frien' to share her journey."

Potter stepped back. "Are you ill, then?"

"Bit o' the influenza. But none too ill for a pin', if yer offerin'."

"Ah—well, now, maybe you'd best get on back to the vicarage. They'll want to know how you're doing."

Reluctantly, the maid agreed and trudged off.

"She looked right peaky," Potter murmured to himself as he went back inside the inn. "Thinner than when she left yesterday. Must be a powerful bad sickness."

He decided to drink a measure of gin as proof against the influenza, in case Barrett still carried about the contagion. It would be only prudent.

The swaddled figure, for the benefit of anyone observing, passed through the vicarage's kitchen entrance, cursing in a thick Yorkshire accent as her gloved fingers fumbled with the latch.

As soon as she let herself inside, she stripped off the muffler and gulped in fresh air. "Hullo, everyone."

Benedict had been waiting at the worktable, feet atop it. They slammed to the floor with an eagerness that made her smile. "Charlotte?"

"The very same," she replied.

Cook and Colleen dropped their utensils and ran over to her. "It's been the most nervous day," squeaked Colleen. "Mr. Frost wouldn't leave the kitchen except to sleep. We've all been that worried for you."

"I wasn't *worried*," said Benedict. "I only wanted to be at hand for the news. So—how did the plan go off?"

Good Lord, it had taken a great many layers to hide the fact that she wasn't Barrett. She was still peeling off shawls and caps and unwinding the endless muffler. "As fine as one could hope. Barrett and I split in Leeds. She went on north in my clothing and the veiled bonnet, with the trunk full of her belongings and money enough to get her to her sister's house."

Cook and Colleen, along with Barrett, had accepted the plan as necessary to protect Miss Perry from someone bad she'd met on her travels. To her parents, Charlotte had been a bit more forthright, admitting that the letter for Charlotte Pearl had made it necessary for that lady to seem to escape.

Necessary for Charlotte, and for their benefit. If she was thought to leave her family behind, Randolph's attention would leave the vicarage.

Once the servants had returned to their cooking, Charlotte said quietly to Benedict, "Potter at the Pig

and Blanket saw me—I mean, Barrett—with influenza.
Only put it about that I've fallen ill again—Barrett,
I mean—and I shall be able to stay in the house
without arousing suspicion."

"The pronouns are perfectly clear," he said drily.
"But what have you gained by this plan, if you're only
to be trapped again?"

"I'm not alone this time. I get to be with all of you.
And together, we'll decide what to do." She dared a
brush of fingertips over his cheek, surprising a smile
from him. "Maybe we'll find that treasure yet."

Chapter Sixteen

Aha. There she was: Georgette Frost. After searching three different coaching inns, Hugo knew at once when he'd found her. That improbable fairy-pale hair was unmistakable, though she'd tucked it up under a cap.

She seemed to think she'd disguised herself as a boy. Not only the cap, but breeches and a strange short jacket. Sitting on her traveling trunk, chewing on a straw, chatting with a grizzle-haired burly fellow in rough workman's clothes.

And she was *spitting*.

Hugo gritted his teeth.

He shouldered through the crush of impatient travelers, grimacing as an inebriated man weaved into him and splashed . . . something . . . onto his coat.

Wonderful. Now he reeked of cheap liquor and his coat was stained. He'd have to return to his town house to change his clothing before his afternoon meeting with Banks, the President of the Royal Society, at Somerset House. Another unexpected errand;

another window of time snatched from his day of scholarship.

Still. It had been unthinkable not to go in search of Georgette. And now that he had located her— well, when he reached her at last, perhaps his hand came down on her shoulder more fiercely than he had intended.

"See here, *Georgie*," he growled. "You can't think to leave like this."

She jerked, the straw falling from her lips to the ground. "Lord Hugo! How—what are you doing here?"

Her newfound friend regarded Hugo with great suspicion. "You know this man, eh, young fellow?" he asked Georgette.

"Of course sh—he knows me." Hugo caught hold of the collar of Georgette's jacket. "He's my nephew." That sounded plausible. There had to be at least ten years' difference between his and Georgette's ages. Warming to his tale, he added, "He stole his dying mother's silver and broke her heart. I've come to bring him home to make amends."

"I never did such a thing!" she gasped, a tolerable impression of a youth with a cracking voice. "Look at the state of him. He's drunk. As usual. He doesn't know what he's saying."

When she started to squirm out of her jacket— wouldn't *that* give the other travelers a show—he put a warning hand atop her cap. One gesture, and all that hair would be falling down around her shoulders.

She knew it, and went instantly still. "So drunk," she repeated, pleading.

The burly man looked doubtful. "But you called him Lord something-or-other?"

"He likes that," she said ruthlessly, "but he's really nothing of the sort. I do it to make him happy so he won't hit me."

"Oh, for God's sake." Hugo folded his arms. "Yes, *Lord*, and here is my signet ring. I do not hit, I am not drunk, and this young criminal ought not to be here."

Georgette coiled as if ready to make a break through the crowd, and Hugo's hand shot out and collared her again. "See? He wants to escape the consequences of his lies. Can't believe a word out of his mouth."

A pretty mouth. He could hardly believe she had fooled anyone into thinking she was a boy. But he supposed people saw what they expected to see; most weren't as skeptical as Hugo.

The chunky gold ring had its usual dampening effect; the grizzle-haired man's sympathy turned toward Hugo. "Look here, young fellow," he said to Georgette. "I can't be involved in the affair of a lord. If he's your uncle, you'd best go with him."

Hugo hauled her to her feet. When she managed to kick him in the shin, he put a warning hand atop her cap again. "Come along now, *Georgie*. No need to make a spectacle of ourselves."

Half walking, half dragging her, they pushed through the crowd—until she set her feet. "Wait. My trunk."

"Go fetch it, then."

She folded her arms. "Aren't you going to help me with it?"

"You can carry it yourself, you strapping lad."

Because she smiled at this—just a touch at the corners of her lips—Hugo took the trunk's handles for her once she wrestled it from the waiting area over to him.

Just for the sake of expediency. His carriage wasn't far, but their progress would be quicker if he carried the trunk. As soon as they came within sight of it, the coachman hopped down and helped them stow it.

They clambered into the carriage and sat facing each other on the soft velvet squabs. In the comfortable interior, Georgette's disguise looked even more pitiful, her ill-fitting boy's clothing shabby and her shoes split and worn.

As the carriage wheels began to turn, Hugo drummed his fingers impatiently on his thigh. "Where did you get the money for the ticket?" The question came out harsh.

She raised a pale brow. "I stole my dying mother's silver, remember?"

Hugo glared.

She rolled her eyes. "I had money enough saved for my ticket and these clothes. Cousin Mary pays me a bit."

"Not enough." Hugo had called at Frost's Bookshop once out of duty to his friend Benedict, and he'd been startled to find the man's sister carrying a stack of books and baby laundry. Again and again, up and down the stairs the entire time he was in the shop. Georgette Frost worked harder than any housemaid he'd ever encountered.

After that, Hugo stopped in as often as he could. After all, a fellow had to buy his books *somewhere*.

"Imagine my surprise," he said, "when I called at

Frost's Bookshop this morning and learned you had left to visit me in the country."

She pressed herself back against the squabs, tucking her chin. "What did you tell my cousin? Did she fret much?" She sounded worried.

Not for herself, but for someone else's sake.

Hugo sighed, his annoyance ebbing as he exhaled. "No, you wretched minx. I told her that my travel plans had changed and that I'd be driving you." He frowned. "Apparently I was so excited about seeing you that I forgot to send a note. My apology was abject."

"She must have been exhausted if she believed all that."

"She was glad to believe it. She wants you to be all right."

Georgette looked out the window. "That makes one person, at least."

"Your brother wants that, too."

"Right." She scoffed. "Benedict is so concerned about my welfare that he can't be bothered to call on me when he's in London." She shook her head, turning to fix Hugo with ice-blue eyes. "And yet I planned to meet him in Derbyshire. I really am as wretched as you said."

"I shouldn't have said that." Hugo had a distinct feeling he'd be missing his appointment at Somerset House that afternoon. "And yes, I know where your brother is. But where do *you* wish to go?"

The week that followed was, Benedict thought, like the eye of a storm. On one side lay the conversation

Charlotte had dreaded; at the end of it would come the exhibition of Edward Selwyn's portraiture.

Tension vibrated in the air, making the fine hairs of his arms prickle and stand on end. It was contagious, Charlotte's worry. Despite her brave words upon her return from Leeds, he could not imagine what they were to do next. She could not leave the house, since she was meant to be both Barrett and ill.

Benedict made his way into Strawfield once, but no matter whom he asked, he'd been unable to find Lilac to ask after the dagger. And there was no purpose to searching for gold alone; it had no smell or sound, and he could be literally atop it without knowing.

So the week felt like a waiting time, with nothing to do but exist. And a waiting time always made Benedict think about leaving. About where he could go next, because going somewhere—even if he turned right around when he reached his destination—was better than feeling the cage close in around him again.

There was no more chance for him to be alone with Charlotte. With Barrett gone from the household, everyone had more to do. Still, one evening, they found a few minutes to settle in the parlor with his manuscript, and she read a bit out to him.

"'Behold me then, in France! surrounded by a people, to me, strange, incomprehensible, invisible; separated from every living being who could be supposed to take the least interest in my welfare, or existence . . . But I had determined not to give way to gloomy reflections.'"

"Pompous ass," muttered Benedict.

Charlotte cleared her throat and continued on.

"'Therefore, I wished my host a good night, and being left to myself, soon regained that contented frame of mind which is indispensable to those who mean to pass smoothly, and happily, through this scene of mortality.'"

He sagged against the rigid back of the sofa. "It reads like it all happened to someone else." He could hardly remember writing those words, could not remember feeling such rootless, determined optimism. Where to be, what to do next—all his own choice.

With no one outside himself caring one bit.

"I don't know," said Charlotte. "I did like the anecdote about the maid in Calais who insisted on helping you undress. This falls closer to my heart, though."

"If it helps, living through the events, I liked the part where the maid helped me undress much more than I liked this part."

She laughed, and read some more, and when she was done he was glad to put the manuscript away again.

Another day, a letter arrived for Benedict. Franked, which meant it was from Hugo.

Charlotte met him near the stable, where the breeze ruffled their hair and Captain barked a greeting, and she read out the letter's contents to him. "He intercepted your sister, Georgette, on her way to Derbyshire, and he is taking her to stay with his mother." She folded the letter with faint rustlings. "Lord Hugo's mother is a duchess. How fancy for your sister. Will she like that?"

"Probably. I don't know." He took the letter from Charlotte and crumpled it, as though he could chastise his sister with the gesture. "She was on her way *here*? *Honestly. Georgette.*"

"I should have liked to meet her," said Charlotte.

"I should have, too," said Benedict. And he meant exactly that: he should have met her. He should have called on her, even if it would have meant stepping into a cage when he did so. "I haven't visited her for a long time. I hate the bookshop."

"Your family's bookshop?"

"Yes." Captain's long chain jingled, and he crouched and held out a hand so the dog might come to him. "I was never able to read worth a damn. I learned the alphabet by heart as a child, and how to spell more useless long words than most scholars. Except Hugo," he added drily. "As long as I worked aloud, I was all right. But on a page, letters squirmed and tipped like drunken snakes."

"Can snakes become drunk?" She crouched at his side, and Captain jingled over to her instead. "Never mind. The image is vivid enough. I do understand, a bit, of—of not feeling like one belongs in one's own family."

"I know." He squinted his sightless eyes toward the sun. "I know you do."

"What about your sister?"

"She was only three when I went to sea, and she was already reading better than I. Georgette is a brilliant girl. She's wasted in that bookshop."

"Does she think so?"

Impatient, he stood, shaking out his legs. "I don't *know.* I don't know what she likes or doesn't like. All I know is she doesn't think I care for her or will provide for her future."

"And so she intends to do it herself. That is admirable."

"How is it admirable?"

She stood too, and Captain gave a whine of neglect. "Benedict, please recall to whom you are talking. I made my own fortune—and before you shudder with disgust, not entirely on my back."

"I am not disgusted by anything you do. Or have done." This was perfectly true, and he hoped she would believe him.

"Yet you would not want your sister to live my life."

He hadn't thought of that, exactly; he'd only been thinking that he ought to take care of his only living relative. But now that she asked the question: "Would you want that sort of life for Maggie, Charlotte? Not only the luxurious bits, but the sad and lonely parts? The parts where you had to say yes when you wanted to say no? Or how it all ended, with you selling off everything you owned and leaving your home of the past decade?"

She kicked at the chain, scooting it over the ground. "No. No, I would not want that."

"Should it please the court," he said, "I'm glad your life brought you to Strawfield so I could meet you. I know it will bring you somewhere wonderful next."

He sighed. "As for my sister—damnation. If she's with Hugo, he'll keep her safe."

He still ought to find the money for her, to secure whatever came next in her life. A visit to a duchess could not last long. One could not live eternally as a guest, sponging off the kindness of others.

As he knew, and felt more deeply every day.

As the week wore on, Charlotte became desperate to leave the vicarage and collect news. She ventured out veiled, in her Mrs. Smith guise, since she could be neither herself or a healthy Barrett.

The arrival of illustrious guests, put up in the grand Selwyn House, had stolen the village's attention from the reward seekers and the missing gold sovereigns. A lord in the hand was worth fifty thousand pounds worth of ephemeral coins with the king's head upon them.

The day before the exhibition, before she ventured into Strawfield, she made Benedict promise to attend it with her the following day. "If it's awful," she said, "at least you will not know quite how bad."

"Why should it be awful?"

She glared at him, which he seemed to feel. "Right, right." He lifted his hands. "Randolph. Devilry. Strange place for an exhibition. It's possible that—"

"Benedict!" She didn't want to be talked out of her trepidation. Or worse, she did not want him to try to talk her out of it and to fail.

Randolph had promised to exhibit Edward's portraiture. But Randolph's promises weren't worth the air it took to speak them.

"We could try to find the coins quickly," Benedict suggested. "I'll go stand outside at night, alone, and when someone comes to attack me, you can lay hold of him and beat the location of the money out of him."

This vision was so ludicrous that she had to smile—for a moment. "You assume your attacker had something to do with the theft from the Royal Mint."

"Stephen Lilac does."

This was true. Yet neither of them had the heart for this plan, or one that made any more sense. What was the point of finding the coins, of collecting the reward and fleeing? As long as she kept ties to anyone, Randolph could find her. He was here, in the village. He was the cat, tail lashing, waiting to pounce. He was the sword of Damocles, waiting to fall.

Was she a mouse, then? Or a would-be queen? A bit of both. It was easier to be brave, to want things, when she was being brave for someone else. But when she thought of Randolph finding out about Maggie . . . she quailed, and she wanted to collect her precious girl and flee that second.

When Charlotte returned to the vicarage later that day, she ripped off her veiled bonnet and turned at once in the direction of the stable, knowing Maggie would be with her beloved dog.

As she rounded the vicarage, she saw that Captain's long chain lay slack. She did not see the dog, but only Maggie's back. Her tangled hair, the back of her blue gown as she lay curled in the dirt before the stable.

Hurt? *Dead?*

Charlotte picked up her skirts and ran flat-out, gasping.

When she reached her girl, breathless, she noticed what she had missed before. Colleen, the kindly kitchen maid, was petting Maggie as the girl had so often stroked the dog. And Maggie was curled around the still body of the hound.

So. It had happened at last.

Knowing the day would come did not make it any easier to experience. Charlotte's throat went tight, her eyes prickling.

Colleen looked up at Charlotte, her sweet face twisted with sorrow. "Poor Captain. Miss Maggie, she found the dog like this when she came out after lessons."

Maggie lay still, her eyes fixed, her expression flat and without feeling. This was somehow more terrible than seeing her wracked with grief.

"Oh, dearest." Charlotte sat in the dirt next to the girl, lacing her fingers through sun-warmed curls. "How sorry I am."

"She was my mother's," Maggie said tonelessly. "My mother loved me, and now I have nothing left of her."

Your mother loves *you,* thought Charlotte, but that same love kept her lips sealed.

Charlotte excused Colleen, who stood with a grateful nod. One's work didn't stop when a child needed comfort.

But if one were a mother, it should.

Maggie made of herself a cradle about Captain's body. The dog's paws were outstretched, head resting upon them. Captain looked comfortable, as though she were resting.

"You made her so happy," Charlotte said. "My sister would have liked seeing how you treasured her pet."

Maggie blinked, setting a tear to welling, and nodded her head. Her fine hair was ground into the dirt with every movement.

"Did you know that I named Captain?" Charlotte took up her favorite pose, knees folded and arms about them, sideways against Maggie's back. In this way, they could see each other's faces. They made a fallen stack of comfort: the old hound, the girl, the one who had been away so long.

"Did you not know she was a girl dog?"

Charlotte patted her feet against the earth, heel-toe-heel-toe. "Oh, I knew. But I wanted her to be in charge. I suppose even at the age of thirteen, I wasn't content with the limits others placed upon me." She smiled. "Or my dog."

"But she was Mother's dog." The first tear slid from Maggie's eye, blobbing across the bridge of her nose as she lay curled.

"She loved your mother with great devotion." Charlotte chose her words carefully. "She was mine, but that didn't mean she was like me. That didn't even mean she could stay with me, or grow older with me. She had to stay here at the vicarage while I traveled. She was better off being safe."

"What if she wanted to go with you?"

"She didn't want to. She wanted the life she knew. But I came back to visit her as often as I could."

Maggie turned onto her back, looking Charlotte full in the face. "Why did you have to go away?"

This was a question Charlotte did not know how to answer. Every time she left, it was harder; every time, the barriers to her return seemed higher. The silence from her parents, the danger of discovery. Of having Charlotte Pearl and Charlotte Perry be identified as one and the same.

And there was a question, too, she did not know how to ask. *Would you have liked me to stay?*

Footsteps crossing the yard between vicarage and stable made her look up. Benedict, wearing the too-short coat, his stern face soft with sympathy.

"Colleen told me what had passed," he explained when he reached the trio. "Miss Maggie, you have my deepest sympathies."

And with this, Maggie sat upright and sobbed for her lost friend with all the pain in her bruised young heart, and Charlotte cried along with her for every missed day.

They gathered to bury Captain that evening behind the stable. After some dithering over whether it would be appropriate, Charlotte's father agreed to say prayers for the dog.

"'Blessed are those who mourn, for they will be comforted,'" he began in a quavering voice, as the sun drooped and sighed its farewell and the sky bled like fire.

"When, Grandpapa? When will it happen?" Maggie's voice was hoarse, her nose red, her hair and face dirty.

"I don't know, child," said the reverend. "I don't know when comfort comes."

The stable had been locked since the half-drowned treasure seeker and his friends had departed, the same day Charlotte met Benedict. She found the great rusty key, shoved open the door, and looked about for a spade. The stable was filled with junk. A cracked vase, a stack of chairs missing their caned seats. A Chinese screen missing a panel. What was a church to do with all that? The detritus was in layers, years of the neglected salves to conscience. *Give it to the church.*

If this building were Charlotte's, she would burn it to the ground.

But it wasn't hers. It was the church's. Her parents had given decades to the church, and all they had was junk. They had cared for their daughters and lost both in different ways. Charlotte had even taken

Barrett from them. And they gave back, in their quiet, unchanging way, a home.

A home for Maggie. A home, when she needed it, for Charlotte.

A home for Captain to rest forever.

There; there was a spade with a broken handle. Enough wood was left that it would be usable, she thought. She took it up and returned to the solemn circle about the dog. Her mother; her father. Colleen and Cook. Maggie, crying openly.

Benedict, who had so quickly come to find a place in this household.

The circle seemed complete without Charlotte.

Charlotte bent, tugged the folding knife from her boot, and handed it to Maggie. "You could bury that with her, if you like. So she'll always be protected."

She had also given her shawl to cover the dog. It had wrapped Benedict's arm, too, after he was cut. For a frivolous garment, it had finally been of some use.

She turned over the first spade full of earth, then the next. Her father was droning something or other, and it seemed Maggie would dry up from all the tears she was shedding, and there was nothing Charlotte could do but set her jaw and dig, again, again, even as the split handle began to blister her palms.

She had hardly begun to move the earth, yet already she hurt. And there was nothing to do but keep digging.

Then a broad hand covered hers, warm and rough, stilling the ragged movement of the spade. "Let me help," said Benedict. "Let me do this for you."

He took the spade from her hand, allowing her

to step back and stand beside Maggie. To slip an arm around her crying daughter.

With smooth, slow movements, he turned over the earth. Quietly, doing what needed to be done with a graciousness that meant everything.

And that was when she realized: she had fallen in love with him.

Chapter Seventeen

The following day marked the exhibition of Edward Selwyn's paintings in the ballroom of the Pig and Blanket. This wasn't the sort of event Benedict felt like racing to attend, and by the time he followed a veiled Charlotte up the inn's stairs to the ballroom, Randolph had already begun a speech of welcome.

"Some might wonder whether it is inappropriate for an art exhibition to be held where an inquest so recently took place." The marquess's voice was cultured. Oily. Like a fake pearl amidst sludge, Benedict decided.

"I say it is not. For what better way to chase darkness from the world but with art? How better to uncover secrets than with the truth held in paintings?"

And with that, Benedict had a feeling this was going to be bad. Very bad.

He had urged Charlotte not to come today; he had offered to go alone, to use his marvelous listening ears to collect every scrap of news possible about the art exhibit. "You could stay with Maggie and comfort her," he suggested, but even this extremely wise and sensible idea had caused her to hesitate no more than an instant.

"He thinks I have left Strawfield, and so he will not be expecting me to be there. I can't pass up this advantage."

But when one was not making the arrangements, one had no advantage.

He pointed this out, and she agreed readily enough. "But it's my choice, Benedict." Her voice lowered, as cast down as he had ever heard it. "Just once, I want to know what they're saying about me as it's said. Maybe then I can fight back."

How could he argue with that?

Selwyn had sent over two tickets to the exhibition, which would otherwise have cost two guineas each— the exorbitance of the price intended to keep out all but the elite visitors Randolph had summoned. Likely, Selwyn thought Charlotte's parents would use the tickets; likely he thought he was about to become beloved and famous among the *ton*. But Charlotte's parents had as little interest in Edward Selwyn's paintings as they did in the fact that fifty thousand pounds worth of gold sovereigns had been stolen, and so they stayed at the vicarage: the father to fret over his congregation, the mother to translate words that would never be read.

Benedict, keeping an anonymous distance from the veiled Charlotte, would have traded places with either of her parents in an instant.

The ballroom was not large, and it was stuffy, as crowded and tobacco-reeking as the inquest into Nancy Goff's death had been. Combined with the usual scents of a country inn, there were the clotted smells of pomade and perfume so beloved by the wealthy. Perhaps four or five dozen were standing about, waiting for the paintings hung around the room to be uncovered. It was quite a feat for Randolph to have drawn so many from London to a plain village in Derbyshire.

Benedict wondered what sort of entertainment he had promised them, or what bribery or blackmail he had practiced.

"And now," Randolph oozed in the oozingest tone that ever oozed, "let us all be enlightened!"

Applause, and a *whup* of fabric as the first covering was dropped.

More applause. Polite murmurs.

Maybe Benedict had been wrong. Maybe this was exactly what it seemed: an exhibition of Edward Selwyn's portraiture, for some reason known only to God, the devil, and Randolph.

And then another cover was removed, and another, and the next—and as cloth after cloth fell around the perimeter of the room, the murmurs changed.

"They are all of *her*," said one female voice. "Did you know—"

"He painted so many? No idea. And all bare, her figure, except for that necklace. Tut! His poor wife." This last was spoken with not a little smugness.

"Randolph." Edward Selwyn spoke above the murmurs. "I understood"—his tone was that of a man who was blinking quickly and trying to smile—"that my portraiture was to be featured."

"Are these not portraits?" Randolph sounded surprised. "I don't believe I said *whose* portrait I would feature. Or what sort of portraits it would be."

So. Yes. It was bad. Very bad.

A tiny piece of Benedict wished he could see the

paintings lined up, Charlotte after Charlotte, all bare and gleaming and cuffed in luxury. But the far greater part knew he must find her. With his cane, he shoved at people's feet until they squawked and moved aside for him. He felt Charlotte's presence as a silence amidst the sounds of the crowd.

Very like the day they had met.

"Mrs. Smith?" he asked when he had reached the side of the silent wintergreen-scented figure.

"If only," said that low, lovely voice that had captured him from the first words she spoke.

"How many paintings are there?" As though it mattered. *Too many* was clearly the answer.

"So many," she whispered. "More than ever I posed for. More than I realized. He painted . . ." Her voice broke. "I did not know he painted all of these."

Seen individually, Benedict had no doubt, the paintings were graceful. Classical. Grouped together, the force of their numbers made them obsessive. Sexual.

Benedict felt the mood of the crowd as a farmer might check the skies. There was an unsteadiness in the movements from foot to foot, a rumbling in the eddies of talk. *Ought they to be scandalized? Ought they to buy something? If Randolph endorsed such things—but then, the artist's wife looked angry . . . .*

At Benedict's side, Charlotte grew smaller and smaller. He wanted to do something to protect her, but anything he did to draw attention to her identity would have the opposite effect. He felt trapped in a smiling statue of a body. Wanting to leave with her. But she stayed, maybe feeling some possessiveness of her own image—and so he stayed, too, his marvelous listening ears catching far more whispering than he wished they would.

And then a familiar voice cut through the rumblings like a bolt of lightning. "Godamighty," shrieked Mrs. Potter. "Those is pictures of the vicar's daughter!"

When the moment came that I had feared for so long, it was not so bad.

Charlotte had heard this saying before, usually at the edges of certain *ton* parties she had attended. It was a phrase beloved by rich young heirs confessing their gambling losses to doting fathers, or fluttery young brides confiding about their wedding nights.

The saying was true for them. It was not true for Charlotte. For ten years, she had been known to one world as a courtesan and to another as the daughter of a simple country vicar.

Now those worlds smashed together.

This was Randolph's plan: not to bare her, over and over, obscenely, but to strip her before those who had known her as more than a courtesan.

Maybe—if she stripped herself, too—if she tried not to be crushed by the collision of worlds . . .

She struggled through the squeeze of people, drew in a trembling breath, and snatched the veil from her bonnet. "Indeed it is Miss Perry," she said. "And it is Charlotte Pearl."

The crowd was silent.

Now that Charlotte looked about herself without the annoyance of her veil, she knew them. All of them. Mrs. Potter was the only villager—well, this *was* her inn. The rest were Londoners, the elite who had known *La Perle* and had probably never thought of what she had been before.

There was a duke she had helped through an erectile problem caused by fear he would have an erectile problem. An earl who had come to her for a listening ear about his fears that he only liked men. The prestige of time spent with *La Perle* had won him a wife five years before, but they remained childless.

There was a widowed countess who had hounded Charlotte for her dressmaker's name. A gentleman who had visited her card parties and recited poems about her eyes. The caricaturist who had called on her every Tuesday afternoon, consuming cakes by the dozen and chortling over the latest gossip.

Public gossip, that was. Charlotte never spoke of her private business. *No one shall know what goes on between us except for us,* she assured them all.

A courtesan was not a whore. A courtesan was a hostess who made discreet arrangements. And a courtesan collected—she thought—many friends. All of these people had known Charlotte, had liked their time with her.

They did not look at her now as though they liked her. They looked . . . disappointed. Mistrustful. Absent of the sheen of her London life and its trappings, *La Perle* was nothing but a speck of sand.

And then there was Randolph, who had slashed her face, and who was smiling at the effect of his little show. Edward, stunned, who had painted her so many times without her knowing it. Which of them had hurt her more?

This was her autopsy. Every time she had been painted, she had been dissected without even knowing it. Yet her heart had not stopped. It kept beating, stubborn organ.

And last, there stood Benedict at the back of the room. Into the silence, he nodded. *Let me love you*, he had said, after he knew everything.

That was impossible now. It had always been impossible.

Yet her heart beat. She could still do . . . something. A bold gesture of her own to counter Randolph's, to wrest away control of the situation.

There was a small dais, used by musicians when this room played host to village balls. Charlotte climbed onto the dais and squared her shoulders. She was *La Perle,* but not the pure sort.

And she was Charlotte Perry, too.

"Thank you all for coming to the exhibition of Mr. Selwyn's works," she said. "I admit, I presumed we would be treated to more variety in his oeuvre, but"— she gave a roguish smile—"one cannot argue with perfection."

A series of awkward coughs. A chuckle—from Benedict, bless him.

"These paintings tell stories, my friends. I have been Nausicaa. Aphrodite. Iris, beneath a rainbow, and Selene with the moon in my hands."

"Why have you always been naked?" called someone at the back of the room. A few laughs followed.

"Besides the fact that such paintings are far more likely to find buyers?" Charlotte managed a smile, knowing it would invite more laughter. Friendlier laughter. "I am bare so you can read into the paintings what you wish. Maybe you will see a bit of yourself in there."

"I haven't had a hope of looking like that for forty

years," grumped the elderly countess who so admired Charlotte's gowns.

The tension was beginning to crack, as Charlotte took it into herself. She ventured a glance at Edward. He looked like a dog that had thought it was about to be kicked, then was handed a beefsteak instead.

At his side, Lady Helena's cheeks had a slapped look, and her nostrils were flaring with deep, unsteady breaths.

Charlotte looked away. Out. Across the crowd. "As you have all traveled so far to attend this exhibition, I hope you will support Mr. Selwyn's work. If you manage to look at the faces, you'll see that they are quite well-painted. Mr. Selwyn has, I believe, a bright future as a portraitist. He *can* paint clothing. Look how well he painted the necklace."

Laughter, thank goodness.

"As a matter of fact," Charlotte added, "if anyone should be interested in purchasing the necklace . . . well. You can say you've seen it in its natural habitat, can you not?"

With that, she curtsied, stepped down from the dais, and slipped away. Quickly, pressing through the crowd before anyone could stop her, hands clenched and fisted together to hide their shaking.

It was done. It was done, and it *had* been that bad.

But it was done.

She found her way into the tiny private parlor where she and Benedict had so recently talked with Mrs. Potter. Someone would find her in a moment, she knew, but she had a few seconds to compose herself. What she wouldn't give for a bit of cool water to splash on her face and hands. She looked about, but there was nothing to use. Plain chairs, a table, a window, a hearth. Not even a pitcher and basin.

When she looked back toward the doorway, Randolph's form filled the space. "Beautiful speech," he said. "I am *so* glad you were able to attend."

She hid her nerveless hands behind her back. "That was a cruel trick you played."

"No more than you deserved for leaving me."

"Not on me." She injected scorn into her tone. "On Selwyn. You embarrassed him."

Randolph gave a careless wave as he stepped into the room. Closer. Closer, bringing with him the scent of bergamot and the unbearable odor of triumph. "He embarrassed himself. Has a bit of an obsession with you, hasn't he?"

Randolph didn't know, then. He didn't know about Maggie. "Can you blame him?" She arched a saucy brow. "You couldn't let me go either."

"I'll always be with you." He stroked her cheek, running a thumb over the scar. "You can't hide and pretend to be someone you're not, Pearl. You can never belong to anyone else."

She set her jaw, refusing to flinch or look away. "Anyone besides myself, you mean? That's true. Though it was always true."

Beneath her brave words, though, her heart quailed at every exception. Because she had belonged to her sister, Margaret, whom she had buried. She was Maggie's, heart-whole, though the girl had no idea. And she was giving herself away to Benedict Frost, a day at a time.

These divisions did not make her feel lessened. But they did make her feel as though she had left the most precious pieces of her soul in places she could never protect them.

Randolph loomed tall, his saturnine features marked with displeasure. "Another fine speech. But it's not for you to decide when our association is at an end."

"Actually, it is." She twisted, seeking to push past him and out of the room.

He smacked her, backhanded, across the face. The emerald ring cracked against her teeth, cutting her lip.

The sound of the blow rang in her ears long after the room had gone silent. Her head reeled; numbness deadened her face, and then it flashed hot and agonizing and her mouth filled with blood.

He smiled.

She spit at him, spraying his impeccable linen shirt with blood where it shone above his waistcoat. "And to think I once called you protector."

His chin drew back. "You dare spit at a peer?"

"You're no peer of mine," she sneered. "I know you care for nothing more than your pride, so maybe this will salve it: you did not lose me, because I was never your possession."

A rap on the doorframe, then Benedict stuck in his head. "Miss Perry. And Randolph, did I hear? You'll be glad to know that idiot Selwyn has already sold three paintings."

Randolph tugged a handkerchief from his pocket with a flourish. Rather than offer it to Charlotte, whose lip was bleeding freely now, he brushed at the specks on his shirt. Of course. "That is odd," he said, "since only one painting was for sale. Mine. The rest were on loan from their owners."

"Yes, well, I gather he won't have any trouble painting more to order," said Benedict. "He seems to have a talent for it."

"Lovely chat, Randolph," Charlotte mumbled thickly. "Or whatever the opposite of loveliness is. I don't expect we will need to speak again for any reason."

"*La Perle, La Perle.*" He looked up from ministering to his injured shirt, and for a second she saw a flash of something besides chill triumph in his eyes. "I could have made something of you."

"I was already something before you met me." She turned away, facing Benedict where he still stood in the doorway. He held out a handkerchief—he must have caught the clotted sound of her voice—and she spat gratefully into it. "Mr. Frost, will you see me home?" This last word caught in her throat.

"Home, you call it," said the marquess from behind her. "For how long, do you think?"

And she realized how tidy his revenge had been. By holding the exhibition in her parents' village, he ensured that even if Charlotte somehow managed to escape, their proper, steady lives were ruined.

He liked hurting, and he had already left Charlotte scarred. Now he intended the next wound to fall upon her family.

She would not even let Benedict take her arm on the way back to the vicarage. "I have to go. I have to get out of here."

She strode, quick and tense, and he tucked his cane under his arm and followed the sound of her footsteps.

He heard no one else on the village street—yet. All Strawfield was in the Pig and Blanket's taproom, all London upstairs. Soon, though, the two halves of society would talk. Likely Mrs. Potter already had.

"You can't run from this, Charlotte."

She halted a few steps ahead of him, whirling in a furious spray of gravel. "What have you to say about it? I can go where I wish . . . do what I wish . . . ."

"Yes, but *is* this what you wish?"

Her breath was sudden and short, a gulp. "It has never been what I wished."

He closed the distance between them and chucked her under the chin with a curled forefinger. "Not even a little bit? Not ever? Not when you first went to London?"

She brushed his hand aside. "Benedict, stop. No. I always left a place when I had to, not when I was ready to. I'm not ready to leave Strawfield now, but . . ."

His hand fell to his side. "Because of the gold?"

"Not because of the gold." More of those terrible gulping breaths, as if she would deprive herself of air before she would give in to tears. "Because . . . I started to think that I could have . . . a family."

"With Maggie?"

"With you." The words were barely more than a whisper; then she laughed, a terrible, grating sound. "There, that's one part of me that hadn't been bared yet today. Have my heart. Pin it up on the wall for the *ton* to ogle and mock."

He hardly knew what to say, how to feel. His own

heart seemed to have stopped beating a while ago, and within he was only numb. "Charlotte."

"Don't say it. I shouldn't have said anything myself."

But it had to be said—for her sake, and for his. "Charlotte, I'm a Naval Knight. I have no home of my own. My income is contingent on my living in a spare, bare room. Alone. A family is the one thing I can never have."

"You could give it up," she said. "And . . ."

"And live on air? The kindness of strangers?" He shook his head. "I'm doing that now, but I can't live like that forever. Besides—I've given up one career after another. I never finish anything. The only thing on earth I'm good at is roaming."

He wanted to be in some far-off part of the world right now, to stop saying these words to her.

He wanted the things he said not to be true. Each word felt like a blow, and when one struck oneself, one knew all the weak spots.

"I understand." She turned away again, her voice dipping. "It was just an idea. I have those sometimes."

"I do, too," he said. "But I know they can't come to anything."

But she was already walking away, and he had to make his way to the vicarage alone.

Charlotte came upon her parents in the front parlor, sharing a rare moment together along with a pot of tea.

"Child!" Her father stood, alarmed. "What has happened to you?"

For a moment, heart-sore, she thought he was

talking about what a fool she'd made of herself with Benedict. Then she recalled the bloodstained handkerchief wrapped tightly in her fingers; the swollen and cut lip that served as end punctuation to her relationship with Randolph.

And then she was heart-sore all over again, in a different way.

"The art exhibition . . ." She trailed off. Tried again. "It was me. All paintings of me." She spared them the details of *what* sort of paintings these had been.

Mrs. Perry caught on first. "Oh. *Oh.* Oh, Charlotte. Oh, now everyone—oh, mercy on us. Who knows? All of Strawfield? Will they—"

"Calm yourself, Mrs. Perry," said the vicar. He took his wife's hands in his, brow creasing in thought. "So, Charlotte. Your . . . London life is known here."

"If it's not already, it will be within the day."

Charlotte's mother groaned.

Her father drew in a deep breath, pulling himself upright. "Well. Then. I shall probably lose the living as vicar, and we shall have to leave here."

He said this quite calmly, as though a crisis had crystallized all his anxieties and fidgets into this one truth.

His wife groaned again.

Charlotte could bear this no longer; she felt like an intruder, a bringer of infinite trouble. "Where is Maggie? I have to tell her. Something."

But she already knew the answer. Without waiting for their reply, she banged out of the front door and darted across the lawn separating house from stable.

Maggie was sitting, knees pulled up and arms wrapped around them, beside the mound of earth that covered Captain. Benedict was there, talking to her quietly, but when he heard Charlotte approach, he stood. "I'll leave you ladies to your own conversation," he said with a ghost of his usual roguery. "Thought I scented some Jacob's ladder near the stone wall. Wouldn't that be a nice bloom for Captain?"

And off he strode, as though he knew exactly where he was going.

Charlotte folded herself next to Maggie in the identical pose. "What were you and Mr. Frost talking about?" Cravenly, she hoped he had broken some news to her.

Thin shoulders shrugged. "He just asked how I was. He said he knew I liked Captain." The girlish voice became smaller with each word.

"He's a nice man," Charlotte said. She summoned her courage. "And, Maggie, I am . . . not a nice woman."

Maggie's arms dropped from about her legs. "What happened? What do you mean, Aunt Charlotte?"

"I did some things while I was traveling that some people don't like."

"What things?"

"Um." Charlotte floundered for an explanation. "I took money to spend time with people."

Maggie squinted, blinking fair lashes over her green eyes. "Like a job?"

"It *was* a job of sorts. Yes. But—"

"Well, that's all right. Lots of people have jobs. Grandpapa has a job as vicar."

"Right, yes. But because of my job—which some

people think is bad—then Grandpapa might have to stop being vicar here."

"I don't understand. What does your job have to do with Grandpapa being the vicar of Strawfield?"

Good question, my girl. "Some people think that a vicar's family has to be perfect."

"That's stupid. Nobody's perfect." Mindful of her spiritual education, she added, "Except Jesus. But even *He* threw things sometimes."

The unassailable logic of a child. "You marvelous girl." Charlotte smiled at her—and after a moment, Maggie smiled back.

She didn't deserve that smile. She had to make this darling child, this wonderful precious girl, understand that Charlotte had hurt her. That she, Charlotte, had ruined everything. Had been in the process of ruining everything since she was a girl of eighteen, and that Maggie was going to lose everything she had ever known, and it was all Charlotte's fault.

So she knocked away the chock that had kept her daughter's heart steady for so long. "There's something else you have to know. Maggie—I'm your mother."

Maggie went still, as still as she had when she held Captain's prone body. "I don't understand. You're my aunt."

"I'm your mother." It was more difficult to say this second time.

"Were you married to my father?"

"No, and that's part of what makes me . . . not nice."

It was so hard to tell this to a girl poised between childhood and the worries of a young woman. Maggie had been sheltered, too much so, from the coldness of being ostracized.

Charlotte reached out a hand. Maggie shrank away from her, toppling sideways onto Captain's grave.

Charlotte tried to explain. "That's why we always said you were my sister's child. She was married. You are baptized as hers, Maggie. In the eyes of the world, you are respectable as I can never be."

Scooting forward on her elbows, Maggie crawled off of the mound over her dog, rolled to a seated position, and stared at Charlotte through fallen hair. "Every time you told me about my mother, it was a lie."

"No, everything I told you about my sister was true."

"But she wasn't my mother."

"No," Charlotte said softly. "No. She wasn't your mother."

"And Captain wasn't my mother's dog. She wasn't left to me. She wasn't a—a sign of someone my mother had loved."

"I always liked Captain." Charlotte's reply was weak. "And she loved you. You were so good to her. You were her friend, and—"

"And she died outside without me." Maggie stood, abruptly as a puppet being jerked upright. "She was my *only* friend."

"I know." Here it was, the punishment that cut her heart. It hurt more deeply than she could have imagined. She had had an idea, she supposed, that she would tell Maggie one day, and Maggie would fling eager arms around Charlotte's waist and say she had known all along.

It was just an idea.

She had those sometimes, and they were always worthless.

"Do you love me?" said Maggie, and her voice was much older than it had been a few minutes before.

"Yes. More than anything. Enough to give you up to give you a better life."

"Then do it again. I want you to leave here."

Turning on her heel, she walked away, thin and small against the gray stone line of the wall between the vicarage and the Selwyn lands.

Charlotte was numb before the pain, as her face had been right after Randolph struck her. Maggie had stabbed her, and if she were lucky she would bleed out before she realized how much she hurt.

But everything she had said had, at last, been true. Especially the last: that she loved Maggie.

And for her child, she would do anything. Even leave, hurting herself, if it would spare Maggie the smallest bit of pain.

Chapter Eighteen

Benedict's search for the Jacob's ladder had been an excuse to leave Charlotte and Maggie alone. He did not truly expect to find any of the strongly scented flowers. They were rare on the edge of the moors, elusive and sweet. Like a feeling he could not grasp.

Under his boots, scrubby grass crunched unevenly. There were spots of bare earth amidst the grass, making him wobble. He trailed the metal tip of his cane along the stone wall, following its line away from the stable.

He *hated* having to admit there was something he couldn't do, even if it had nothing to do with being blind. He couldn't give Charlotte what she wanted of him. He couldn't even *think* about what *he* wanted. Had he thought he could escape from the cages of his life? This was but a reprieve before the door crashed shut again.

Crash.

The sound was so sudden and loud that he halted in surprise.

And then he realized it had come not from within, but from the direction of the stable, and he hauled up his cane and raced back the way from which he had come.

Finding the splintery wooden wall of the stable, he ran fingertips along it until he came to the corner. A few more steps, and he reached the door. It gaped open, dust filtering free and tickling his nose.

Another crash, several thumps, a muttered curse.

He stepped within the stable's coolness, inhaling the scents of hay and old wood and rot. "Hullo? Does someone need help?"

"It's just me, Benedict. I'm trying to find a trunk." Charlotte's voice, muffled by stacks of things and the stretch of effort, issued from about two yards ahead.

"Why do you need a trunk?"

Charlotte exhaled hard; he imagined her blowing hair out of her face.

"Barrett took mine."

"Nice sidestep, but you know what I mean."

"Because I am *leaving*. People need trunks when they leave."

"What? *No.* No, you don't." He took a step forward, kicking something flat that slid lightly away. A picture maybe, or a screen. "You can't leave Strawfield just when your parents' lives are about to blow up in their faces."

She heaved something aside, and her voice came more clearly. "Can't I? How will it help them if I stay? How will it help any of us to have to look each other in the face and see how much we've hurt each other?"

He kicked at the flat picture-thing again. "They didn't take the news well, then."

She hesitated. "I don't know, actually. I've rarely seen my father so calm, and that includes at ordinary mealtimes when the beef is a little tough."

Another thump and totter and tumble, as a stack of entombed rubbish tipped over. "But that doesn't matter. I'm not leaving for my own sake. I'm leaving for theirs." Her voice wobbled and broke on this final word.

Shite. "You're leaving for Maggie's sake, aren't you? What happened? Did someone tell her about you?"

"I told her. Everything."

He had to sit down. Unfortunately, he happened to be in front of a pitchfork, and he quickly stood again. "You told her you're her mother."

"Yes. And she asked me to leave."

He whistled. "Well—you mustn't. Children will say the worst things, but they don't mean them."

There followed a crash so loud, glassy and shattering, that he suspected she had shoved something over just for the sake of breaking it. "You say I *cannot* leave for the sake of my family. My parents say they *must* leave because of me. And Maggie says she *wants* me to leave. Just me.

"The voting is against you, Sailor Boy, and we haven't even polled the good people of Strawfield yet. What do you think Mrs. Potter would say when she passed me in the street, when she was so harsh about Nance meeting a young man? Do you think I'd be allowed in the village's only taproom? Do you think anyone would sit in my father's church?"

"Do you care?"

"Yes, I care. Because Maggie will have to hear whatever people say about me. Today she lost a mother she'd thought of as a perfect angel, and in return she got me."

He kicked at the hard-packed dirt floor. Where was that picture? He wanted to kick something more. He wanted to rail and howl.

In case Charlotte could see him through the labyrinth of fallen items, though, he smiled. He couldn't be a beast. "You *are* accomplished at virtuous works. That's even better than being angelic."

"Don't, Benedict. Don't. She's always been better off without me, and now she knows why. They'll all be better off without me." A heavy thump, and a few words that were little more than a whisper. "I owe them this."

And he understood. That was what love did, wasn't it—left when it was one-sided? He had loved his parents, and he hadn't known if they could ever love him back. Not completely, not as he was. So he left when he was little older than Maggie was now, and he went to sea.

In the end, it hadn't solved anything. It separated him from Georgette. He didn't want Charlotte to lose the only family she had, too.

But she had had enough difficult choices piled upon her today, and he couldn't argue with her. If Maggie wanted her to leave, and she wanted to honor that request, then they ought to be allowed to go their separate ways.

"I'll help you find a trunk," he said quietly. "If you'll quit shoving things about. I can use my cane, and I'll find one by the echo of it, and you can—"

"No! Don't. Don't help me leave. Don't ask me to bear that, too."

His temper flared. "Well, then don't leave me before you have to!"

"Benedict, stop." She had gone still behind some barrier, something solid as furniture. Her voice was quiet and low. From the first time he'd heard her speak, he had taken a little thrill from her every word. "If you know you must be done with me, then be done with me. Don't drag out this pain. Don't make me lose you bit by bit."

As he had lost his sight.

The realization rooted him, lost amidst unseen trash or treasure. She was right. It was worse, losing something or someone bit by bit. Knowing the end would come, being tortured by the anticipation of what must happen and the hope that it would somehow pass one by.

His heart was a hard pit, knowing that he had added to her sadness. That the family she'd hoped to form was now being wrecked. But she wanted it for Maggie, and he wanted to stand on his own two feet, and so they just didn't *fit,* no matter how sweetly Charlotte's head tucked, in quiet moments, into the hollow of his shoulder.

Voting, she had made mock of. Who would vote that a blind explorer and a lapsed courtesan would be able to make a go of . . . anything?

He would have liked to, for a while. But he wasn't a landowner, and she was a woman, and neither of them had a vote. The question fell dead to the floor.

"All right," he agreed. "You're right."

He turned to make his way back to the stable door, but there were so many things over which to stumble. His eyes, never any help now, were bleared and wet, and somehow his ears weren't quite working right, and his cane was a dead stick in his hand. Then someone was talking to him—a man's voice, from right before him, and he shook his head, not listening, not understanding.

Dimly, he heard the clean snick of a blade, and the wetness of blood slid down his right arm and he dropped his cane.

Blood.

Not much, but still. It snapped him rudely back to the present. "What the hell! Who is there?"

"What are you doing here, blind man?" The growl was familiar.

Benedict grimaced. "Let me guess. My little friend from the street. And how are you?" He talked loudly, willing Charlotte to hear and hide and be silent.

"What are you doing in here?"

Benedict held up a quelling hand. "Wait. Did you just cut me with my *own knife?*"

"You took mine," came the growl.

"Likewise. Isn't that delightful? We have a tradition." *Damn.* He had neither knife nor, at the moment, cane. Where was it? He couldn't feel it with his boot; it must have rolled. At this close distance, he could smell the assailant, all beer and sweat. The man was no taller than Benedict, but he had the stiletto. He might have a gun. Who the devil was he?

Mind reeling, Benedict stomped as hard as he could, willing the world to vibrate into order. About him was a tangle of unknown objects.

Oh. But nearby was that pitchfork. Yes. "Don't cut me again." He sidled to one side, hoping he'd made it look like a stumble. "This is a borrowed coat. Friend, you are hell on coats."

Aha. He closed his hand around the handle and

hefted it, then gave it a toss in the direction of the assailant.

It hit nothing. Thumped to the hard-packed dirt floor.

But where was the man? Wasn't he here to hurt Benedict?

Crash. A tumble of heavy items that seemed to fall and echo forever. Benedict clapped a hand over his mouth to keep from calling Charlotte's name. Was she hidden? Would she stay that way? Stay safe?

"Do you have a gun?" Benedict called. "I think it's been so sweet of you not to shoot it."

"I don't use a gun," growled the voice.

Aha. Benedict got an idea of where he was. He shifted closer, a cautious quarter step at a time.

His foot bumped against something—that flat thing, that screen or picture or whatever it was. He bent, picked it up, and whipped it in the direction from which he'd heard the voice.

The guttural curse told him he'd hit his mark, but the man didn't come after him again. Instead, he shifted something heavy. Then something more.

"Friend of mine," Benedict called. "What are *you* doing here?"

Another heavy piece went scraping and sliding, hitting the fallen items knocked free by Charlotte.

"You're searching," Benedict realized. "Aren't you? What did you hide in here?"

He remembered the Bow Street Runner's words. Stephen Lilac thought the attack on Nance was connected to the gold sovereigns. And Benedict was sure the attack on himself was connected to that on Nance.

Which meant . . . "You hid . . . what's the word?

Evidence? You hid some evidence in here, didn't you, friend from the street?" *Hear me, Charlotte. Go for help.*

"Shut up, blind man."

"Not that we have been introduced, or that I wish us to be, but the name is Frost." Benedict found the nearest thing that he could sit on—it turned out to be a saddle—and sat with seeming unconcern. "I'll just sit here and keep you company. If you feel like cutting me again, you can try, but I don't intend to let you. Anyway, it seems you're busy right now."

More shifting. More cursing. The man had an impressive vocabulary.

A grunt as if he was pulling something heavy—and then came a dull thump, a groan, and the thud of something falling to the floor.

"This is the loudest building," Benedict muttered. "Hullo there? Friend from the street?"

"No, it's Charlotte," came her voice, a little breathless from exertion. "Nicely done. He must have sneaked in after we stopped talking. With all your distractions, he didn't realize I was in here."

He stood up, craning his neck to find the source of her voice. "And you hit him with something?"

"In the back of the head. A cricket bat. Broken, of course."

He managed a tiny smile. "It seems to have done the job."

"Are you bleeding?"

Oh. His arm. He toyed with the rip in the coat sleeve. "Are you?"

"No. He didn't hurt me, but I cut myself on some broken glass. I'm not bleeding anymore."

"I'll be able to say the same soon enough. What do we need to do now? Tie him up in case he wakes?"

"Right. Yes." She directed Benedict around a few fallen items so he could reach them: cricket-batter and former assailant. "You ought to have his knife."

"*My* knife," he said with covetous glee. When Charlotte placed it in his palm, he ran his fingertips over it, cataloguing every nick and dip in the bone handle. "Well met, old friend."

He slipped it into his boot. "Do you see rope anywhere in here?"

"Something useful, you mean? Ha, no."

Benedict retraced his steps to the saddle, wrenched free a stirrup, and also snapped off the cinch. He brought them back to Charlotte. "The leather's old and rotten, but it's better than nothing. Can you bind him?"

"Believe me," she said drily, "I know how to bind a man."

The wink of her Charlotte spirit made him smile. "Excellent. I'll sit on him while you go for Lilac. If our friend wakes up again, I'll hit him with something."

"Here, use the cricket bat. It worked well enough the last time." She pressed the split but solid wood implement into his hands. "Benedict—what was he looking for?"

"Something you covered up looking for a trunk." He felt grim. "Something he didn't mind using a knife to find."

She swallowed heavily. "The gold sovereigns."

"Go get Lilac," he said, then sat on the yielding back of the man who had twice slashed his arms, and who had probably ended the life of at least one person.

He made a more comfortable seat than a broken-down saddle, for what that was worth.

* * *

Charlotte didn't have to go far to find Stephen Lilac. The Bow Street Runner, hat at a jaunty angle, was just crossing from the road onto the vicarage land.

"Mr. Lilac! I was coming in search of you," she called.

The expression on his bearded face sharpened. When he drew within a few feet of Charlotte, he said, "The same to you, Miss Perry. I was about to pay a call on you at the vicarage."

"Me?" She pressed a hand against her side; she had a stitch from all the running and whapping of intruders. "I—why?"

"Ah, well." He looked at her, not unkindly. "Bit of a to-do in the village today, wasn't there, and you at the heart of it. Mrs. Potter was determined I come learn your remaining horrid secrets."

"Oh. That. There aren't any more, at least not the horrid sort." How long ago that all seemed. "Mr. Lilac—do you have a gun?"

He looked wary. "Is there some need for it?"

"Someone came into the vicarage stable. He attacked Frost with Frost's own knife, which means—"

"He attacked Frost the first time, too." Lilac caught on at once. "Which means—"

"He might be the same man who attacked Nance. Which means—"

"Means he'd be worth meeting, doesn't it?" Lilac smiled thinly. "As a matter of fact, I do have a pistol. And a pair of shackles."

Charlotte blinked. "Are you in the habit of carrying shackles?"

"All part of the work of an Officer of the Police, Miss Perry. Wouldn't want to need them and not have them."

When they returned to the stable, Benedict was still sitting on the unknown man—who was now awake, alert, and extremely disgruntled. Lilac threw the stable doors open wide, and Charlotte got her first good look at the attacker's face.

"Why, I know this man." She shook her head. "That is, I've seen him before."

"And when was that?" Lilac crouched, replacing the worn-out leather bindings on the man's wrists with a pair of iron shackles he pulled from a coat pocket.

She thought about it. What was her association with that face? A short beard . . . straw-colored hair . . . For some reason, she imagined the expression sloppy and lolling. Hmm.

Benedict stood, and together he and Lilac hauled the scowling man to his feet. The sharp, stale odor of beer struck Charlotte, and the memory clicked into place. "The afternoon on the day Nance died. He was in the Pig and Blanket. He . . . bothered me."

"I never seen yer before, bitch," the man spat.

The local accent clinched it. She hadn't Benedict's memory for voices, but she recalled that one. "Bitch *courtesan*," she said crisply. "I was wearing a veil at the time. I told you I didn't want your company, and when you didn't believe me, I had to convince you with a knife."

"Awful fondness you people have for knives," Lilac said. "It's really not right."

"It's not," Charlotte agreed. "But I remember that he called Nance over as though he knew her."

"Nance." The ruddy face sagged. "She was a righ' nice girl."

"Who killed her?" asked Lilac.

The man shut his eyes. "She wasn't supposed to die. I just wanted to shut her up . . . give her a warning. We needed people to come, but she was going to say something too much."

"Needed people to come—for what?" Benedict said sharply.

The man tried to fold his arms, defiant, but the shackles stopped his movement. "I'm going to swing no matter what, so why should I say more?"

As a vicar's daughter, Charlotte supposed she ought to appeal to his immortal soul. But instead, she worked at that kernel of feeling he'd shown. "For Nance. Because she *was* a nice girl, and you can help see justice done for her."

For a long moment, he stared—first at Charlotte, then, bowing his head, at the iron bands about his wrists. "I was drunk," he whispered. "I didn't mean to kill her."

"Did she know it was you?" Charlotte asked softly.

He shook his head, eyes reddened. "I wore a cloak. Just meant to put a scare into her. She saw my dagger but that's all."

"Cat eye," murmured Benedict. "I thought it was a rich man's toy."

The man recovered a bit of spirit. "Was before I stole it off him."

"You said Nance was saying too much." Charlotte considered. "About the gold coin she'd received?"

"I give it to her," said the man. "She was supposed to show it around, like, so people would get excited and come here to hunt for the coins."

"But why?"

"Hidin' new faces among other new faces. Who'ud notice four strange men in the village if a hundred came to town?"

"Clever enough." Lilac had been listening, head tilted, to the impulsive questions of Charlotte and Benedict. Now he went into action, all peppery professional. "Name?"

"Smith. John Smith."

Another Smith. Charlotte rolled her eyes.

"So there were four of you involved in the death of Nance Goff?" Lilac asked.

"No. That were just me. Four of us in the theft from the Royal Mint."

Lilac had pulled forth a pocket-book and stub of pencil from his seemingly infinite pockets. "Four. Alllll right. You and your companions stole fifty thousand pounds worth of gold sovereigns, shooting four guards in the process."

"I didn't use no gun! I don't use no gun."

Lilac lifted the pencil, fixing the man with a stern gaze. "Hardly makes you innocent, does it?"

The man looked again at his shackles. "Guess not."

"Why steal the gold sovereigns before their release?"

"I di'n't know what they were. Thought anything from the Mint'ud be worth somethin' big. Didn't know until we left and opened the chests what we'd got, and then we knew we couldn't spend it until the new coins come out. So we had to hide it until it were safe."

"So you brought the stolen money here." Lilac was writing again.

The man shrugged. "I grew up not far away. Lots

of places to hide things in the Peak. Nice an' far from London, too."

"And now it's here. In the stable."

Brow knit with distress, the man twisted around before Benedict took hold of his shoulder. "It ought to be. We moved it a few times, like. I don't know. Didn't trust each other."

"Fancy that," murmured Charlotte.

"Had it in the icehouse on the rich nob's land for a while, but the weather get warm and the groundskeeper come around too much checking for strangers. Had to move it."

Charlotte remembered—a trio, crossing the Selwyn lands, laughing. One of them had reminded her of Randolph, making her quail. "Is one of the other thieves a big blond fellow who moves like a snake?"

"I don't know about the second part. But Smith's blond."

"Another Smith?" Lilac looked up sharply. "What's his full name? And that of your other partners?"

"Smith." A slow smile showed brown teeth. "And Smith, and Smith. John Smith is all we ever called each other. If they has other names, I don't know 'em."

"And you? Is it your real name?"

Another shrug. "It'll do for me, too."

Lilac looked amused. "We'll see about that, Mr. Smith. But on with your tale. After the icehouse, then you moved the coins to this stable?"

"Yes, but then the blind man come to visit and we know he was lookin' for the coins."

"It's *Frost*," said Benedict. "And there was not much danger of me spotting the gold."

"No, but yer can't blame us for worryin' with yer so

close to it. I said I'd try to find out what he wanted and put a scare into him."

"You do like to do that scaring sort of thing," Benedict said.

"A scare worked well enough. No need to kill yer, blind man."

"Frost," said Benedict in a freezing tone. "And I fought you twice. Won, too."

Charlotte hated that he'd had to hear those belittling words. Hated that anyone could see him as other than, well, *Benedict*.

"Still," the thief said mulishly. "Yer left the gold alone."

"Only because I never thought of searching for six trunks of gold in a building."

"Probably not six now," admitted the so-called John Smith. So many Smiths, none of them real. "The others each took a trunk, but the coins is heavy. Before we could move 'em all, there were this dog outside the stable that bark every time we come by."

"Captain," Charlotte realized. "She stayed outside all the time."

Lilac had a few more questions, but Charlotte drifted away, touching fallen stacks of random items. Captain and her friendly soul; Captain and her barks of greeting. If there was gold still hidden in this stable, it was because of Captain.

"What a good old soul she was," Charlotte murmured.

So Randolph had come to Strawfield because of Charlotte. Charlotte had come to Strawfield because of the gold coin. And the gold coin had come to Strawfield because Smith—one of four—had lived near here at some point in his life.

And they'd hidden the coins in the stable because it was so full of rubbish that no one used it. Except someone had, a few times. To pray over a half-drowned man; to look for a trunk.

She hadn't found a single useful thing. Certainly not treasure.

"What now, Lilac?" Benedict was asking. "Do we need to find the remaining coins to prove the truth of his story?"

"The Royal Mint would appreciate that, yes," the Runner said drily. "Smith, any hints?"

"I'll help yer look if you undo these shackles."

Three disbelieving glares speared him.

"Hold fast to him, Frost, if you will," said Lilac. "Miss Perry, if you'll help me scout around?"

Charlotte agreed; she could tell the Runner which items she had shifted in her search for a trunk.

"Shall I encourage Smith to tell us where they put the chests?" Benedict called. "I do have my knife back."

"You people and your knives," sighed the Runner. "Come, Miss Perry, let's check this way. They'll be little chests, so we must be careful not to overlook them."

"They'll be little," she repeated. She hadn't thought about how the coins would be stored—but of course they were heavy and couldn't all be tipped into, say, one large box. "Little chests," she said again. "Oh!"

There was a box, metal and worn, beneath a basket made of an elephant's leg. She had hated to touch the basket earlier, and why should she? She needed a traveling trunk, not an elephant's trunk or any other part of its unfortunate body.

And she had not been looking for a small metal

box. Or . . . *ugh,* the elephant leg was unpleasantly yielding about its armature . . . or . . . yes, there were two more little chests, shoved behind.

"Mr. Lilac," she called in a voice that was not quite steady. "I think I have found them."

The Runner was at her side in an instant, knocking the elephant leg aside with an elbow and hauling forth the small boxes one at a time. Each was smaller than a hatbox, but the wiry man half slid, half carried them, teeth gritted with effort. "Good sign," he managed, "how heavy they are. Each trunk from the Mint weighed one hundred fifty pounds, full."

"Full," she whispered. "Imagine that." She traced the top of one box, brushing dust and grit from its lid. The crowned royal arms were stamped on the top.

"Mr. Frost," she called. "Do come help Mr. Lilac move these boxes, will you? I will guard our guest."

"Take my pistol." Lilac handed it over. The weight was unfamiliar in Charlotte's hand, but she understood readily enough how to use it.

Much shuffling of items brought the three little stout metal boxes within the entrance of the stable, mere feet from the shackled, glowering Smith.

"Let's have a look, then," Lilac said. "Is there a crowbar about?"

"Anything useful?" Charlotte said. Together with Benedict, she chorused, "No."

"But I've my knife again." He unsheathed it from his boot. "You're welcome to it, Lilac. Only, you must give it back."

"I'll do that." A few pries at the seal of the first chest, and the Runner had it open.

And inside: gold, bright and shining and warm,

coin after coin after coin. The king's face, stolid as though his image had never caused anyone to hurt or die.

"That's it." Charlotte's throat was dry. "That's it, Benedict. These are the coins. You must—you ought to touch them."

She held the pistol on Smith while Lilac pried at the other two chests. Benedict crouched before the first, trailing gentle fingers across the gold surface. Bump-bump-bumping over the tiny surfaces of each coin. He picked up a few, rubbing a thumb across the face. Learning the shape of the coin, the feel of it.

"It'll all have to be resealed and counted at the Mint," said Lilac. "But from a guess, this is fully half the money—minus a sovereign or two handed to unfortunate serving girls."

Smith ground his teeth.

"So." Again, the Runner took up his pocket-book and pencil. "Once that's all settled, someone will receive half the royal reward. Who was it who found the twenty-five-thousand-pounds worth of gold sovereigns?"

Benedict let the coins slip through his fingers back into the chest before standing. "Not I. I'm blind. I can't tell one trunk from another."

"Benedict!" She knew, she ought to be calling him Frost. But who cared now? What did it matter?

"It's not mine," he said. "It's not my reward." His expression was perfectly calm, but there was something unyielding in the crease of his brow, the jut of his jaw. "You found the chests, Miss Perry. You take it."

Take it. Let me love you.

She wished he had meant that when he said it.

Let me leave you. That was what she had to say instead.

And she would, just as she'd planned.

"Since the sovereigns were found on the land occupied by my parents," said Charlotte, "I rather think the reward goes to them."

Lilac's shrewd eyes, she was sure, missed nothing. "Two thousand five hundred pounds. In the funds, that'll be one hundred a year. Not a bad income for a couple looking to retire to a new home, say, if things get a bit too dramatic for them."

"Not a bad retirement," said Charlotte. "But not a good one, either."

The gold was found, and it wasn't enough to change anyone's life—except for that of those who had stolen it, those who had died for it. The sovereigns were pure and perfect and new, yet there was not enough good in them to make up for all the harm tied to their existence.

But she had one more idea, before she left. One more way to help her family.

And then, she really did need to find a traveling trunk in all this mess, and she had to be on her way.

Chapter Nineteen

"'I strongly believe,'" Maggie read aloud to Benedict and her grandparents, "'that Lady Helena Selwyn will purchase this necklace, if only to destroy it. Do not accept less than seven thousand five hundred pounds.'"

Charlotte had left that afternoon, alone, with a trunk so broken that she had to fasten it shut with the cinch of an old saddle.

So Benedict had been told by the Reverend John Perry. "I asked her not to go," he said, "but she said she must. She would take nothing, no money at all, except a little for her coach fare."

And then Maggie had found the note on the dining room table—and alongside it, Benedict gathered, a spill of gemstones that proved to be a necklace.

The necklace, he realized. The one that had collared *La Perle* in painting after painting. It had lost its mystery and its sting when Randolph caught up to her, then revealed her identity to her home village.

The bastard. Benedict wondered if he was still here or whether his crested carriage had trundled off, work accomplished.

"Your daughter means to take care of you," said Benedict. "With the reward money, and the money from the necklace, she has arranged a comfortable income."

Four or five hundred pounds per annum if they chose to invest it in the funds. Enough to pick up stakes, certainly, if they decided to do so. Enough that they would never have to worry about money again.

There were always other things about which one could worry.

With a gentle pat, the reverend splayed his hands on the table. "I am sixty-two years old. It's time one started thinking of retirement."

"What do you mean?" said Maggie.

"Indeed," sniffed the vicar's wife. "If—but—Perry, I thought you would never wish to leave here."

"I would rather not *have* to leave." Ah, the familiar fidgeting movements of his hands, dry and faint on the tabletop. "But I have been thinking of retirement. An impossible idea, it seemed for a long time. But—well."

"Oh, Perry—I did not realize."

"Well, now. You've been in ancient Greece for a long time." Benedict could imagine the sad smile that touched his host's face. "You won't mind a retirement, will you? It does not matter to you where you live, or even in what century."

"It matters to me if it matters to you."

"It matters to me," said the vicar. "Very much. To have you with me."

Benedict began to feel highly superfluous, and one step at a time, he sidled toward the doorway. The last thing he heard before reaching the stairway was the vicar's voice: "This all would have been much more difficult without Charlotte."

And Benedict was glad he had said this, when her parents could also have said the opposite.

The sound of tears, muffled and sniffled, interrupted Benedict in his packing.

He stepped across the corridor; though the door was open, he knocked on the wooden frame. "Miss Maggie? Would you like some company?"

"I don't have any company," she said. A tiny voice, low to the floor. She was sitting on the carpet before the hearth, Benedict guessed, where Captain had been used to curl.

"You can have some for a while," he said. "If you like. I'm just a rough old blind sailor who couldn't even find any flowers today, but maybe I'm better than nothing."

She sniffled. "You are." *Sniffle.* "You can come in if you want to."

He plumped right down in the doorway, leaning his back against one side of the frame. "What's bothering y—"

"Why does everything have to change?" The words were thick and bitter.

"Um," Benedict began. "I don't know. Some changes, I don't like at all." Some he did, of course, but this was obviously not the time to mention such things.

"She left me the ribbons." The identity of *she* was quite clear. "Green silk ribbons. I thought she forgot about plaiting my hair, but she remembered. She just didn't do it."

"Or maybe," Benedict tried, "she wanted you to have a way to remember her."

"No. It's easier to leave something behind than to stay and care for someone." Maggie sniffled. "What if someone else asks that first someone to leave?"

Wrong answer. Wrong question, rather. This earned him a fresh burst of tears. *Shite.* What did he know about talking to a ten-year-old girl?

He patted his pockets until he found a handkerchief. His last one. These Perry women were rough on his handkerchiefs.

On hands and knees, he reached out and set it beside Maggie on the hearth rug—then, tentatively, he seated himself nearby. "You know," he said, "I met a lot of people when I traveled the earth. In . . . Tahiti . . . there was a family with a daughter. Two daughters, actually, but one of them had left that island as soon as she grew up."

The sniffles had subsided a little; she had plucked up the handkerchief. Encouragement enough to continue, then. "The second daughter always wanted to come home, but she could help her family more by staying where she was. She sent them money and food and other things that were difficult for them to get. If she'd come back to them, she would have felt like a burden."

"But one of the sisters got to stay."

"She was the lucky one," said Benedict. "But then, the second sister got to see new things, and learn about different parts of the world, so maybe she was lucky, too. They were both exactly where they needed to be."

A long silence followed.

"You made that up," Maggie said, and for a moment Benedict heard Charlotte in her tone: half-laughing, half-exasperated.

He grinned. "Perhaps. But wasn't it a good story?"

Tiny picking sounds, as though she were plucking at loose bits of the hearth rug. "Do you think it's true? That a person can love someone even if they aren't there?"

"For some people," he said carefully.

"For me," she whispered.

"Yes."

"For you?"

This, he was not expecting. "I don't know. I only have one sister, and so we don't fit the story, and—"

"Mr. *Frost*."

He sighed. And thought about it.

Since the age of twelve, he'd been used to looking after himself. But he never expected the same of Georgette, and he didn't want to. He didn't want his only remaining family to feel she couldn't count on him, or that he wouldn't care what became of her.

But he'd had the treasure in his hands for her, and he'd let it slip away. Literally. Because he knew, he could find another way to secure Georgette's future. He'd give her the money from the sale of the family's bookshop.

In that moment, he'd known Georgette would find her own future. In the present, with Charlotte feeling so alone, he'd wanted her to have the reward. Just one way to show her she *wasn't* alone, even if she left.

But she had left, and she'd left the reward behind, too. And a fortune in jewels. And the family she'd said she wanted.

She'd left *him*.

Because giving people things—that wasn't enough, was it? It wasn't enough. He had a sister he hardly knew, and he'd been beside a pile of gold, and now he was just as alone as Maggie.

"I think the sisters should have switched places sometimes," he decided. "Then they'd both get to be with family and they'd both get to see the world."

"Or the whole family could travel," said Maggie. "If it were a real family."

"It could be real," he murmured. "For the lucky ones."

Pick pick pick at the rug. "Sometimes there's a sister no one needs."

"What do you mean?"

"Someone like me." She gulped against another swell of tears. "Grandpapa and Grandmama don't need me."

"There are a lot of ways to need someone besides relying on them to shelter or feed you. You might not bring them money, but you bring them joy. They take care of you because they want you to have a good life."

"My . . . mother. She doesn't need me. She didn't want to have me."

At times like this, he was almost glad he could not see. He feared the pain on her young features would break his heart. "She *never* said that," he told her. "Your mother has loved you every day of your life." He flailed for some evidence that would convince her, then remembered. "The day I met her—and you—I knew she was your mother just by hearing her speak to you. Because she loved you so much, she couldn't hold it in, and it just shone out of her voice."

"I didn't hear it shine," she said.

"Well," he said modestly, "I'm used to listening for these things."

Pick pick pick. A long silence. "My mother made this rug. Both of my mothers."

"Ah." Benedict decided against saying more.

"They wanted me to have a good life, too, didn't they?"

"Yes. They wanted that more than they wanted their own happiness. And that's love."

It hurt so badly to be the one left behind. In his travels with the Royal Navy and on his own, had he ever left anyone feeling like this: scooped hollow and grieving?

No, because no one knew him well enough to love him.

He had come here for treasure, and he had found it, and he had given it away, because he wanted Charlotte's happiness more than his own.

And that meant—good *God.* He really *had* found a treasure, and it was Charlotte, and he was *stupid,* so stupid, to tell her he couldn't accept it. To tell her he couldn't make a future with her, because of—what? Money? Obligation?

Pride?

If he gave up his wandering life, his post as a Naval Knight, he would lose everything he'd earned from the last seventeen years of his life. He'd lose his income, his connection to the navy, his right to call himself a lieutenant. There would be so many ties, snapped irrevocably. Ties for which, as a boy, he had traded a home and family.

But what might he gain instead? If his travels led him not *from* but *toward*? Might he get that home, that family, back again? Was there a chance?

He wanted Charlotte's happiness more than his own. But how much greater would his own be if they were together? Somehow, sometime—maybe when she flirted with him over sour ale, maybe when she bandaged his arm—she had come to rest upon his heart.

Somehow, he had come to love her.

The thought was as clean and resonant as his metal-tipped cane striking solid marble. How ringing; how obvious. Yes.

"Miss Maggie," he said. "I seem to have made a horrible blunder."

She sniffled.

He smiled.

She giggled, a little.

"Will you help me send a letter?" he asked. "No—a parcel."

A month after Charlotte had left Strawfield, she had achieved a state of tolerable contentment.

Benedict had suggested she write a memoir, and she did just that. It was a short one, and highly specific. Not intended for publication.

Charlotte had become popular and respected as *La Perle* in large part, she thought, because of her loyalty. Her skin was all on display, but her private business remained exactly that: private.

The Marquess of Randolph also held the esteem of others; maybe due to his reticence, maybe because of a fist of fear. But if the world really knew him . . .

When she finished her work, she made two fair copies. She placed one with a solicitor in London, one with a solicitor in Edinburgh, and sent the original to Randolph himself.

The accompanying note was brief.

If you approach me again, these papers will be released. What do you think of yourself?

His reply was just as terse.

Madam, but return the items I gave you and I will consider our arrangement dissolved.

Always the last word. Always the win.

She remembered the *items* to which he referred: a few baubles, nothing of great value. The gifts of a man testing how little he might get away with giving.

In her haste to sell everything and flee London—flee Randolph—she had only received a few pounds for the trinkets.

I sold them, she wrote back. *Here is the amount I received.*

When she sent it off, cutting the final tie with the marquess, she felt free.

He thought he had won. But she felt that she had, too.

Without the need for haste and panic, she was able to sell her house in Mayfair for a good price. For a fraction of the money, she bought a cottage in Edinburgh. So it was called by the seller—but the word *cottage* made her laugh. It was sturdy stone, two stories high, with a walled garden and plenty of space for servants' quarters.

She liked the idea of living outside England—even if only just. Benedict had planted the notion, with his travels and his medical studies here, and so, so, many jokes about the virtuous works she was meant to have performed in distant parts of the world. The weather in Edinburgh was not so different from what she was accustomed to, yet the *climate* of life here was a new thing entirely.

Once she had a settled address, she had remembered to write to Barrett, asking the maid to return from Yorkshire to work at the Strawfield vicarage. But the Reverend John Perry and his wife were gone from Strawfield, Barrett replied, so the servant came to her instead.

Gone from Strawfield, and her parents hadn't even written to her.

This put a severe weight onto her state of tolerable contentment.

With the exception of the crushed-almond tart, she didn't miss Strawfield, a village to which she had never quite felt herself to belong. But as worn as her parents had become, she'd never thought they would leave it.

She sent a letter to Stephen Lilac to see what he could find out. The wiry Runner had confirmed the receipt of the Strawfield treasure by the Royal Mint, and he had seen half the reward issued to her parents.

They had gone to Bath, he wrote back, with their granddaughter. Had sold some jewelry and he had given up the post as vicar of Strawfield.

So. At least they were cared for, even if they could not forgive her.

As for the other half of the Royal Mint's stolen sovereigns?

Charlotte had laughed to read the news. Lord Hugo Starling had had a hand in their recovery. She never had met the man, but maybe someday she would.

No. She wouldn't. She didn't mix with the elite anymore.

Be that as it may, the gold sovereigns were released

on schedule in July. The king's face was everywhere across his realm, not that the poor madman knew it.

And at some point during the month, her courses came. A relief, of course. She had established herself as Charlotte Perry, an unmarried woman of means.

No more lies.

And nothing of Benedict. Which was good. She had grown used to not having him, her heart hollowed in one terrible wrench. Eventually it would fill.

"I am tolerably content," she insisted every time Barrett asked. "It would be greedy to hope for more." Barrett said nothing, but sent out tear-spotted pillowcases for laundering.

At the end of the month, Charlotte began writing again.

Not a memoir of her time as a courtesan. Something new. Something fresh.

This time, she would write a love story, and she would give it the ending she wished.

The knock at the door came too early for the mail and too late for the fish. And it should have come to the servants' door either way.

"Barrett!" Charlotte called.

Barrett was everywhere at once, as usual, which meant the chances of her being exactly where one wished were low. With a rueful sigh, Charlotte set aside her paper and quill. Her hands were inky; well, it couldn't be helped. Whoever was at the door would just have to understand.

It was Benedict.

Benedict Frost, looking gruff and big and blunt, wearing a dark blue coat that fit him perfectly.

"Benedict," she breathed, as though she could not quite say his name enough.

When he smiled, he was the handsomest man she had ever seen. When his smile fell and turned tentative, he was even more so.

"Miss Perry." He made a proper bow. "You see before you a complete and total civilian."

"Why do I see such a thing?" She fumbled to understand his appearance before her. "How did you find me?"

He straightened up. "After a staggering amount of negotiation, I gave up my place as a Naval Knight, which"—he waved a hand—"meant I couldn't live in a castle anymore. Always sounded better than it really was."

"Right." She hesitated. "Yes." It meant much more than not having a room in Windsor Castle anymore, she knew. As a civilian, without the income from his pension and half pay status, he was penniless.

"As for finding you," he added, "I requested your direction from your parents. I left Strawfield after you did, once they had decided where to go."

"I see." Which was true—almost. He was not the sort to throw himself upon her charity. And that was quite the elegant coat he was wearing. "Out with it, Frost. What have you done?"

"Ah." He looked a little guilty. "Something I swore I'd never do, but I did it for a good reason. I sold my memoir to George Pitman—or rather, I paid Pitman to publish it on commission. He advertised it as the wildest of novels, and it is doing quite well. I've made several hundred pounds already, and Pitman is asking me for another in the series."

"But . . ." She fumbled for understanding. "You worked so hard on it. It was your *life.*"

"Just a little piece of it." He held thumb and forefinger a wee distance apart. "I'll have more. It's doing much more good this way than by taking up space in my trunk."

"What of your sister?"

"I sent her half the money I received from selling the bookshop to our cousins. She had more than a few travel expenses to cover." With a little smile, he added, "Georgette took care of herself. When I found her, she informed me that she hadn't taken any help from me yet, and she didn't need to now. But I reminded her the inheritance was from our parents, and that it was terribly unfair everything had come to me as the eldest. Eventually she accepted the money—on the condition that we visit one another several times a year."

"Are you . . . all right with that?"

"She's happy. So—yes." He cleared his throat. "But I'll tell you about all that later. For now, may I come in?"

He was asking to take a step over her threshold. To become part of her life again.

Her heart hammered where she thought only hollowness remained.

"There is something I ought to tell you first," she said.

"Your favorite sentence." He paused. "Who are you now?"

"That's just it. I'm Charlotte Perry, a respectable spinster. I have friends and a subscription at a lending library and accounts at the local shops." She shook her head, though he couldn't see the gesture.

"I can't allow you in if you're only going to leave again."

"Indeed." He tipped his head, a sly expression crossing his features. "It's remarkably easy to get married in Scotland. None of this fuss about expensive licenses and waiting for banns and whatnot."

"Are you asking?"

"No." He dropped to one knee, right there on the stone stoop. "I'm begging. I know you've a home here, and a new life, and you don't need me—but I need you. My heart has a space in it, just your size."

"Your heart is very large," she said faintly.

"I never thought it was, particularly," he admitted. "I've been a selfish sort of fellow, wanting to be alone and go alone and . . . alone, alone. Tedious stuff. You seem to have made me rethink a few things."

Oh.

"Get up off your knees," she said. "That must be so cold."

He clambered to his feet, pulling himself up with the hickory cane that, she now noticed, he had leaned against the side of the house by the door. "Does that mean you're saying yes?"

"Not quite," she said. "What of the man who felt England was too small for him? How can I know life with me won't become a cage to you?"

"Because I choose it—that is, if you'll have me. It makes all the difference to leave when one wishes, and to go where one wishes. Not to be getting away from something, but to be going somewhere you want to be." His hands worked nervously about the cane. "To a home. With someone I love."

Oh.

"Also," he added gamely, "we aren't in England. I

can almost hear the sea from here, and if you want to, maybe someday we can cross it. I was happy in Edinburgh when I lived here before, studying medicine. If you'll allow me to be with you, I think I'll be happier still."

"You're babbling," she said. "Go back to the part about making a home with someone you love."

His lips curved. "Did you like that part?"

"I did," she admitted, "like that part."

"Good. I like it, too." He rested the cane against the side of the house again. "I was such a fool, Charlotte. I loved you long before I realized it, long before my pride allowed me to sort out a new way to live. I love you now, and I don't intend to stop, and I hope you'll give me another chance to make a life with you."

She smiled, catching his hand and bringing it to her face so he could feel her expression. "Tell me the part again about love."

His fingers were gentle, learning the shape of her all over again. *Charlotte, there you are.* "I love you. A Charlotte by any other name is just as sweet, but yours is the one I love best."

"Don't get too fond of it," she said. "Because soon it will change to Charlotte Frost."

"That's a yes, then?"

"That's a yes. And an 'I love you, too.'"

Despite her joy, a tiny piece of her heart still ached, incomplete. Until he added, "If you'd want Miss Maggie to visit us—well, that would be nice, wouldn't it?"

"It would," she agreed. "It really would."

And she pulled him indoors, kissing him so hard that, for a sweet and seductive interlude, there was nothing else in the world.

Epilogue

As summer turned to autumn, the fame of Edward Selwyn's paintings of *La Perle* grew, rippling across the border to Scotland. Edinburgh had its own society, its own wealthy who enjoyed the symbols of fashion and acquisition. It was inevitable that someone would seek out a painting of the nude Nausicaa or the bare Boadicea.

Charlotte knew this. But the days passed in waves of light and dark, work and play, and it was easy to forget there had ever been another life.

One day Benedict returned home, half-dismayed and half-laughing. He rested his cane against the back of Charlotte's writing chair, kissed her on top of the head, and handed her a small parcel. "The new quills you requested, Madam Shakespeare."

"Thank you," she said. Now filling some two hundred sheets of foolscap, her novel had consumed every pen in the house. She set aside her work and shoved back the little table on which she wrote. "Wherefore art thou smiling in that odd way, Romeo?"

"Ha. Yes. I encountered the keeper of the Rose and Thorn while I was running your errand."

The closest inn, with a pleasantly clean and warm taproom. Charlotte had a nodding friendship with the publican's wife, and Barrett went there several times a week. Sweet on one of the ostlers, Charlotte suspected.

"It seems," Benedict continued, "that the Rose and Thorn has acquired a painting of Charlotte Pearl in a trade from a patron with a bar tab the size of a king's ransom."

"I have been traded for ale? How lowering."

"A *king's ransom* worth of ale. That's . . . I don't really know how much ale it would take to ransom a king, but surely a lot." Benedict grinned. "Here's the best part, though: when he hung the painting in the public room, he said someone told him the picture looked a little like Mrs. Frost. So he wanted to know if I thought that improper."

She considered. Her life was so different now, resting little on the past. Many people in Edinburgh were passing through or had come from somewhere else. The water was nearby, and it was wide.

"I don't think it much matters at all," she decided. "But what did you say to him?"

"I said I couldn't speak to the resemblance myself, but by all accounts *La Perle* was a great beauty and so is my wife. Of course, my wife is a respectable married woman."

"With a scar on her face, who rarely if ever appears outdoors in the nude," Charlotte added.

"All true," said Benedict. "The publican agreed that you were a right handsome woman, and that the painting was right handsome, too. And that was that."

"And that was that," she repeated. "Perhaps I have left behind the nude wanton in those paintings."

"A nude wanton? I hope not entirely. You make me wish you had been sculpted, my dear, so I might enjoy these portrayals."

"Ah, but you can run your hands over the original inspiration."

And he did.

Charlotte had wed Benedict the day after his arrival in Edinburgh. The day after that, she wrote to her parents at the Bath address collected from Stephen Lilac.

The letter of congratulations, signed by both parents, came as soon afterward as the Royal Mail could speed their good wishes along. They were happy for her; they thought Benedict a good man.

They thanked her for her help. They were happy in Bath, in a retirement she had not known they coveted, and Maggie had befriended several girls near her own age. Mrs. Perry was working on a new translation.

Best of all was the end: the promise that they would write again soon.

To Charlotte, the letter felt like a bandage around some wound within her. Maybe her parents, like she, had been waiting for the other to write the first letter. To make the first gesture of forgiveness for all those years apart.

Yes, they were still apart, but it felt different now. A carriage ride, and a bit of time, could bring them together, and the togetherness would be welcome.

She missed Maggie, of course, but that was an old familiar ache. She had been missing Maggie in some way or another since she first put her infant into her sister's arms.

And then came a letter from Maggie herself.

The first one was short.

> *Dear Mr. and Mrs. Frost,*
> *I am well in Bath. I have begun a translation of* The Odyssey *from the Greek into English. Grandmama says it is a favorite of hers.*
>
> *Maggie Catlett*

Charlotte was tempted to write back a great screed of delight, but she restrained herself. With Benedict's aid, she crafted an affectionate reply that invited more letters.

The next letter was longer. Most intriguingly so.

> *Dear Uncle Benedict and Aunt Charlotte,*
> *Grandmama told me the rest of the story. Penelope did not forget her husband even though he was gone for twenty years. She said she thought he was not true to his wife and I asked her what that meant and she got very red but she told me. I think I understand now. Not everything he did was good but that didn't mean he didn't love her. I think he still loved her even though he was away for so long.*
>
> *Yours,*
> *Maggie Catlett*

When they invited her to come to Edinburgh for a visit, the reply came with no salutation at all—which Charlotte hoped was a sign of confused excitement.

I may come for a visit. Colleen will bring me, and we will be there in a month's time, and I can stay through Christmas if that is all right with you.

Of course it is all right, Charlotte wrote, though she wanted to write *Never leave at all.*

The day Maggie and Colleen were meant to arrive, Charlotte watched out the front window of the cottage all day.

"I could just tell you when their carriage is coming," Benedict murmured as he scratched out a line on his noctograph. A new scene for his next novel about the blind traveler. Unbounded by fact, this time he was really enjoying himself. "I'll hear it. You could hear it, too, for that matter, if you could settle. Come, write beside me."

This was a habit they'd got into in recent weeks, as each worked on a novel. Charlotte was not sure she would ever finish hers, as all her characters wanted to do now was kiss and cavort. Writing it had soothed some need within her during a lonely time. Now she was more apt to peek at Benedict's straight-ruled work and contribute saucy anecdotes in which the fortunate traveler could take part.

Today, though, she sprang from her chair as soon as she touched the seat. "I can't settle," she said. "I can't—I need to *do* something."

Striding through the front parlor, through the corridor, through the kitchen, she made her way into the kitchen garden plot and ruthlessly weeded everything that dared poke through the soil in the wrong space.

She had had to learn their shape and type, sometimes through error. Different plants grew here than in London or Derbyshire. But when one matched a fruit or a flower with the right type of soil, it thrived.

She worked her fingers into the cool earth, trying not to think too much. Her heart was divided, part at her husband's side within the front parlor, part on the long road north, and she ached with wanting all the pieces together.

Behind her, the kitchen door opened. One of the maids, no doubt, coming to pick the herbs and vegetables needed for dinner.

But the footsteps that approached were light and hesitant. Not those of a bustling maid, but of a girl.

Even before Charlotte turned around, she was smiling. And then came the loveliest sentence she had ever heard.

"Hullo, Mother."

Author's Note

The truth is often more marvelous than anything a fiction writer would dare dream up, and the historical figure on which Benedict Frost is based is one such example. James Holman (1786–1857) was a lieutenant in the Royal Navy who, as a young man, caught a mysterious disease that took his sight. He was given a pension, attended medical school, traveled the world, and wrote books about his experiences. He was in the habit of carrying a metal-tipped cane, which he used to learn the shape of his environment through a sort of echolocation. I have given this hard-won skill to Benedict, along with much of Holman's career path.

The quotes from Benedict's memoir are taken from Holman's first published book, which is now in the public domain and can be read online. The full title is *The Narrative of a Journey, Undertaken in the Years 1819, 1820, & 1821, through France, Italy, Savoy, Switzerland, Parts of Germany Bordering on the Rhine, Holland, and the Netherlands; Comprising Incidents that Occurred to the Author, who Has Long Suffered Under a Total Deprivation of Sight; with Various Points of Information Collected on His Tour!* Whew!

Please read on for an excerpt from
Theresa Romain's next Royal Rewards novel,

PASSION FAVORS THE BOLD,

coming in March 2017!

Late May 1817
London

As one would expect of a young woman raised in a bookshop, Georgette Frost was accustomed to flights of imagination. But not even in her most robust fancies could she have dreamed of her present situation.

Not because she was garbed in boys' clothing. Many the blue-blooded heroine of a *conte de fée* had disguised herself to escape the cruel predations of a wicked relative.

True, Georgette's veins ran with the ink of her family's longtime bookshop rather than blue blood. And Cousin Mary was not wicked; merely overwhelmed by the endless demands of the shop and her multitude of children.

Nor was Georgette dismayed to set out on her own, with all her worldly possessions in a small trunk. Freed from the endless shelves and endless demands of starched-collar customers, she had felt gloriously unfettered as she sought a coaching house and prepared to join her elder brother on his travels for the first time.

There was only one problem, but that problem was a significant one: six feet tall, hawkish of feature, and stuffy of temperament. Lord Hugo Starling, the youngest son of the Duke of Willingham. Friend of Georgette's elder brother Benedict. Representative of everything chill and sterile about the life of the mind: study, solitude, and sternness.

Unfortunately, Lord Hugo had encountered Georgette at the coaching inn before she could board the carriage. After a public spat which did credit to neither of them—though far less to Lord Hugo, who ought to have kept his high-bridged nose out of her business—Georgette had grudgingly scrambled into his carriage.

She now faced him, glaring, as he settled against the soft velvet squabs. "How can you say what I want is impossible? You *asked* where I wanted to go."

"I asked, yes. But I didn't say I would take you there. It would be wrong to send you to the wilds of Derbyshire."

The wilds. She almost snorted. Likely Derbyshire, all grasses and livestock, *did* seem wild to a London-bred noble with a perfectly starched cravat. Georgette was London-bred herself, but with an elder brother once in the Royal Navy, she felt she'd seen a bit of the world, if only through his letters.

This carriage, though, came from a world of luxury she'd never known. Scrupulously tidy, the wood shone with lemon-scented oil. Within sparkling-clear glass globes, the wicks of the unlit lamps were trimmed. The velvet squabs were brushed clean and soft.

Her second-hand jacket and cheap boys' shoes had seemed the perfect disguise when she was outdoors. Now she felt shabby and false, her pale blonde hair falling in drab strands from beneath the cap.

Rapunzel, back in a different sort of tower. *Cendrillon*, doomed to a new sort of drudgery.

In retrieving her—no! *abducting* her—Lord Hugo had been splashed with mud and cheap liquor, his fine coat stained and reeking. Somehow he still managed to look confident and unbending; like the carriage, tidy and elegant save for his encounter with Georgette.

She set her jaw. "I wish you'd left me alone. I was going to find my brother."

He muttered something that sounded suspiciously like *fool's errand*. "You want to seek the royal reward, don't you? Your brother is sure he'll find it, and you want to help him."

She waved a hand. "Of course. Who wouldn't want five thousand pounds?"

For such was the reward offered by the Royal Mint to anyone who located fifty thousand pounds worth of missing gold sovereigns. New coins, not yet circulated, they had been stolen from the mint in a mysterious and violent rampage some weeks before. Since then, no evidence of them had been found—until one gold sovereign was spent in a Derbyshire village, drawing the curious and the treasure-mad from all corners of England.

That was where Benedict had gone as soon as he returned to England from his latest voyage. And so that was where Georgette would go to find him, and her fortune.

"Until I can write your brother, I shall take you to

stay in my parents' townhouse," Lord Hugo decided. "You shall be with the Duchess of Willingham. Won't that be . . . er, nice?"

She could almost hear the gears of his mind grinding. *Smile! Present single option as though it were appealing while giving no choice!*

"No." She folded her arms. Rude, yes; but he had been rude in taking Georgette away from her coaching stop. Her ticket, purchased with scraped-together savings from her salary at the bookshop, was now money wasted. "None of your behavior has been nice at all. I cannot *believe* you told a crowd of strangers that I was your criminal nephew who had stolen silver from my dying mother."

Instead of looking chastened, the cursed man shot her a grim smile. "And you told them I was drunk. *And* you told your own cousins at the bookshop that you'd been invited to stay with my family. Won't it be agreeable to convert one of your lies into the truth?"

"Certainly. You have my permission to get drunk. As soon as you return to me the price of my wasted ticket, that is."

He scrubbed a hand over his face, then sank back against the squabs with apparent weariness. "I took you up, Miss Frost, because your brother would want you to be safe. And that is the end of the discussion."

"Oh, good! Then you agree with me." She bared her teeth in a grin. "You should let me go to Benedict."

"I can't let you go alone, Miss Frost." He shook his head. "It wouldn't be right. A woman alone . . . there are those who would hurt you."

Thus my disguise as a boy. She rolled her eyes. "If

your conscience won't permit me to travel alone, you may accompany me to Derbyshire."

"Out of the question. My business holds me in London."

"What business?"

"Endless business. Only today, I have an appointment at Somerset House with the president of the Royal Society. Then I must review a new treatise on infection at the Royal College of Physicians."

"Say royal once more."

His dark blue gaze snapped to meet hers, suspicious. "Why?"

"Because I hadn't quite got it into my brain that you're a lord who moves in exalted circles and can do whatever he likes."

The carriage rocked on its well-oiled springs, swallowing the roughness of London's roads. Twisting and cornering. Taking her away from the coaching inn. Was she closer to Derbyshire now, or farther away?

Farther. Definitely farther.

She sighed. "Lord Hugo, I don't want to stay with your mother. I want to go to my own family. Surely you can understand that."

He lifted a brow. "Such desires are unfamiliar to me. But then, my family is ashamed of me."

Dark images of hidden chambers and monstrous deeds flooded her mind. Now it was her turn to ask, with some suspicion, "Why is that?"

"Because I went to medical college instead of into the clergy. Because I call upon ill people and sometimes perform surgeries."

Georgette released a caught breath. "How terrible. I can understand why they are disgusted by you."

He winced, then tried to cover it by adjusting his starched white cuffs.

Oh, dear. "I'm *teasing*, Lord Hugo. I can understand nothing of the sort. To me, such behavior seems . . ." She cast about for the right word. "Acceptable."

"Acceptable," he repeated drily. The carriage gave a sway, and he steadied himself with a broad hand against the fabric-softened ceiling.

"Is that why you're going to all those royal locations? To learn something about patient care?"

"Nothing so admirable. I'm looking for a patron for a private hospital." He lowered his hand, regarding her narrowly. "You're about to ask why again, aren't you?"

"I would never intrude into a matter that was no business of mine." She fired a pointed stare at him.

"Right. Of course you wouldn't." The curve of his mouth was distant and haughty, the sort of not-quite-smile worn by classical statues. "Surgeons with little knowledge cut and operate, while the physicians with the most medical training drone and profess. I think the best of both roles should be blended. I intend to do so."

"So your meetings are to ask important people to give you money because your family will not support your scheme?"

"Indeed. Honesty is the most expedient way of getting what one wants."

"When one is dealing with the elite?" She hooted. "Not likely. I've changed my mind. Take me along with you. I want to watch this."

"Ah—well. No. This is a delicate matter. If I hope to persuade them this time—"

"*This* time? You've asked before?"

His gaze slid away. "Twice."

"So you'll batter them with arguments and proposals they've already rejected. Twice."

"Because they are *wrong*."

"Say no more. That would convince me."

"I ought to put you out of the carriage right now," he muttered.

"If you'll give me coach fare to Strawfield village in Derbyshire, I'll be on my way."

It wouldn't be the first time she'd left before being evicted. Cousin Mary and her husband had bought Frost's Bookshop from Georgette's brother Benedict with the understanding that they'd house Georgette until she turned twenty-one. But in the cramped family quarters above, Mary needed another day maid much more than she needed Georgette. And Georgette's wages, meager though they were, would easily hire Mary the help she needed.

Better to leave now than to find herself cast out— with kindness and apology—in a few more weeks. Better to descend from Lord Hugo's carriage before she found herself in a world she knew not at all.

She had raised her hand, prepared to rap on the ceiling and bring the carriage to a halt, when Lord Hugo spoke: "Wait. Please."

She glared at him.

"Miss Frost. Please do not make yourself unsafe."

His tone was stern, but not unkind. How odd. She let her hand fall to her lap, fingers twisting together. "My lord, I don't wish to be unsafe. I wish to go to my brother."

This observation seemed to strike the high-handed man in the solar plexus. "I am trying to *help* your brother. And you. Why do you think I visited Frost's Bookshop so often?"

"Because you wanted books."

"I could buy books anywhere."

Her mouth opened—and then, uncertain, closed again.

He turned aside, working at the latch on the carriage window. "Warm day," he grunted. "Some air would be—*ah.* There. Isn't that nice?"

The gruff tone of his voice had gone tentative.

In fact, the air was humid and close outside as well as in, and with the window open, smuts wafted in like a sprinkling of black snow. It freckled his features, making him blink.

If his expression were always thus—a little weary, a little fuddled—he would be quite handsome.

Digging her split-seamed shoe into the mat cushioning the floor of the carriage, she looked down. "Thank you for your concern."

"If you were my sister, there is no way in heaven I'd let you run off and seek treasure."

Quickly as that, the moment was spoiled. Her head snapped up. "Let, let, let. Just *stop.* If I were your sister, I wouldn't need the money, so the point is moot. If I were your sister, I'd have been raised on clouds of spun sugar and dined off dishes made of carved diamond."

"That is ridiculous. Diamond is far too hard to carve for use as crockery. Too small as well." He tipped his head. "However, my sisters-in-law are remarkably fond of spun sugar."

"Hugo." She used his name without the honorific for the first time, and his brows lifted—surprised, but not, she thought, displeased. "You asked where I wanted to go. Besides the cousins I have left behind, my brother is the only close family I have left in the world. I do not know him well, and I do not know what his life is like. But I know being in his company would be better than being alone."

And then an idea struck her. A marvelous, wonderful idea, worthy of a heroine of a fairy tale. "You really could come with me," she said. "Leave your business with Royal This and That behind and try something new. Pursue the royal reward instead."

Impossible. Illogical. Yet as Hugo turned the suggestion over in his mind, it did not seem inconceivable.

He bought a bit of time. "Not while you're wearing those ridiculous boys' clothes. I can't imagine how you fooled anyone."

She shrugged. "People see what they want to. I couldn't have deceived Benedict, of course."

This was undoubtedly true. Her brother had lost his sight due to a tropical illness during his stint in the Royal Navy. Ever since, Benedict had navigated the world—including medical college alongside Hugo—through hearing and touch, and there was little nuance that escaped his notice.

"There's an idea," she went on, sounding pleased. "If you don't like my boy's costume, I can travel as your sister."

"I never said I would travel with—"

"It's *perfect*." She leaned forward, eyes wide with enthusiasm. The already precarious cap tumbled from her head, allowing all that fairy-pale hair to fall. Down about her shoulders; down, down, to her waist. "If you help me, I will take the reward and you may take all the credit. You can use the popular notoriety to gain acceptance for your pet project."

Hugo bridled. "*Pet project* is hardly the way one ought to refer to a private hospital with the potential to save many lives. And why should I not set off on my own and have both the acclaim and the reward?"

"Because that would be horrid of you. And if you have the acclaim, you won't need the reward."

His brows lifted. "So you say. Another thing I won't need is the scandal of being thought to have abducted an ungrateful whelp."

"I give you my word, I won't tell a crowd of strangers you're trying to abduct me. As long as you don't try to abduct me," she added. "Again."

Abduction. *God.* This was his thanks for rescuing her from a crowd that, if they recognized her as a gently-bred young woman, would have turned on her every way imaginable.

"If you accompany me to Strawfield," Georgette added, "I shall behave properly."

Feigning docility, she lowered her eyes. Light eyes, like the pale of a summer sky. Pale hair and skin too. Seeing her among the endless shelves of Frost's Bookshop, Hugo had always thought she looked as though she were half-faded into the pages of a story.

A fanciful observation. Most uncharacteristically so. Especially since, as his visits to the bookshop stacked in number, he saw how hard and how prosaically she worked. As Hugo was a friend of her brother's, she seemed not to regard him with the formality she would a stranger. In his presence, she carried garments for the laundress, scooped up her cousin's wayward toddlers, marked accounts, stacked books—and so on, in ceaseless motion.

"Do you want to search for your brother, Miss Frost? Or for the stolen coins?"

She considered. "First the second thing. Then the first thing second."

"I should have guessed," he murmured. "Do explain to me. My family already disapproves, and my would-be patrons have already declined. How would notoriety for finding stolen coins increase my credibility in medical circles? And better still, how would it translate into financial support for my hospital?"

"Finding the coins would make you *ton*nish. Then everything you said and did would be all right with people of influence." She spoke matter-of-factly, as though this were obvious.

And maybe it should have been. These people of influence—of which his father was one, and of whom his family was constantly aware—were unimpressed by logical argument. By tales of infection, of suppuration, of dirty wards, of lives that should have been saved.

Accompany me to Strawfield: the words painted a lovely picture such as he had not seen for years. A wide sky, absent the caustic smell of chloride of lime and the heavy odor of ill bodies, often beyond help. People who listened to him simply because they thought him worth listening to. Not because they *had* to, because his father was a duke. Not dismissing him, either, as a younger son with wild ideas that trespassed against the upper class's notions of suitability.

When influenza broke out among the dukedom's tenants, Hugo's own father, the Duke of Willingham, had called Hugo mad to quarantine ill tenants away from their healthy relatives. Everyone knew that influenza came from an imbalance of humors, said his

father. But when the spread of illness was halted and
the outbreak ended almost as soon as it began, the
duke granted that perhaps Hugo had been right.

Not right enough to support his other medical
ideas, though. Not right enough to grant that Hugo's
chosen field was a worthwhile way to spend one's life.

"Think of all the people you could help with your
hospital," Georgette coaxed.

Hugo folded his arms. "One. You."

She beamed. "You only fold your arms when you're
about to change your mind."

"I do not." He unfolded his arms, but they snapped
back into a cradle about his midsection. "How did
you—why . . ."

"I learned such signals working in the family bookshop. When to push someone a bit harder. When a
bit more coaxing would help me to make the sale."

She had sorted him out, that was true enough—
though he wasn't quite prepared to tell her he'd give
in. Despite himself, his mouth curved up at one
corner. "All that fluffy blond hair covers a diabolical
mind."

Her brows knit. "What is diabolical about both of
us getting what we want?"

To this, he had no answer: only a question. In this
agreement, would he be the devil, or poor Faust who
sold his soul?